PIECES OF ME

A CARRIGAN RICHARDS NOVEL

PIECES OF ME Copyright © 2013 Carrigan Richards

ISBN: 1492146536
ISBN-13: 978-1492146537

All rights reserved. No part of this book may be reproduced, scanned, or distributed in any printed or electronic form without permission. Please do not participate in or encourage piracy of copyrighted materials in violation of the author's rights.

This is a work of fiction. Names, places, characters and incidents are the product of the author's imagination and are fictitious. Any resemblance to actual persons, living or dead, events or establishments is solely coincidental.

Cover art and design by Judy Gibson and Ryan Gibson.

To learn more about author Carrigan Richards, visit her website at www.carriganrichards.com

CARRIGAN RICHARDS PUBLISHING, LLC

Also by Carrigan Richards
Standalone Novel
Pieces of Me

Elemental Enchanters Series
Under a Blood Moon
Under the Burning Stars
When Darkness Fell
Under the Winter Sun
Under an Onyx Sky

January Dreams Series
January Dreams

ACKNOWLEDGMENTS

First, and foremost, I want to thank you, the reader, for giving this book a chance. If it weren't for you, my dream would not exist. As with any novel, there are so many people to thank and I couldn't have done this without their help.

Jennifer Watts – the world needs more friends like you. Thank you for your incredible support throughout the years, for reading countless revisions, and for your brutal honesty. You are the best.

Lydia Senn – I can't tell you how much I appreciate all your help! You're an awesome cheerleader and I'm grateful for you.

To Mom, Dad, Patrick, and Morgan. Thanks for all your support in making my dream possible and for cheering me on. I love you!

And last but not least, thank you to Laura, Judy, Ryan, Derrick, Danial, Chandra, Alan, Colleen, Marcia, Lisa, Rachel, and Angie for all of your incredible support and for not getting annoyed by my endless questions!

DEDICATION

In memory of my grandmother.

PROLOGUE

The leafless trees swayed in the breeze as the darkening clouds moved across the sky. I pushed open an iron gate, cutting my wrist on a jagged edge. I ignored the trickling blood as it steered toward my fingertips and dripped onto the dead ground. I followed a narrow dirt path up a hill to a large oak tree. My hands touched the cold bark and I rounded the tree to the other side, stopping short when I saw hands on the ground. Narrowing my eyes as if it would help me see better in the dark, I moved closer.

The hands moved and suddenly *he* stood before me. A glare in his blue eyes. A scowl on his mangled face. His hair was caked with dried blood. His hands curled into fists. My breath caught in my throat.

"D-David."

"Look what you did to me." Anger and hatred in his voice.

"I-I'm s-sorry."

"This should be you. You should be here. Not me."

He looked larger than I remembered him. His stance was like a lion about to attack a gazelle. I stood frozen, afraid to look at him. He was always protective of me. But I couldn't protect him.

I closed my eyes, waiting for what I deserved to come to me.

CHAPTER ONE

Dad never cried. But as I peered into the rear-view mirror from the back seat, I saw tears in his brown eyes. An uneasy feeling returned in the pit of my stomach. My hands clasped together as I held the tears back.

Dad, who resembled a young Warren Beatty with his brown hair and easy smile, winked at me in the mirror. Daddy's little girl. The one who used to make breakfast in bed for his birthday every year since I was six. And in return, he read stories to me. Made sure the room was safe from all monsters. Held me during my first heartache over a guy. Always looked out for me.

I glanced over at Mom who sat in the passenger seat. Her usual dyed blond hair was now brown with gray roots. The first time she ever dyed her hair, people thought she was my sister. And there were a few times when we got along, that she did feel like my sister.

The whole drive she would softly cry. Stop. Then cry again.

I didn't understand it. If they were both so sad, why were they making me leave home? I wanted to scream at them to take me back. I was fine. I could prove to them that I wasn't insane. I could be friends again with Mom. I wouldn't yell at her anymore. I could be the perfect daughter.

But I never said a word.

No one did. Just the sound of the wipers swiping across the windshield and the annoying pitter-patter of rain. I hated the sound. I gripped the handle on the door, wishing I could claw my way out of the car and run.

I hated being inside a car. It was like a trap—always taking me back to that fateful day. I leaned my aching head against the cool window, hoping a panic attack wouldn't come, and watched the trees pass by in a blur of green.

The hospital was an hour away from home in a quaint little town called Fairview. It wasn't known for much—just the fact that it had a mental institution. Dad kept a steady forty-five miles an hour down the two-lane road. If Mom were driving, she'd be doing eighty. The faster she could get me away, the better for her.

The storm had ended but the dark clouds remained. As we turned into a parking lot, knots tied in my stomach. I arrived at Fairview Mental Institution. It looked more like a university campus than a hospital.

"You don't have to do this," I whispered so quietly that I wondered if they heard me. It was a hopeless attempt, but I had to try.

Dad shut the engine off and sighed. "Sweetie, maybe being away from everything will help you feel better." He twisted around and his gaze met my water-filled eyes.

As I got out of the car, I looked around at the serene campus. Water dripped from the tall oak and pine trees and onto the perfectly landscaped rose bushes and perennials. Steam rose from the pavement. There were no sounds except for Dad removing my suitcase from the trunk and Mom complaining about the humidity.

Maybe Dad was right. Keeping me away from everyone, including the memories, would help.

We made our way toward the two-story brick building that looked like it had been built in the seventies, and I gritted my teeth together as my mouth salivated uncontrollably. I was going to be sick. The uneasy feeling was trying to escape but I swallowed constantly, keeping it down.

The sterile scent of the hospital and the stark atmosphere was all too familiar to me. After the long trip, I was tired and wanted to sleep but as usual, I was afraid to sleep.

Dad walked up to the counter and spoke to a woman who looked to be in her mid-twenties, and had brown hair like mine. She smiled at us and was way too energetic. Even her ponytail bounced as she walked out from behind the counter.

"Hi, you must be Corinne." She held out her hand and Dad nudged me. I took her hand and she squeezed it so hard I thought my bones would break. "I'm Nurse Smith, the head nurse of the ward you'll be staying." Her high-pitched voice irritated me. "You'll enjoy it here."

So easy for her to say. She gets to leave every day.

After we signed admittance forms, she showed us around the ward to the cafeteria to the art room to the library, which looked like a high school. As we walked, she talked about each room and what patients could do during their stay, like it was a vacation resort.

"Each floor has its own ward, and we put those with certain disorders together," Nurse Smith said, and opened a door that led outside. "Unfortunately, new admissions aren't allowed many privileges in the beginning, for safety reasons. Corinne will have to have a chaperone for the first few weeks. We have someone on staff here all day and all night, so if the patients need anything, we have a rotating staff that's here twenty-four hours," she assured my parents.

We followed her on a sidewalk path that was lined with holly bushes. Tall maples and oaks shadowed the large campus-like yard. The sun came out, but it was hot and too bright.

"What about interaction with other patients?" Mom asked.

Of course she'd ask that.

"It depends on if they want to interact, really. A lot of the girls keep to themselves, but some have made really good friends here." She acted as if this was the best place to live.

"What she means, is that she's afraid I'll lash out or attack someone."

"Corinne, that's not at all what I meant. I'm concerned for your safety."

"Doubtful," I mumbled. "You're just trying to get rid of me."

Mom halted and twisted around. "Corinne, that's enough," she snapped. The whites around her blue eyes were red and the vein on the right side of her head protruded. "We are putting you here so you can get help. End of story."

So she says.

We went inside another building that had closed offices lining the hallway. Nurse Smith led us into a vast office with a window that spanned the entire left wall. A large desk sat in the center of the room with a leather armchair resting beside a matching leather couch. Psychologists and their leather. Yes, I know you're rich.

A woman with thin, curly red hair leapt out of her leather chair from behind her desk and warmly smiled. I looked at the tall, slender woman that stood before me. She wore a dark pantsuit with a cream blouse under the jacket.

"Good afternoon," she said. "I am Dr. Meisner." She shook my parents' hands and then mine. Her hand was soft and warm. "You must be Corinne." She kept smiling. "Please, have a seat." She offered and we sat on the couch and Nurse Smith left. "I know this is all overwhelming for you and I just want to assure you we will make this as comfortable as possible."

Wasn't that something doctors told patients who were going to die?

"I only know a little bit about you. I would like to ask questions so I can get a feel for the situation," Dr. Meisner continued. "Is that okay, Corinne?" Her gray eyes focused on me, asking my approval.

I was taken off guard. No one ever *asked* if they could question me. "Um, sure," I quietly spoke, feeling my parents' eyes on me. I crossed my arms in front of my chest.

"Okay. Some of these questions might be too much for

you now, so if you don't feel like answering, I ask that your parents answer for you as best they can."

Great. I was sure Mom would have a field day with that. The tightness returned in my stomach, and my heart pounded. I didn't want to be here. And I didn't want to tell this stranger anything especially with my parents there. Judging me.

"Have you ever experienced any trauma before this?"

"No."

"What are your symptoms?" Her voice was articulate and calm.

I bit my lip. "I can't sleep. I have nightmares. I see things from the accident." I tried not to sound crazy. But as the words left my lips, I knew I was giving my parents proof that I was insane and needed to be here.

"Any other symptoms?" She probed.

"I'm sad all the time. I can't remember a lot except for the accident. No matter how hard I try to forget, it's always there reminding me, like it's torturing me." I let the words flow freely. "I feel guilty for what I've done. I feel numb all the time. The absence of him is so overwhelming and I feel as if it would be easier for everyone if I weren't here. To not be a burden." Heat rose to my cheeks, and I bowed my head.

I surprised myself at how honest I was being with her because when I told my friend, Lisa, she stormed out on me.

"I imagine these feelings disrupt your everyday life."

I nodded. "Yes."

"You were hospitalized for a suicide attempt about a month ago in April, correct?"

Why was she asking me this if she already knew? I didn't want to talk to her anymore. It was ridiculous and pointless.

"Corinne, answer the question," Mom said.

I sighed. "She obviously knows the answer."

"Adjust your attitude."

I rolled my eyes.

Dr. Meisner flipped the page in her notebook. "Do you have any physical pain?"

"This is stupid."

"She has headaches from an injury she sustained in the crash," Dad answered for me.

"She hasn't been herself for months." Mom chimed in. "She doesn't listen to music anymore or read. Anything and everything will startle her. I accidentally dropped a ketchup bottle one time and it splattered everywhere, and she started hyperventilating. She's always afraid of being in the car. She quit school, work, hanging out with her friends, and broke up with her boyfriend. I guess that's a good thing because they were too serious and I think it's best that she not focus on that right now."

I glared at my mom. "Because you know what's best."

"You need a friend, not a boyfriend." Mom turned back to Dr. Meisner. "She constantly stays in her room, moping. She's angry a lot and takes it out on us."

I grinded my teeth, ignoring the ache it brought my jaw, and tried to keep my breathing level. I clenched my fists.

Dr. Meisner nodded. "I've gotten what I need for now. Corinne, you and I will meet every day for an hour each session. You will have group sessions three times a week from 9 a.m. until noon. And you'll meet with your case manager once a week."

"Do I have to?"

"These sessions are optional, however, if you do not attend, you won't get any privileges nor will you get well enough to leave here."

"How long do I have to stay here?"

She gave me a pitying look. "As long as it takes to get you better."

My eyes watered and I refused to look at her. I had to sign more forms, which felt like I was signing my life away. My parents hugged me goodbye, and promised to visit.

Then, they left me.

CHAPTER TWO

The sky rumbled like a rubber mallet hitting a drum and heavy rain pelted the windows. The security light's blurry orange glow seeped inside the room, shadowing the bars from the window on the tiled floor. I closed my eyes tight knowing something bad was about to happen. And then I was back there again.

I jerked the wheel but the tires refused to grip the road. I lost control. The car acted as a magnet to the great oak. It slammed into the tree, crushing itself. Glass exploded all around me as the metal crumpled. My body jerked forward but the seatbelt held me back. My hands flung to my face, covering it from the flying glass.

I screamed.

With an intake of breath, my eyes opened wide. My heart beat against my chest like rapid fire. I gasped for air and trembled as a tingling sensation scurried throughout my arms. Tightness developed in my throat and my body heat rose. The dark room swam before me and I clutched the sheets, waiting for it to end.

When it finally did, I collapsed back on the lumpy bed. Another vision. And then I would panic. Like some unfortunate doom lingered over my head. I didn't know what it was.

A feeling of dread washed over me as I realized I may

have actually screamed aloud. Lovely. I was sure Emma was glad to have some crazy roommate who screamed randomly. I sighed.

Just twenty-four hours ago, I was in my own bed, angry that my parents packed a suitcase for me. I missed my room. It wasn't drab. Or so small it could make someone feel claustrophobic. It definitely didn't have stupid floral pictures on the walls. They weren't a boring white either. I couldn't believe I actually started feeling homesick.

I wanted to sleep, but I knew the nightmares or visions or whatever would prevent me. So I lay there and gripped the itchy blanket, wishing for the storm to pass, like some little kid. I jumped at every flash of lightning and every explosion of thunder. I was seventeen years old and scared of storms. How pathetic.

The early morning sun shone through the high window and into the room. The silhouette of the metal bars swept across the floor. I must have fallen asleep but it wasn't restful.

I noticed Emma's bed already neatly made. Why was she in this hellhole? What was wrong with her? She seemed fine to me.

I stared at the wall and then realized the frames of the floral paintings were actually glued to the wall and no glass covered them. The pictures were plain. Like the colors had faded. The pale pink and green colors almost looked black and white.

The door opened and I jumped.

A tall, dark haired nurse with a small harelip emerged from the doorway. "Come on, dear. Shower time." Her hair looked like a boy's cut and she seemed rather nonchalant. Her white scrubs were just as bleak as the whiteness in the room.

"Where's my stuff?"

"We had to go through your suitcase. Your clothes are in these three drawers." She pointed to the left side of the mirror-less dresser. "I grabbed your shower things out of our cabinet and it's in this." She held up a plastic bag.

"I don't want a shower."

"Come on. Out of bed."

We stared at each other until I angrily pushed back the thin blanket and got out of bed. I figured she would end up using her burly arms to force me and I didn't want her touching me.

I got some clothes out of the drawers and then she followed me into the tiny private bathroom. A toilet was in front of a sink stand with an aluminum mirror and a shower next to it.

"I think I can figure it out from here," I said as she shut the door behind her. There was hardly any room to breathe.

"I have no doubt." She pulled out a worn romance novel from her scrubs pocket.

"Are you seriously going to watch?"

"I'm going to be reading. But when you need some shampoo or soap, I'll pour some in your hand. You have fifteen minutes, so I'd hurry up if I were you." She leaned against the door and opened her book.

I glanced at my reflection in the mirror and stopped. A tired, miserable girl looked back at me. Dark circles pasted beneath her blue eyes. Her shoulder-length brown hair that surrounded her petite shoulders was matted. Her large gray t-shirt hung on her like a small dress over her red shorts. And no smile stretched across her downtrodden face.

I didn't want this woman, this stranger, here with me. Seeing what I was seeing.

"Can I use the toilet?"

"Absolutely," she said, her nose still stuck in her book. She wouldn't leave.

"Is this going to be an everyday thing?"

"Yep." She turned the page.

Humiliated, I slowly sat on the toilet and did my business. Afterward, I turned on the shower and undressed quickly before stepping behind the dark curtain. There was just enough room in the shower for me to turn around. Like Nurse Harelip said, she handed little amounts of the soap and shampoo.

The water was cold and my body shook violently. "Is there any warm water?"

"Sorry."

"Guess you don't care if I get hypothermia."

I hurried through the achingly cold shower and dressed while the nurse stayed glued to her book. I brushed my teeth and didn't notice a change in my appearance by taking a shower.

"Can I ask Dr. Meisner that I never do this again?" I handed her my toothbrush in its holder.

"Every patient has to take a shower every day." She placed all my toiletries back into the bag and then opened the door for me. I hugged myself from the cool air and tried to get warm. She walked out of the room, closing the door behind her.

I didn't want to leave the room and have people talk to me. I probably would lose points since I didn't go down to breakfast. But I didn't care. I sat on the edge of my bed, ignoring the water dripping from my hair onto my jeans.

I jumped again when the door opened and Emma walked through balancing a glass of orange juice and a muffin in one hand and a glass of water in the other.

"Morning." She smiled a little. "I kinda figured that you really didn't want to eat with everyone so I brought you a muffin and some juice." She handed it to me.

I looked up and met her brown eyes. Dark half moons clung underneath them and she had high cheekbones that made the side of her face rather sallow. A silver stud adorned her left eyebrow. Her thick hair was mostly brown but the ends were black from the dye growing out. The sun made her olive complexion glow. Her black sweatshirt and matching pants swallowed her emaciated body.

I took the muffin and juice from her and nodded. I never really liked orange juice, but I was rather parched. Orange juice was always David's favorite.

"It's really not bad," Emma said. "Everyone tends to keep

to themselves, but they're nice. Except Tracy, and I think it's because she's lonely or just demands attention."

Ahh, Tracy. She had stared at me all through dinner last night and kept asking why I was here.

"I can stop talking if you want."

I shrugged. Her voice was soft and calming so I didn't mind. But I didn't talk because every time I wanted to speak, the words just wouldn't come out right. I sipped the pulpy orange juice, and hid my grimace from Emma as the acidic drink moistened my dry throat. I set the muffin down on the nightstand.

"Did you sleep well?" she asked. "I know I did. Apparently, it stormed last night pretty badly, but I never heard a thing."

Did she really not hear me scream? Or was she just being polite? Then again, if I did actually scream, I'm sure a nurse would have come to check on me. "I slept okay," I lied.

Emma plopped down on the bed. It made an awful sound as though she was going to fall through. She was small, like me, however. Beds must be old or just shabby.

"It'll get better," she said. "I see you met Nurse Whitman." Emma rolled her eyes. "She can be annoying. But I promise the shower thing won't last long."

"Why do they do that?"

"You're new. So you're on suicide watch."

"So they have to watch me in the shower?"

"Apparently. We all went through it though. Just follow the rules and you'll be okay. Don't get mad or they'll send you to hell. At least that's what we call it. Oh and do not, under any circumstances, get involved with any of the guys. They freak out when that happens."

"Does that happen often?"

"Tracy's done that a few times. I'm sure it happens more than we hear though. People are lonely."

I couldn't imagine hooking up with some guy in a mental hospital. Then again, I never imagined I would ever be in one.

"Where are you from?" she asked.

"Birmingham."

"Ooh really? I'm from there, too. I miss it. I can't wait to go back, but who knows when I'll get out of here?"

"You seem fine to me."

"I have my good days and bad days. Plus, it's nice to have a roommate. Haven't had one in about five months." She brushed her hair behind her ears.

Five months? How long had she been here?

I finished my juice, propped myself against the headboard of the bed, and pulled the covers up to my stomach. I couldn't seem to get warm enough. "What do you usually do all day? Do we just sit around doing nothing? How is that supposed to help us?"

"No. For most of the day, we have therapy sessions. I like going to the library and getting a book. Sometimes we'll watch movies out in the common room. It's all optional—even the medication part. They want you to make the choice to get better. The more you follow their rules, though, the better your chances are for getting out."

"Doesn't sound too optional to me."

"I know. But if you're like Tracy, she's been in here like three or four times. Since you're new, you'll be busy with evaluations and therapy for the first couple of days."

"More evaluations? What do they need to evaluate? They already know I'm a nutcase."

The door opened and startled me.

Nurse Smith held a clipboard and stood in the doorway. She smiled brightly in her baby blue scrubs. "Good morning, Corinne. Are you ready for your therapy session with Dr. Meisner?"

"I already met with her yesterday."

"Well, that was yesterday. Now it's today. Eat your muffin and I'll take you over in a few minutes," she said and then closed the door.

Reluctantly, I pushed the covers off me and stood from the bed. "I don't see why I have to keep talking to these people. They don't ever solve anything and they haven't *made me better*. They certainly can't bring him back. What do they know about pain?" I said aloud as I pulled socks from the dresser and slid them forcefully on my cold feet.

"I'm sorry," Emma quietly said.

Heat rushed to my cheeks as I remembered I wasn't alone. I jammed my feet into my tennis shoes and walked past Emma's bed to open the door.

Nurse Smith waited, just like she said. I followed her outside to where the bright sun greeted us. I immediately started to thaw from the warmth. Everything was still damp from the storm and I inhaled the sweet sickly scent of honeysuckle. But the smell didn't put a smile on my face like it always had before.

"Did you sleep well last night?" Nurse Smith asked.

"Sure," I mumbled.

We reached Dr. Meisner's office and Nurse Smith opened the door for me.

"Thank you, Nurse." Dr. Meisner smiled and then the nurse closed the door behind her. "Have a seat, Corinne."

The big cushiony couch squeaked as I sunk down into it. I crossed my arms, waiting.

"How are you today?" She took the seat across from the couch.

"I'm okay, I guess."

She had a notepad, just like my previous doctors. Writing down notes that would be on my permanent record. *Corinne needs to be locked away for good*. Couldn't they save all the time and energy and just let me go? Why wouldn't they just let me die?

"Did you sleep well?"

"Same as usual."

"What's usual for you?"

We locked eyes. I hoped she wasn't serious with that question. Did she forget everything I told her yesterday? Was this why we had therapy every day? "No, I did not sleep well."

"Not many patients sleep well on the first night. But you'd mentioned yesterday you haven't been sleeping well in months. Did you have any nightmares?"

"Of course." Not like they ever went away.

"Can you describe them?"

"Being here is a nightmare. Why am I even here?"

"You tell me."

"My parents made me come. Didn't you just talk to me yesterday?"

"Yes, but now it's just you and me. Why do you think your parents put you in here?" she asked in a calm voice.

I peered out the massive window at the cherry blossoms. The white petals glided in the air like snow. As if they were carefree. Like they were pieces of me drifting away.

"Corinne?"

I turned and looked at her. "Do you think you can fix me?"

"I'm going to do my best, but I will need your help."

"You can't fix me. Nobody can. My parents put me here because they couldn't deal with me."

"They want to help you. You've been through a lot but I'm here to help you cope with it properly."

"Is that what all your books tell you to say?" I nodded to the bookshelf. I wondered if she had the same ridiculous books as all the other doctors.

She smiled slightly. "The books don't really talk."

Touché.

A few seconds of silence filled between us, and I didn't want to be there anymore. I usually sat in the other doctors' offices, silent. I never wanted to talk to any of them.

My head felt as if a hammer were smashing my skull. My eyes felt as if they would pop out any second.

"You never described your nightmare."

They never let anything go. "I have a headache."

"Do you have any other physical pains?"

"No."

"I read your charts after your attempt and you admitted to

having a fast-beating heart and tightness in the chest sometimes. And your mom mentioned you hyperventilating."

"Well if you know this, then why are you asking?"

"Do you still have these symptoms?"

"Yes."

She scribed more in her notepad. "What do you feel when your heart races and you have the tightness in your chest?"

"Like I'm going to die. Or that something bad is going to happen."

"Does it end?"

"Eventually."

"How do you feel when it's over?"

"Tired. I want it to end permanently. But it's the same every night. I fall asleep, have a nightmare, and wake up in a panic. Or hallucinate in the middle of the day. It's like I'm actually there again. It feels so real. That's why I don't want to be here anymore. You think I want to live like this? You think I can cope with that *properly*? You're the expert."

"I believe with time, yes, you will learn how."

"You already know everything that happened to me."

"No, I don't."

"You have all my charts. It's pointless to meet. Why don't you just give me the drugs, then we won't have to meet again."

"Drugs can't fix everything. What are you feeling right now?"

"That I want to leave." Anger was seeping through my voice, but hers stayed the calm voice.

"What are you *feeling*?"

"I don't know," I snapped. "Stop asking me." I looked away.

I heard her pen scrawl across her notepad, noting every little gesture or comment I made. The less I said, the less she could write about. I watched the trees outside. They were motionless—numb.

"What is going through your mind right now?" she asked.

I shifted uncomfortably, and held my aching head in my

hand as my elbow rested on the arm of the couch.

"Try not to push those thoughts to the back your mind. If you are able to release them, you won't put so much stress on your head."

Like talking about it was really going to help.

"I'm going to place you on an antidepressant."

"And is that the magic drug to cure me? You know, I've taken it before and it didn't work."

"This is a different one."

"Whatever."

"I am also going to prescribe an anti-anxiety, a mood stabilizer, and an anti-psychotic for the time being. These medications will help treat depression, anxiety, improve your sleep and decrease nightmares. They will also help diminish the flashbacks."

I doubted that. Just as I thought. Pump me full of pills.

"I think we made good progress today." I thought she was delusional. "Let's go back and get you some medicine." She stood from the chair, and placed her notepad and pen on her desk.

I got up from the couch and Dr. Meisner followed me out of the office and locked her door. We walked back to the main building in silence. I hated having escorts wherever I went. As if they were the hawk and I was their prey. But at least Dr. Meisner didn't attempt to make small talk.

Dr. Meisner walked to the nurse's station and wrote on a chart for my medication. She then gave me a small plastic cup with a white pill.

"This is for your headache. If you have any problems of any kind be sure to let me know. Sleep well tonight and I'll see you tomorrow."

I swallowed the pill and folded my arms across my chest as I walked to my room.

Emma lay on her bed, reading again, with ear buds in. I retreated to my bed and lay down on my side, pulling my knees up to my chest. The demon inside my head was pushing my skull apart, splitting it right down the center. My hands, on either side of my head, tried pushing my skull back together. The pounding wouldn't stop.

"How was it?" Emma asked.

I hugged my knees tightly. "Fine."

"You'll like her eventually," she said. "She's my therapist, too. Do you wanna go for a walk? It's a beautiful day."

I shook my head. I closed my eyes and fell asleep.

CHAPTER THREE

When I woke, I saw Emma lounging on her bed, still reading and listening to music. I wondered if she had even moved while I slept. I turned over onto my back and rubbed my eyes.

She closed her book. "How was your nap?" She lay on her stomach with her feet in the air, facing me.

"Good." I sat up. "What time is it?"

"It's almost dinner time. I'm not in the mood to go tonight. Maybe we won't have to sit next to Tracy."

"Maybe. How long have you been here?" I asked Emma shyly.

She hesitated. "Seven months." She sounded disappointed. "But I left and came back."

My heart sank when I heard her answer. How long would I have to stay here? They already knew what was wrong with me. Could they really take away my pain? How was keeping me here going to fix any of that? Would I have to come back after I left, too?

"I know it seems like a prison," Emma said. "But they really do help you."

I looked up. "Are you some sort of advocate for them?"

She smiled and rolled her eyes. "I should be. How old are you?"

"Seventeen, but I'll be eighteen next month. You?"

"Sixteen. Couldn't even finish up junior year of high school because I wound up here. Mom told me I needed to grow up and stop all this nonsense. But she doesn't get it." She rolled her eyes. "Sorry. It just pisses me off sometimes when I think about it."

"It's okay." Her thoughts were similar to mine. What happened to her that forced her into this place?

"Are you ready for dinner?"

I nodded and got out of bed.

We both walked sluggishly down to the cafeteria. There was already a line and I felt like I was back in high school with everything on a schedule. We got our food and sat at an empty table that would soon fill up with others from our ward, and of course, Tracy.

"Wow, two nights in a row for you, Emma," Tracy said, and sat across from her. "Quite an accomplishment." Her long wavy red hair parted on the right side and covered her left eye. Dark eyeliner circled her brown eyes and she wore three necklaces.

"Shut up, Tracy."

"Oh are you going to cry? You know, you looked so much better before you started eating. Very pretty and very thin. I wonder what your mom will say once you've gained all this weight."

I couldn't believe she was saying those things. Emma ignored her, but I could see tears in her eyes.

"Tracy, I wonder what your mom will say when she has to pay for another year here," a boy with sandy blond hair said. He sat catty-cornered from me at the end of the table. His brown eyes looked up as Ginger sat next to Tracy. Ginger wore a hooded sweatshirt and I could barely see her blue eyes from the heavy dark eye makeup she wore. I liked her short messy hair that went from blond to black. Her skin was milky like mine.

"Whatever, Scott," Tracy said. "If I wanted out of here so bad, I could easily make up lies and have those therapists eating out of my hand. You'll be back in here again once you realize the world out there is filled with stupid people. I am so much better than any of those assholes."

For a while, we endured Tracy's dominating conversation, pointing out faults of everyone who sat at the table. Veronica was a fake. Ginger deserved her abuse, though she admired the scars on her arms. Emma was fat. Todd really did hear the voices and that he should listen to them. And Scott was pathetic. I remained quiet but she didn't skip me. She just kept telling me she'd figure it out eventually. She reminded me of Lisa Hazel. Lisa was my friend, the closest one I had. She had been there for me when no one else had and never left my side, until I told her what I did.

At one point, Tracy started talking to this boy with black hair and left us alone. She never pointed out his faults. I couldn't concentrate on Emma and Ginger's conversation because Tracy and the black-haired boy were noisy. A loud bang sounded and I jumped, knocking over my soda all into Scott's lap. He leapt up, letting the brown drink drip onto the floor.

And I started to hyperventilate. I wanted to leave, but didn't know where I could go hide. I felt arms around me and someone crooning in my ear. But I only focused on the one voice that always helped me. I remembered his words. *Focus on your breathing. Breathe in. Breathe out.* A few seconds later, I calmed down.

"Are you okay?" Scott and Emma asked simultaneously.

"Wow. So you freak out over people dropping trays?" Tracy said and then she howled in laughter. I could feel blood filling my cheeks and tears clouded my eyes. I bit my lip as I grabbed some napkins and handed them to Scott.

"I'm so sorry. I don't know what happened. I—."

"It's cool. Really." He smiled.

"I should go." I grabbed my tray and stood.

"You don't have to," Emma said. "Come join us in the common room." Scott, Ginger, and Emma followed me with their trays and emptied their trash.

We went to the common room to watch a movie, after Scott changed. The room was actually quiet with plenty of seating for everyone on the ward, and then some. A couple of lamps filled the room with yellow light. A long gray fabric couch rested in front of the television while a matching loveseat sat to the left and a recliner on the right. The faint light of dusk leaked through the windows behind the large television. I was surprised that the walls were a light coral instead of the usual boring white. Though it still had the same floral paintings that were in our rooms.

Scott put in a movie while Emma and I sat on the couch. Ginger reclined in the chair and Scott spread out on the loveseat, his long legs rested on the opposite arm and his feet dangled.

They never asked about my stupid episode, which I was glad. And they didn't seem to make a big deal out of it either, which was nice.

The movie started, which was a rather dumb movie. I wondered why Tracy wasn't in there tormenting us, but glad she wasn't. I half paid attention to the movie and somewhere in the middle of it, Scott and Ginger started making fun of it.

"I think I can actually feel myself getting dumber," Scott said. "I even used to smoke pot, but this is ridiculous."

"What, you never had five hot chick aliens merge into a giantess while you were baked?" Ginger asked.

"Not that I recall. But maybe seeing a giantess eat people." I smirked.

"I could use some pot right now," Ginger said. "I once set my bangs on fire while trying to light a bowl."

Scott belted out a loud laugh. Emma and I snickered.

"One time I was so high with some friends and I went down to get some food, and I think I fell asleep on the couch or something. The next day my mom was doing laundry and wanted to know why I had a peanut butter and jelly sandwich in my back pocket of my pants."

We all laughed. And for a moment, I felt like a normal teenager. I couldn't remember the last time I felt that way, but it didn't last.

"Wow." Ginger shook her head. "I'm going to have a smoke. Anyone wanna join?" She set the recliner back to its normal position and stood.

We left the lounge and walked out into the hallway. As we passed the nurses' station, a short Hispanic nurse with pink scrubs came out with a clipboard.

"Where are you all going?" she asked.

"Outside to smoke," Ginger said.

"Don't worry, we'll make sure she doesn't do anything," Scott said, placing an arm on my shoulders.

"Arm, Scott." The nurse warned.

He immediately removed it. "Sorry."

She nodded and walked in the opposite direction.

We snickered as we walked out into the cool night. The bullfrogs croaked from the pond next to us. It was dark and because we were out in the boonies, the stars were incredibly bright. We were away from everything. There were no houses or subdivisions around us. It was almost like we had our own community for a few miles.

The brochures advertised that our facility was on 14 acres of land. Private! Quiet! But did it mention in the small print that it was a place to keep all the crazies away from the rest of the world so everyone could feel safe not being near us?

"So how's your first full day?" Scott asked.

Ginger pulled a cigarette from her pack, lit it, and then took a long drag.

I shrugged. "I guess okay. I definitely didn't like taking a shower with that nurse this morning."

"Oh man. Nurse Whitman." Ginger shook her head.

"Sometimes I wonder if she was a bouncer previously," Scott said.

Ginger flicked her cigarette forcing the ashes to fall. "She certainly has the body for it. I was on that suicide watch crap, too. Don't worry, she's way too involved in her Fabio romance to even pay much attention to you."

"I was on suicide watch, too," Scott confessed.

"Thankfully, I only have two weeks left of this place."

"Ugh, stop talking like that. I will seriously miss you."

I wished I only had two weeks left.

"Who's your therapist?" Scott asked me.

"Dr. Meisner."

Ginger exhaled smoke. "I heard she's good. I have Dr. Creephead. He just stares at me like he wants me."

Scott laughed. "Gin, he doesn't want you."

"Whatever. He's Tracy's doctor, too. Wonder if that means I'm going to turn into her."

"That's ridiculous," Scott said.

Ginger shrugged. "Do you like Dr. Meisner?"

"She's okay," I said. "I got mad at her today."

"I've gotten mad at her, too," Emma said. "Like, I'll get better, but something puts me right back to the beginning."

Ginger exhaled the rest of her cigarette and then stubbed it out on the wooden railing. "Same here. I hate group because it's like they all talk about us afterward. 'Ginger did this today. Ginger slept too long. Ginger fraternizes too much.' Ugh, what do they expect us to do? Just sit around in our rooms all day until therapy? I'm not going to group tomorrow."

Scott sighed. "Gin, you should go. Don't start skipping."

"I don't see how it helps. All they ever talk about is stupid stuff. No one ever talks about their issues."

"So what's the point?" I asked.

"Exactly."

"Because if you go, they'll see you participating. And if you follow the rules, you'll get out sooner."

Ginger grimaced. "I've been here for a year, Scott. Nothing I've done has gotten me closer."

"We should probably go," Emma whispered to me. "We're gonna head back to our room. We'll see you tomorrow."

"Goodnight," Scott told us.

Once inside, I turned to Emma. "Are they secretly dating?"

"No. They're just really good friends. Ginger sorta latched onto him when he arrived. I'm afraid she'll fall apart when he leaves, though."

We got back to our room and Emma took a shower. I didn't have any books to read, but I found some pictures in my dresser that apparently Mom and Dad had packed.

The one on top was of David giving me a piggyback ride. I almost didn't recognize the happy girl in the photo. My eyes watered. I stopped again at the last picture in the group. I stared at it, still shocked that my mom put it in there, since she was the one who decided we needed to break up. It was of James and me hugging and smiling. My finger carefully touched the photo over his short brown hair and sapphire blue eyes. I lay on my bed and let my thoughts drift back to James. My eyes stared at the ceiling, but all I saw was James, my sweet James. He was the only one I could think about who didn't make me completely lose it.

I wanted everything to be normal. I wanted him to be holding me. Or my brother telling me jokes. I just wanted to be myself again. I turned over on my side, facing the wall, and let the tears out.

Everything was so normal then, but that was two years ago. It was impossible for the guilt, the emptiness, and the pain to go away.

CHAPTER FOUR

I survived my first week of living in a crazy house. It had started off better than I ever expected. Though, in group I didn't say anything and just answered some questions from Dr. Meisner in our sessions. My parents didn't come back, though Emma told me that we weren't allowed visitors in the beginning. Fine by me. All Mom would do is yell until she was blue in the face anyway.

A day trip to the mall had been scheduled, but since I had no privileges, I couldn't go. The ward was quiet with most everyone gone. I was bored and couldn't do anything unless I had a chaperone. It just didn't seem worth the trouble. Besides, I was safe in my room. No one could see me panic over something stupid.

I picked at the little clumps of lint on the blanket and dumped them on the floor. When I heard a soft knock at my door, I raised up on my elbows and answered.

The door opened, and Scott peaked his head in. "Hey, sorry I didn't know if you'd be asleep. You wanna go to the library?"

I shrugged. "Sure."

The moist hot air clung to me like an invisible wet blanket once we walked outside. Birds flitted around and a squirrel stopped on the sidewalk, looked up at us, and then scurried away. The library was in the old building on the hill, not far from our ward. It was nice that I didn't need a nurse. Scott acted as my chaperone and he didn't make me talk. It was a nice comfortable silence.

When we entered, Scott returned a book and I found myself in the S aisle in the fiction section. I grabbed the new Nicholas Sparks book but my eyes also swept across *The Notebook*. I pulled it out from the shelf and stared at the cover. I sat on the floor and opened it. As I read the first opening sentences, my eyes watered. I could hear James's soft voice reading me the story. Sitting with me and comforting me. I couldn't hold the tears back. My hands drew to my face to cover it and I felt the book slide to the floor.

"Corinne." I heard Scott.

I removed my hands and wiped the tears. Scott sat down next to me and wrapped his arm around me. He rubbed my arms while I softly cried.

"Sorry," I said, and pulled away from him. There was a strict no-touching policy and I didn't want to get him in trouble.

"You don't have to apologize. It's the nature of the beast."

"I hate it. I hate the constant pain. I hate being reminded of everything I've lost. Don't they realize I would be better off dead?"

"Personally, I don't think you would be."

"How did you manage to survive this place?"

He gave a slight smile. "I haven't yet. But this place is nothing compared to facing my own struggles. When I first got here, I was like you. I didn't want to talk to anyone and I held a lot inside. I didn't think they could really help and figured they'd just pump me full of pills and hope for the best like most doctors I'd been to."

"Of course."

"For years, I've wanted nothing more than to end my misery. I tried to shoot myself but the chamber locked. Call it a sign or whatever, but I told my dad and we came to the decision to bring me here."

"That's terrible. Your dad seems very supportive. Mine is too, but I think part of him doesn't want to get too involved because of my mom. She hates me."

"I doubt that. She could have just abandoned you and wanted nothing to do with you."

It was true. But I never saw it that way. "She just doesn't understand me. She says I'm the one always getting mad at her, but I know she's disgusted with me for what I've done."

"A lot of people don't understand what you're going through and may not know how to act around you. I lost my mom a few years ago to cancer, and I guess it put me in a bad place. Just couldn't get over it. And then you get to hear endless people talk about how you're a coward or weak because you're taking the easy way out."

I looked up into his brown eyes. I couldn't believe how much we had in common. "My best friend did that."

"Called you a coward?"

"Among other things."

"One thing I've learned is that those who won't support you aren't worth your time."

I bowed my head and focused on my fingers pulling off and on my white gold ring. It was a slender ring that carved in a small, intricate pattern containing a round sapphire with two round diamonds on either side. I loved it for its beauty and because of who gave it to me.

"It's not that Lisa didn't support me. She did. Until I tried to kill myself. She had come over to talk to me after she got back from her beach trip with her boyfriend Jack. It was the first week we had been apart since all this started." I shook my head.

"It's okay, Corinne."

"We were in my room, and I was trying to tune out her loud voice. As usual, she was irritated with me when I got sad or whatever."

She asked me what was wrong and I said nothing.

"That's a lie," she said. "You're not yourself. I mean, things were fine for a while when we'd go out all the time, but then you just stopped altogether." Her raspy voice turned cold and stern.

Lisa wasn't exactly drop-dead gorgeous, but she sure acted like it with her robust body and thick long blond hair. She had brown eyes that could intimidate a lion. I'd always known her as sort of a man-eater, for lack of a better word.

Lisa kept talking, but I wasn't listening. Her loud voice drowned out my thoughts.

I looked away from her intense stare and focused outside at the wooded backyard. I watched the wind rustle the green leaves on the trees. The rain poured down the window in squiggly lines. Lightning flashed followed by the roaring thunder that rattled the windows, and I closed my eyes and prayed I wouldn't have another flashback. Or flip out and scare her. It was so hard not to think of that day.

"I mean, why are you always so depressed lately?"

She reminded me of Mom giving me the third degree. Why couldn't they leave me alone?

"Talk to me, Corinne." She raised her voice. Her hands molded on either side of her wide hips.

"What do you want me to say, Lisa? Everyone hates me because of what I've done. Not that I blame them. I hate myself."

She groaned. "Back to that again? This is so irritating. Is that why you just up and stopped hanging out with me and broke it off with Will?"

"Lisa, no. Will and I were never together. He was just some guy I met at a party. A distraction. It was a mistake."

"Mistake? He was so much better to you than James ever was."

"No, he wasn't. But that doesn't matter. James and I are done." I sighed. My head began aching. "Leave me alone, please." I didn't know what to say to her.

"I'm not going to leave you alone until you tell me what's going on."

I looked at her reflection in the window as she towered over me. I wanted to distance myself from everyone. I didn't deserve them. They couldn't take away my pain. I turned around and saw the confusion in Lisa's immense eyes.

I sighed.

Lisa furrowed her eyebrows.

I wiped the tears from my weary eyes. I knew I was about to lose my friend, but she needed to know. I bit my lip. I rubbed the sweat from the palms of my hands onto my jeans.

"Imagine diving into a swimming pool on a hot summer's day," I said and she listened intently. "The cool water rushes over you like a blanket. You come up for air, but suddenly something pulls you under. You can't breathe. Your heart suddenly loses a beat. It feels like a snake wraps around you. Constricting you of any happiness you might have had. You lose hope. Nothing's the same anymore and it never will be."

"What the hell are you talking about? What's all this gibberish you're spouting about constricting and swimming?" She jeered with a bitterness lingering in her voice.

I knew these subjects angered her. "Lisa, do you know why I dropped out of school?"

"Wait—you did *what?*"

I exhaled. "I dropped out of school right when you left to go to the beach."

"What the hell have you been doing for the past few weeks? I thought you were sick. So now, you've been *lying* to me?" She scowled.

I moved to my desk and for a moment, we were silent, and all I heard was the pattering of the rain outside. "Lisa, I have been sick."

"What's wrong, Corinne? Why are you crying? Why don't you ever want to do anything anymore? Is it me?"

"No." I took a deep breath and let it out. "Lisa, I dropped out of school because I can't deal with this. I-I tried to kill myself," I said, barely above a whisper.

"You're kidding right?"

I shook my head.

"That's what you had to tell me? That you're a fucking psycho and you just can't take it? You're just like my father.

Killing yourself and leaving me behind. You think killing yourself is really going to help?" she screamed. Her words spewed from her mouth like a champagne bottle opening for the first time. She towered over me, making me feel smaller than I already was. Heat filled my cheeks under her glare.

I saw her eyes move to my wrists, and then widen. Lisa saw the scars. "You've lost your mind, Corinne. You're so selfish. I can't believe you would do this to me. Why are you doing this? Why are you being so selfish?"

"Stop it, Lisa!" I covered my ears.

"You're so weak. A joke. No wonder they all left you. I hope you're satisfied with what you've done," Lisa yelled and then left.

"I was too stunned to move or say anything, so I let her leave," I told Scott. "It took me a moment to actually realize what had just happened. I didn't know what to do."

"Wow. Sorry, but Lisa's a bitch."

"My life fell apart right before my eyes because of one mistake and I couldn't stop it. People don't respect you if you want to make things right. I don't want to live with this anymore." I wiped tears from my cheeks and felt the hollowness inside my chest once more. "Don't they know that they'll be better off without me?"

"No, the world is not better off without you." He pulled me closer.

"How am I supposed to trust anyone after I told Lisa? If she was one of my best friends and left the second I told her, how would a complete stranger react? One that happens to be a psychologist in a mental institution, nonetheless."

"It's hard to trust, believe me. I told some friends what happened and they just kinda gave me this look like I was crazy. And suddenly they treated me so different. Like they had to walk on egg shells around me. It was awkward for them, I know, but it was for me, too."

"That sucks, I'm sorry."

Scott shrugged. "Some people will lose respect for you because they think you're being selfish. But you get so lost and feel like you're bothering everyone and feel like it would just be easier to end it all. But it really isn't the best way. I've come to realize that my father would be devastated if he lost me. And some of my friends, the good ones, have actually done some research to comprehend what I've been going through."

"It's just hard. I never want to go anywhere or do anything because I'm afraid. I can't get through one day without jumping at the smallest sounds. Or panicking over something."

He squeezed my arm. "It'll come. Just keep talking about it. I talked about every little thing, with my doctor. Besides, you've already done well today. You came to the library." He smiled.

"And had a breakdown."

He raised an eyebrow. "I hardly consider crying a breakdown. You wouldn't be normal if you didn't cry. And I can understand how the attacks make you feel insecure. But think of it as an added quirk. Like, I count my steps everywhere I go. Unless I'm talking to someone. No lie. It's just something I do. Which I'm not comparing that to your attacks."

I nodded. "I get it."

Talking with Scott helped me see things in a new perspective. I wasn't alone and there were people here just like me. Lost and trying to find their way. Too bad he was leaving next weekend. I could see how Ginger might fall apart when he left.

When we got back to the ward, Emma had given me a sweatshirt that she got at the mall. I couldn't believe she'd given me something after only knowing each other for a week. But it was something to keep me warm in the freezing hospital.

We went to dinner, and over the week I noticed she ate the weirdest things, like ketchup on a salad. Tracy didn't sit with us. I guess she was off tormenting someone else. Afterward, Emma and I walked outside. The sun was barely visible through the trees as it dissolved into the horizon in hues of pink and orange. I listened to the crickets chirp loudly and the cicadas call their mates. The cool breeze slightly lifted my hair, tickling my face. The half-moon began to creep through the thin clouds above and I could hear the small creek that was just beyond the woods.

"How do you like it so far?" Emma asked as we took a seat on our favorite wooden bench. We'd been taking walks almost every night during visiting hours, since neither of us had visitors.

I sighed. "I don't know. I really don't think we've made any progress. Dr. Meisner bugs me with all her questions. I mean, she knows everything about me."

"I know I hated her when I first got here. And not to sound like a repetitive therapist, but it really does take time."

"How did you overcome that? Or anything. I mean, aren't you frustrated that you're still here?"

"Of course I am. But I'm working on that. I overcame it because I started telling Dr. Meisner everything. Everything I felt and why I felt it. She just listened."

"That's what Scott said. I don't see how it helps. I can't relive this, Emma. No one understands this pain." I leaned forward and gripped the edge of the bench.

"No one has to understand it. No one will probably know exactly what you're going through. But there are a lot of us who are in pain. It's just nice to tell someone and have them not raise an eyebrow like you're nuts. Like I said, it will take time."

I looked back at her. Her dark eyes peered off through the trees, as if she were in deep thought. Her mocha hair slightly swayed in the breeze.

"Can I ask you something?" The lump was back in my throat, as I feared her reaction to my question. I was afraid of how *I* acted when people asked me.

"Sure," she said.

"How did you end up in here? You seem fine to me." Heat filled beneath my cheeks and I looked away.

She chuckled. "Oh, that's the medication taking over. It works wonders."

Was it really something to laugh about? Then again, it could have just been her way of dealing with it.

"They say if it continues to work well, I'll be on my way out of here." She paused for a moment. "That and if I continue having positive thoughts. I'm bulimic."

She didn't look bulimic, but maybe she had been eating lately. I realized that the large clothes she wore was to hide her thin body. It occurred to me that I really didn't notice anything else, except what was going on with me, and it only made me feel guiltier. "I'm sorry."

"It's not your fault. It started two years ago when I was fifteen. I was at my parents' wedding, and my cousin, who I'm close to, came up and told me I looked like I was gaining weight. She said I should start working out in order to make the cheerleading team. So from then on, I worked out constantly and would eat a lot of food, but then throw it all up."

"That's awful."

"My doctor put me on some medication but I didn't want to be on it for the rest of my life. Always controlling me. I wanted to control myself. I'm always tired of people telling me what to do and when to do it. But I'm learning that they're only trying to help."

Maybe she had a better support system than me.

"After a long time of dealing with this and losing my friends, I just didn't want to deal with it anymore. One thing led to another and I honestly just wanted it to end." She hung her head. "No one understands the pain you're going through or how much their words can really have an effect on you. I blamed my cousin for the longest time. We got into a huge fight. But it's really my own fault. I should've known better—but I didn't."

"Do you and your cousin still talk?"

"We're getting there. You're easy to talk to. A good listener." A moment later she uttered, "Well, now you know about me. Can I ask about you?"

I knew she would ask. My body tensed. The darkening sky reminded me that we'd have to go inside soon, though I didn't want to.

"I understand if you don't want to tell me."

My hands were clammy and I clasped them together in my lap.

"I-I." The words caught in my throat. It was like my mouth wouldn't cooperate. Of course I feared her reaction, but she had been through it, too. My body slightly quivered and the nervousness settled in my stomach again. "I slit my wrists."

She smiled sympathetically. "You're braver than me. I just swallowed a bunch of pills. Of course I'm not exactly sure that's a compliment."

I relaxed a little. She didn't run. Or yell. Or tell me what a weak loser I was.

"That must have hurt," she said. "They say that's the most painful way to do it."

"I didn't really think about it. I remember being in pain in the hospital."

"I bet."

"Did your friends freak out when you told them?"

"I didn't really have any friends at that point. I had pretty much pushed everyone away and was so focused on my weight. That was the only thing on my mind. What about you?"

"Yeah. I told my friend Lisa and she flipped out and left. It's been a while since I've talked to her."

"Maybe it was best that she didn't stay. I mean, she's obviously not a good friend if she just left you like that."

"She was there for me though."

"What about your other friends?"

"They don't know because I haven't talked to them in months. Ever since everything happened."

"That's terrible. Did they all abandon you?"

I bit my lip, and cleared my throat, pushing back the tears.

"I made a terrible mistake. They had every right to abandon me."

"I'm sorry."

"It's not your fault." I faked a smile. "I just feel so exhausted. I can't seem to find that happiness I once had. It's like a dark cloud is hovering over me and all I see is darkness. I have a hard time concentrating. The nightmares make it so hard to sleep. I get headaches all the time."

"Headaches?"

I nodded. "From the accident. Doctors think they can help me, but I don't see how. I can't forgive myself for what I've done. And neither can my friends or family. It just wouldn't be right. I just feel so empty, but I deserve this."

"I don't think anyone deserves this."

"I constantly have nightmares and it's hard to think about anything else."

"I can relate. The only thing that surrounded my mind was that I needed to work out and lose the weight. I was on the scale all the time. My schoolwork started suffering, but none of that ever mattered. I was more concerned with how I looked. And when I got really stressed out, I'd gorge myself on so much food in one sitting. But it's nice to have a clear head now, and you'll get there someday."

"Maybe."

"So, is that an engagement ring?"

I nodded as I looked at it. "The last time I saw him was before my attempt, and we fought. Mom made him leave, and he tried calling but I never talked to him. It's better this way. I've already hurt all of them too much and this way I can't hurt them. That's why I tried to kill myself."

CHAPTER FIVE

Just tell Dr. Meisner everything I'm thinking and feeling. It will help. Emma and Scott both told me that. So I did, but I didn't feel any different. Dr. Meisner listened and scribbled on her notepad. But sometimes she asked questions, and I hated that.

"People don't realize that you can't just snap out of it," I told Dr. Meisner. I talked, but it was just the ramblings of a crazy person. I never really talked about my life.

"You're right," she said. "Sometimes people don't want to understand."

"Like my mom."

"Why do you say that?"

"Because it's true. She has barely talked to me since this whole thing started and when she does she yells."

"She's hurting, too."

"I know that," I snapped. "It's my fault she's hurting. Why everyone is hurting." My eyes blurred from the tears and I looked away.

"Why do you think that?"

I glared at her. "Because I killed him. Is that what you want to hear? So you can write it down and use it against me later."

"It wasn't your fault."

"Don't say that. You can't pretend that it's okay."

"You can't punish yourself for something that was an accident," she said.

"Well, you weren't there, so you don't know what happened." Heat spread throughout my body and to my palms and under my arms.

"No, I wasn't there," she coolly stated. "But it was an *accident.*"

"I fell asleep at the wheel," I yelled. "How is that an accident?"

"It's easy to blame yourself. But you should not be so hard on yourself."

We stared at each other for a while. The large clock on the wall slowly ticked away the seconds.

Tick. Tick. Tick.

"Corinne, do you like it here?"

"Why do you care? All you care about is getting your money. You'll tell my parents that I have some kind of condition, just to keep me here, feed me your psychobabble, and get paid. Isn't that it?"

She didn't seem surprised by my attitude. I guessed she expected it. "I care because you're my patient and I want you to be comfortable."

"I've heard that before." I was tired and didn't want to talk to her anymore. "I have a headache. Can I go?"

"You can't always use that excuse. One day you will have to stop being silent." She looked at her wristwatch. "And we still have thirty minutes."

I sighed and looked outside. It was dark, like it would storm any second. I was so sick of the rain. I swear it had rained for six months straight.

"Corinne, tell me about Lisa."

"What?"

"When was the last time you saw her?"

I looked at her. Why did she want to hear about Lisa? "A couple of nights before I came here."

"Does she know you're here?"

"No. If she knew I…" I shook my head.

"What?"

"Nothing."

"What were you going to say?"

"If Lisa knew I was here, she would laugh."

Dr. Meisner placed her notepad on her desk. "Why do you think she would laugh?"

"She just would."

"That doesn't sound like something a friend would do. What happened the last time you saw her?"

"I told her about my attempt. She said I was weak and pathetic among other things."

"She doesn't sound very supportive. Has she always been like that?"

"Sometimes. She has her reasons," I said, swallowing back tears. "She took care of my family, day in and day out. I can't believe I'm telling you all this."

"Why is that?"

"Don't you understand it's painful for me to talk about? Telling you things you already know won't miraculously cure me. No matter what, the pain is still there."

I wanted to be angry with her for making me talk to her. But truth be told, I wanted to get rid of this pain. I wanted to get rid of the nightmares.

"I realize nothing will mask the pain or stop it. But I will try to help you make every day bearable. A lot of this has to come from you. You need to decide what is best for you and what *you* want. I'm here to help along the way and to help you release a lot of the built-up anger, pain, and stress."

"I've been talking to you for two weeks, and I don't feel any better."

"With your condition, the most important thing is for you to come to terms with what's happened, and to accept it. Talking about it will also help your nightmares."

"I'm not going to talk about it."

"I won't force you. Let's talk about your friend, Amos."

"What about him?"

"You're good friends with him, is that right?"
"I used to be."
"And why aren't you now?"
"Because I pushed everyone away." My eyes blurred again. Did she enjoy seeing me cry so much?
"How did you meet Amos?"
"He went to school and worked with me."
"Would you like to rekindle that friendship?"
"I'm not sure he'd want to. Or anyone. Not after the way I hurt them. Besides, they've all moved on."
"Maybe you could call Amos and perhaps he'd visit you."
"What? No." I shook my head. "No. No one can see me in here. They can't come."
"Are you afraid of what they might say?"
"Yes. I don't want them laughing at me. I don't want to hear their angry words."
"Would Amos laugh or lash out like Lisa?"
I wiped a tear. "I don't know."
"You're allowed to have visitors now. I believe Amos cared about you and having friends through this process helps nourish you."
"I don't want people thinking I've gone crazy. I told Lisa and you know how that ended. I can't let that happen again. That is, if any of them would even come."
"Have you told Emma or any of the others here?"
"Emma and Scott."
"Did they run?"
"No, but they know what it's like."
The room darkened and I turned my head toward the windows. The trees shook from the brisk wind.
"How do you feel about Scott leaving Sunday?"
"Fine. I'm glad for him."
"Do you want that to happen to you someday?"
Thunder clapped and I jumped. My heart unsteadily beat fast. I gripped the steering wheel, closed my eyes, and tried to catch my breath. The glass collapsed all over me.
"Corinne. Corinne, look at me." I heard Dr. Meisner

demand.

"Make it stop! Make it stop!"

"Corinne, relax. Take a slow deep breath. You are only having a panic attack. Breathe in, breathe out."

With my lips pressed tightly together, I opened my eyes and locked mine with hers.

"It's okay," she said. "Just stay with me."

I nodded, focusing on her gray eyes.

Lightning flickered and I flinched. I grabbed my tightening chest and trembled as the room spun.

"Keep focusing on me. Slow your breathing."

I did as she suggested, but another explosion of thunder rattled the windows.

"David," I screamed as his body flew through the windshield. The terrible crunch made me nauseous. I could smell the blood.

"Stay with me. Stay with me," Dr. Meisner repeated calmly.

Her voice brought me back to the room. Slowly, the flashback began to disappear. I opened my eyes and Dr. Meisner had knelt down in front of me. I could feel the blood had drained from my head.

After several minutes passed, my heartbeat slowed, and she sat back in her chair. "How long have you been having panic attacks?"

"Since the accident," I mumbled.

"Were you experiencing a flashback?"

I shrugged. "I don't know.

"You mentioned seeing him go through the windshield."

I swallowed hard. "I did?"

She nodded. "Yes."

Tears welled in my eyes. "I don't remember that happening. What is wrong with me?"

"Corinne, you have Post-Traumatic Stress Disorder," she said.

"What? Aren't I just depressed? That's what the other doctors said."

"Depression is associated with PTSD. I'm not sure the other doctors really took the necessary time with you to diagnose you properly."

"So I am crazy."

"No, you are not. Your symptoms are caused by a biochemical change due to the trauma you experienced. Your condition can be treated and you will get better."

"What is it?"

"It's a severe anxiety disorder that can develop when a person experiences an overwhelmingly stressful event or abnormal situation. It overwhelms the person's ability to cope properly. In your case, the accident was so traumatic that your mind shut down. The guilt, fear, depression you feel is known as negative automatic thoughts."

"Automatic thoughts?" I leaned forward, resting my elbows on my knees, completely absorbed in her words. It was the first time someone diagnosed me with something other than depression and anxiety.

"A thought that is automatic. For example, if a boy you liked did not ask you out, you may assume you will be lonely forever. Because you experienced such trauma, your mind is rather distorted by the event that it perceives things differently than it should. It assumes things. Making you only think of negative thoughts. Or how things should've gone and what went wrong, only focusing on the negative."

"So my mind has been making me think these bad things?"

"Yes. It doesn't know any other way to function because of the trauma. Was it thundering when you had your accident?"

I nodded, and my cheeks warmed. "It woke me up."

"And now whenever you hear thunder, what goes through your mind?"

"I start feeling like I'm back in the car. Like I'm really there."

"The thunder is triggering your memories which causes your mind to re-experience the trauma. Are these flashbacks similar to your nightmares?"

"Yes. But why do I panic like that? I sometimes feel like something bad is going to happen and I can't seem to control it. I'm always on edge and it feels like I'm having a heart attack."

"You're having a panic attack."

"How can I make it stop?"

"Let's try a technique. Close your eyes and take a deep breath. Relax your muscles."

I closed my eyes, listened to the rain softly bounce against the window like tiny pebbles. My fingers unclenched the couch as I inhaled slowly and then exhaled. Thunder rumbled in the distance. I opened my eyes

"Each time you feel anxious, or fearful, just remember to take a deep breath. How do you feel?"

"Better."

"I know the world can become a frightening place after traumatic events, but you're safe here. I am here to listen and to get you through this. Our session is over for today. You are making progress, Corinne."

I nodded, and then left. Strangely enough, I actually didn't want to leave. I went back to my room and napped, something that was becoming a habit. I ate dinner with Emma, Scott, and Ginger, and then we hung out in the common room again. I never felt ashamed in front of them, but I wasn't sure I wanted Amos or anyone to visit.

The next day I returned to Dr. Meisner's office for therapy. I wasn't angry, which was a first. It wasn't raining, finally, but I still felt embarrassed that I had a panic attack in her office and tried to think of ways to avoid having another one, like always.

"How are you today?" she asked.

"I'm okay."

"Did you sleep well?"

"Yes."

"Good." She jotted down a few notes, and then placed her notepad on her desk. "Did you think about inviting Amos to visit?"

I shook my head. "I don't want visitors."

"Okay."

I took a deep breath. "I want to remember what it's like to be happy."

"What made you happy before?"

I chewed on my lip. "I had friends. A fiancé. I was close to my family."

Dr. Meisner didn't seem to be watching my every move. She looked as if she were really just listening to me. "Was James your fiancé?"

"Yes."

"Were you in love?"

I swallowed my oncoming tears. "Yes."

"How did you meet?"

My mind immediately flooded with the memory. "He went to my school. He was a senior and I was a junior. All the girls had been constantly talking about him ever since he started the previous spring. He was tall with short brown hair that he sometimes spiked, and had a cute boyish face. He was adorable. Especially when he smiled because it was so genuine. And sexy. So when he walked into Precalculus class and took the seat next to me, my heart banged against my ribs.

I wanted to talk to him, but what would I say? *Hi, I'm Corinne. I think you're hot.* Ugh. Why did I have to be so shy?

I stole a glance at him. Wondering if he had a girlfriend from his previous school because with the way girls around here pounced on men, I was surprised he wasn't dating any of them. It shouldn't have mattered anyway. I was done with dating. The only guy I dated ended badly. He could have won Asshole of the Decade.

"Hey, do you have a pencil I can borrow?" James asked.

I looked up and for a moment, our eyes met. I couldn't tear myself away, because he had the most beautiful Mediterranean blue eyes. They were captivating. And then I felt the familiar heat reach my cheeks. *Just don't choke on your saliva.*

"Um, yeah." I reached into my backpack, grabbed a pencil, and handed it to him.

"Thanks." He smiled. At me. And there went my heart again. Beating erratically like I had just run a mile.

"You're Corinne, right?"

Omigod. He remembered my name? My mouth went dry. I cleared my throat. "Yeah. And you're James?" Of course I knew he was James Arion, but I didn't want him thinking I was obsessed. Which I wasn't.

"Yeah. I'm surprised you remembered me since we never talked last year."

How could I *not* remember him? "You have a recognizable face," I said, and then wanted to hide. Recognizable face? What kind of statement was that? God, why was I so socially awkward? Talking to cute guys turned me into a bumbling idiot. I was so envious of my best friend, Abby. She was never shy and always seemed to know how to act. She was a tough chick and a little spunky. Once she beat up some boy in her gym class because he wouldn't stop calling her 'flabby Abby.' She was not nor has she ever been flabby. A week later, they started going out, but I think it was because he needed a protector.

He nodded slowly. "I hope you're good at math."

"Why?"

"I might need a study partner."

I blushed. Was he serious? I opened my mouth to speak, but a couple of loud guys walked into the room. And when I looked up, I stiffened, hoping he wouldn't sit near me. But as my luck would have it, he did, and his friend sat in front of James.

He turned around in his seat, and I avoided his eyes. "Well, if it isn't the slut herself." Mike Malone. Asshole of the Decade.

I wanted to tell him off. But he was so not worth the breath.

"Did you have a good summer?" Mike asked.

Why was he even talking to me? He hadn't said two words to me in a year and a half.

"Yeah." I glared, hoping he could see my hatred for him. His blond hair hung over his dark eyes. His square face set in a menacing look. I realized, now that David had graduated, Mike felt free enough to talk to me.

He smiled, but it repulsed me. "Heard you hooked up with several guys." He laughed, and so did his buddy.

I chewed the inside of my mouth, hoping the bell would ring soon. I hadn't even lost my virginity. Why were people so cruel?

"Why don't you leave her alone?" James asked.

"Dude, you trying to get with that?" Mike asked. "Bad idea. She'll sic her psycho brother on you."

"Sounds like you deserved it."

"Whatever, dude. Why don't you mind your own business?"

"Why don't you apologize to her?"

Mike laughed. "Yeah, okay." He turned around, and that was all he said. I don't think I'd ever seen someone shut him up like that. Except for my brother, and yes, he did deserve it.

Finally, the bell rang.

I felt the release of tension. I tried to stop my hand from shaking. This was not going to be a good year.

After class, I had the liberty of being the library aide. It was basically a study hall for me and my lunchtime. I didn't really have any friends since David and Abby started college. And the worst feeling was walking into the cafeteria and not seeing a single person to sit with. So I ate my lunch in the library. Can we say loner?

Although, Amos and I did go to the same school, we never had any classes and mostly talked at work. We didn't really hang out either which was a shame because he was really funny.

I pulled out a book to read and took a bite of my peanut butter and jelly sandwich. The door to the library opened, and I expected it to be one of the librarians. When I looked up, I froze. James saw me and walked toward the desk.

"Hey." He smiled.

"Hey." I blushed.

He chuckled a little, and I assumed it was because of my reaction. Great. "Do you always eat your lunch here?"

I smiled. "No. I'm a library assistant and I have lunch this period. Might as well eat in here."

He looked around. "Want some company?"

"Sure." I couldn't believe he even wanted to sit with me. He came around the desk and pulled up a chair. He set his backpack on the floor and I noticed he didn't have anything to eat. "Do you not have a lunch?"

He shrugged. "I'll eat when I get home. Besides, the food is in the cafeteria and you're here."

My heart stopped and I looked away. I wasn't sure what he meant by that, but I couldn't let him starve. "Here." I offered him the other half of my sandwich. "You should eat."

He smiled. "Okay. Thanks."

"Thanks for sticking up for me earlier."

He took a bit of the sandwich and chewed it. "It's nothing. I take it you two have history."

"You could say that."

"What are you reading?" He pointed to my book.

"I'm afraid you'll laugh if I tell you."

"Try me."

"*The Notebook*."

"Ah. The ultimate love story that no guy could ever possibly live up to."

"You never know. It's my go-to book when I haven't found something to read. So, what brings you to the library?"

"Looking for a book. Got any suggestions?"

"What do you like to read?"

"Depends on my mood, really. Right now, I'm interested in learning about this girl, but I'm not sure I can find her in a book." He smiled again, showing his perfect teeth. His smile made me feel warm inside and had a certain sweetness and innocence about it. Yet, it had a sense of trust and comfort. It was sexy. *He* was sexy.

I blushed, again, and avoided his gaze. Why couldn't my cheeks always be red? Then, no one could see each time I got embarrassed. I cleared my throat. "Oh."

"I actually saw you heading in here and I sorta followed." He sheepishly grinned.

"So we're stalking today?" I asked.

"That sounded bad," he said, and grabbed the back of his neck. "I just meant that I'd like to get to know you more."

"Oh." I hoped he couldn't hear the constant rapid beating of my heart.

"Are you sure you don't mind me being here?"

"No. Not at all. It's always good to get to know somebody new."

"I agree. I always wanted to carry on a conversation with you in class, but Ms. Edwards would've given me detention for just looking at you. That and it was hard to find the courage. But as I'm talking to you now, I find it very comfortable."

Courage to talk to *me*? That was a first. "So, how was your first summer in Birmingham?"

"It was pretty good. It's better now." He winked, and heat rose to my cheeks. Would it ever end? "How was your summer?"

"It was good. Went to a few concerts and hung out with my brother and best friend."

"Cool. I haven't been to a concert in so long. Last one was Foo Fighters."

"You like Foo Fighters?" I asked. "They're like one of my favorite bands and I've never seen them."

"They're pretty amazing live. They played for three hours."

"Ugh. You suck," I teased. "I'm so jealous."

He chuckled. "I'll take you the next time they come to town."

"Okay. What about Tori Amos?"

"No. I've not seen her. But she's not really someone I'd go

see."

"Why?"

He shrugged. "She's not really my type of music."

"Why? She embodies female empowerment. She's passionate and unique and elegant. And seeing her live, the songs carry throughout the audience and swathes you in awe." I shook my head and felt my face turn red.

A hint of a smile played on his lips. "Sounds like we have a couple of shows to attend. But I know what you mean. I don't think I could live without music."

"Oh me either. I love that you can listen to a song and it'll bring back a memory and make you feel the same way you felt when in that memory. It's amazing to hear a song on a bad day and it help you through. Music's gotten me through a lot."

"Me too. Sometimes, when I listen to a song, it's like they went through exactly the same thing as me or they wrote it just for me. It's sort of like a universal connection. Makes me feel like I'm not alone."

"I know. I am constantly listening to it. I even sleep to it, or read with it on. It sucks sitting in this building for eight hours without listening to it. But sometimes when I get bored I actually write lyrics to some of my favorite songs." And now I was sure he was going to think I was weird.

James smiled. "I know what you mean. I have to listen to music when I write."

"Really? What do you write?"

He hesitated. "Uh, some poetry, but mostly stories. Psychological and fantasy." He seemed as if he was nervous to tell me. But I could understand why someone wouldn't want anyone knowing such things.

"That's really cool. I'd like to read some."

He seemed to have relaxed. "Sure."

When the bell rang, I silently groaned. I didn't want him to go, which was silly.

James stood, and swung his backpack over his shoulder. "Are you busy Friday?"

"No." It was very rare that I had a Friday night off from work.

"Great. What time can I pick you up then?"

"What?" He did not just say that. He couldn't have.

"You heard me. I want to take you out."

"You're sweet, but-."

"You have a boyfriend?"

"No. But-."

"You're grounded?"

"No. You're going to be late to your class."

"It can wait. Seven? I need directions and a phone number. Y'know, just in case I get lost." He grinned.

I sat quietly, hesitant to answer and I guess he saw that in my eyes. I wanted to go out with him, but I was scared.

"Just a date. No pressure. But it would really be fun."

I didn't want to set myself up for heartache, but then I argued that I can't shy away from the world, so I agreed. I wrote down my number on sticky note and then handed it to him with a shaky hand.

The late bell rang.

"See ya tomorrow," he said, and then walked out.

My heart wouldn't return to its normal rhythm. I couldn't stop smiling. Nor could I concentrate on my book. I immediately sent a text to Abby, and she was all encouraging. I couldn't wait to tell David, but I'd have to wait until I got home. He was probably cracking out on video games with his friend Charles.

I was in complete bliss.

When I got home, I tried calming Booger, my black Labrador-Chow mixed dog. His body was Lab, but his fur and curled tail was Chow. His brown eyes were wide with happiness. He always got excited when any of us came home. So much so that he would pee on the carpet. After jumping on me and wagging his tail frantically, he finally calmed down and went to grab his unstuffed squeaky hedgehog. I was surprised it still squeaked after a week of him owning it.

I walked upstairs and dumped my backpack on the floor.

Booger followed me to David's room where he and Charles were intently playing a video game. His room was a bit barren now that he had removed his Led Zeppelin posters and M.C. Escher drawings from the walls. Boxes were stacked along the wall. I was surprised he'd already packed so much since he was such a procrastinator. I hated seeing the boxes. I was happy that he was going to college, but I hated thinking about not having him around.

"'Sup?" David said, not veering from the game.

"How was your first day back?" Charles asked. His brown eyes widened with exaggeration. All through school, people thought Charles and David were brothers from their identical attitudes and appearance: Same brown hair that came just above their eyes, though David always hid his under a navy blue Auburn hat. Their faces were round and David's eyes were a baby blue, but that was the only difference in the two boys.

"Oh, it was awesome." I could feel the wide smile on my face, but neither of them saw it. "First, I found out I have a class with Mike." Both David and Charles groaned. "And apparently I slept around this summer, so now I'm a slut."

David paused the game and his face twisted in disgust. "What?"

"That's what Mike said."

He shook his head and clenched his teeth. "Can't you switch classes or something?"

"I don't think I want to."

"What's with the grin?"

"I got asked out by James. We talked the whole lunch period."

He raised his eyebrows as if to say, 'excuse me?' "Uh huh. Can't go unless I give the approval." David teased. But I'm sure there was some truth to it.

"Yeah. Like you needed my approval for dating Abby?"

"Burn," Charles said.

"So, who's this guy?"

"He just started going to our school last semester. He's

from Atlanta. He stood up for me against Mike."

"I think I like him already. He had better treat you right or I'll have something to say," David said.

He was always protective of me. But I couldn't protect him.

CHAPTER SIX

I wished I could remember what that bliss felt like. Nothing made me feel like that now. Definitely not even memories of David. But thinking about him almost made me feel as if he was right next to me. Talking about James helped, but it still left me depressed and guilty of how I had treated him.

"Why were you so hesitant when James asked you out?" Dr. Meisner asked.

"I had a bad experience."

"When was the last time you spoke to James?"

I froze. Why would she bring that up? Anger simmered inside me. I clenched my teeth. I didn't know why I was suddenly so angry, but I exhaled and relaxed. "I-I don't want to talk about it."

"I want to suggest something to you that I truly believe will help." She stood and walked to her desk and pulled out a notebook from her drawer. Walking back to her seat, she handed the green covered notebook to me.

I opened it to a blank page. "Okay. A notebook."

"I want you to start writing your thoughts down. No one will read them, unless you want them to. This is for you. Write down anything you want. Your anger, your sadness, your fears, anything. Write in it at least three times a week. You need to let your feelings out and learn to process them gradually. If you start writing something that gets too uncomfortable, stop writing. Go at your own pace."

"Okay," I agreed slowly.

I left therapy with my new notebook and went back to the room. I took a nap, and when I woke up, I joined Emma, Scott, and Ginger for dinner. I could see, each day closer to Scott's release, Ginger was on the verge of crumbling. Nobody knew where Tracy was, but assumed she had a breakdown and was now in 'hell' as they called it. The four of us actually had a nice conversation without Tracy butting in.

After somewhat forcing myself to eat peas, mashed potatoes, and chicken fingers for dinner, we all went for a walk again. It was still hot even though it was night. But at least the sun wasn't beating down. I could hear the cicadas and bullfrogs from the pond nearby. Emma and I sat on our bench, while Ginger and Scott stood.

"How was your session today?" I asked Emma.

"It was good. Little by little, I am starting to understanding things clearer. But it's still hard to let old habits die hard, y'know?"

I nodded. "Yeah."

"How was yours?"

"It was okay. I talked about James."

"Really? That's great."

"I still feel guilty about how I treated him."

Emma gave me an apologetic look. "I know. Just keep at it."

Ginger lit a cigarette and groaned. "They aren't going to help."

"Stop." Scott warned.

"And you're leaving, so who's going to take care of me?" A tear slid down Ginger's face. "Everyone hurts you and then leaves."

"Don't do this, Gin."

"Leave me alone." She tossed her cigarette on the ground and angrily walked inside.

Scott ran his hands down his face and then sighed.

"She's not your responsibility," Emma said.

"I might need to hear that more."

"Is she going to be okay?" I asked.

He nodded. "I hope so. She makes me feel so bad about leaving. It's like she wants me to fake some sort of breakdown just so I can stay with her."

"She's probably having a hard time letting you go," I said. "I know what that's like."

"I know."

"Just remember, you have your own life to live," Emma said.

"But I will visit. You guys are my best friends."

"That's kinda sad that your best friends are mental patients," I said.

They both laughed.

"It's all right." Emma smiled. "We're all messed up. But at least we have each other."

It was a comforting thought. "So did either of you get a notebook from Dr. Meisner?"

"Oh yeah, like a journal?" Scott asked.

"Sure."

"Yeah, I did," Emma said.

Scott rolled his eyes. "You should see all the crap I wrote."

"I've never written a thing in my life. What exactly am I supposed to write?"

He shrugged. "Just whatever comes to your mind. It gets easy because sometimes you realize you've filled like two pages without thinking twice. No one reads it."

"So my parents can't read it? I don't have to turn it back into Dr. Meisner?"

"No. It's for you and you only. Unless you want to share," Emma said.

The thing was, I didn't want to share whatever was going on inside my head. I didn't want to talk about it. So how was writing it down going to help? Just so I could actually see how crazy I was on a page?

Though Emma and Scott seemed pretty together. At least,

Scott was leaving. And I definitely didn't want to stay here forever, but I also didn't want to go back home. Nothing at the hospital reminded me of my past.

The three of us walked around campus a little more. It was nice to talk to people actually. People who had experienced the same things as me. And they didn't always ask how we were feeling. We ended up in the common room, since I couldn't leave the ward for more than thirty minutes, and joked around until about midnight.

Back at the room, I propped myself against the headboard and stretched my legs out on my bed. I grabbed the green notebook and pen from the nightstand, and opened it. I brought my knees closer and rested the notebook against them. I placed the pen's tip to the blank page.

So, I'm supposed to be writing in this thing. Write what, I don't know. It's May and instead of beginning my summer, I'm stuck inside this hospital of insanity. But after what I did, I deserve far worse. The nightmares are still there, but not as much. And I still have panic attacks. Which is embarrassing. Talking to Emma and Scott helps a lot. We've all attempted suicide and have very similar thoughts. It's nice to talk to them.

Today I told Dr. Meisner about the first time James and I met. I miss him so much, but he's long forgotten about me. I remember when I first told you about him. All you cared about was that he treat me right. You were always protecting me.

I wish I could talk to Abby. She was always by my side, until I made the biggest mistake of my life. You and Abby helped me through so much.

But she will never forgive me. Neither will Mom. And neither can I. They say I have post traumatic stress disorder. Scott and Emma tell me to just talk about everything. Tell Dr. Meisner everything that's bottled up. I just can't go back. If it hadn't been for me being stubborn and reckless, you would still be here. I called your name, but you never answered. I'll never hear your laughter or your stupid little jokes. See your smile. Every day I wake, hoping it never happened. Hoping I'll see your face or hear your voice. These words are never enough to bring you home. I just want to close my eyes and sleep forever. I'm so sorry.

The words just flowed out of my mind and onto the page. I really didn't know what I was writing and I didn't go back and read it. I wrote every time I was despondent or angry. I wrote to *him*. Writing became my crutch. I could vent and no one would be there asking questions. No one was there judging how I felt. However, no one could see the pain that spilled onto every page and the guilt and sorrow that was left inside me.

Since talking about James with Dr. Meisner, I couldn't stop thinking about him. It was like I had poked a hole in a beehive and all the memories flew out.

I remembered his poems. Especially the ones he wrote for me. He never wanted to get them published because it was something for him to release his inner thoughts. James always shared his thoughts with me. He wanted to be a writer, but decided he wanted to focus more on teaching. He wanted to teach people the importance of literature. I wondered if he still wrote and what it was about.

My stomach clenched at the thought that his poems were of how he hated me and how I had treated him so horribly.

James was all I could think about. It was like I lived in a fairytale—where the prince would always receive me with open arms, and he still thought about me and loved me.

I remembered our first date. These were the memories I wanted to relive…

James was definitely like no other guy I had ever met, which meant a lot to me. He seemed to have more character than most people I had met at that age.

My stomach twisted and untwisted. I couldn't calm my heartbeat and I fidgeted. A part of me was afraid to be alone with a boy, but the other part gave me confidence and strength. I also felt a bit more comfortable after talking with James on the phone during the week.

I wore a dark blue halter dress with wedge sandals. It fit my petite figure so perfectly. I curled the ends of my hair. It was a different look for me, since most of the time I wore it straight.

Mom came into my room as I was putting mascara on with shaky hands.

"So you're still going?" she asked.

I rolled my eyes and glanced at her through the mirror. She sat on the edge of my bed and nonchalantly picked up a magazine. "Yes, I'm still going." She'd given me the third degree about dating a guy who was a year older, but also after what happened with Mike she didn't want me dating at all.

"I just don't think it's a good idea. What is gonna happen when he goes to college?"

I sighed. "It's just a date. Who says we'll even be together that long?"

"Do you have your cell phone on you?"

"Yes."

"All right." She said it like she was exasperated with me. I was surprised she didn't make David come along like she normally did with anything I did, but he had already left for college.

When the doorbell rang, my nerves acted up again. Dad called my name from downstairs and I gripped the edge of my dresser and took a deep breath. I opened my bedroom door and walked down the stairs to the kitchen where I saw him smiling as my parents tried to contain Booger from jumping on him. James looked so handsome in his khaki pants and light blue button up shirt. He'd spiked his hair a little. I couldn't believe I was about to go out with him.

I felt my lips stretch into a wide grin. And of course I knew I was blushing. "Hi," I said. "Sorry 'bout my dog. He loves people."

He petted Booger. "It's cool. What's his name?"

"Booger. Don't ask, my parents named him."

"Hey, it's a perfect name for him," Mom said.

"Mom, Dad, this is James."

They shook hands.

"Nice meeting you," James said, while making eye contact with each of them.

"You, too." Mom smiled. I could tell that they were

impressed, by the look in their eyes.

"Sorry you don't get to meet David," I said. "He already left for college."

"Oh, where?"

"Auburn."

"Ah, a fellow Tiger, eh?"

"Yeah. Are you a fan as well?" I asked.

"I am indeed."

Dad cleared his throat. "Oh, I think you should leave now," he joked. He and Mom were Alabama fans, which was a huge rival of Auburn's.

James chuckled. "I'm sorry to have let you down. My dad went to Auburn."

"This'll be an interesting season this year."

I silently groaned. I knew that if we didn't leave then, Dad would hold him hostage and discuss every single statistic or strategy or game with him. "You ready?" I jumped in.

"Yes."

We said goodbye and left for the evening, though not without a slight grumble from me when Mom said I had to be home by 10:30. I never understood her curfews, since I worked later than that most nights.

James took me out to dinner first, to an Italian restaurant. We got a table outside with a single votive candle that flickered from the gentle breeze. The night was rather cool for August, but I was burning up from my anxiety. The waiter took our order and gave us our drinks.

"Are you trying to impress me?" I asked.

"A little. By the way, you look beautiful."

"Thank you. I'm sorry about the early night."

"It's okay. I'll take what little time I can get." He gave a half-smile. "I love that."

"What?" I asked, trying to ignore my pounding heartbeat.

"You're cute when you blush."

My face warmed even more and I sipped my cold water.

He chuckled. "Do your parents always make you return home at that time?"

I sighed. "No. It changes almost every day. It's annoying."

He looked at his phone, and then put it back in his pocket. "Unfortunately, I don't think we can go see the movie. I think it's kinda long."

"Oh." I said, trying to hide my disappointment. I sipped more water and cursed my stupid curfew.

"How about a walk on the lake? Starlit Lake—isn't that the name?"

"Yes."

"Yes to both?"

"Sure." I dropped my gaze. Alone on the lake? Would he try anything?

"Are you okay?"

"Yeah. Sorry. I'd love to go." I knew I had to stop being so guarded around him, but it was hard. David had sent me a text earlier telling me to relax and enjoy myself.

"Cool."

"So you mentioned writing. Do you write often?"

"I suppose. I don't write as much as I want, though I did write a lot over the summer. Mostly songs for my brother. He loves to play the guitar."

"Oh wow. Talented family. You'll have to let me read some sometime."

He looked away with a meek grin. "Only if you're lucky."

"Okay. What do I have to do to get lucky?" I immediately covered my face. "Oh god, I did not just say that."

He laughed. "You did."

I shook my head, and then cleared my throat. "Is English your favorite subject?"

"Yes. You?"

"I like reading the books in English, but I really hate writing essays. I suck at it. I might need a tutor."

"Sounds like we need to plan some study dates." He gazed into my eyes, and I wanted to kiss him right then.

When the waiter brought our food, we both had to back up, as we'd been leaning forward.

"What's your favorite subject?" he asked.

I thought for a moment. "I guess Psychology. How the brain works and how people interact certain ways or why something makes them who they are fascinates me."

"Like lifespan development or abnormal?"

"Mostly abnormal, but I like all of it. How we learn, grow, and handle certain situations. How each of us is so different yet similar in some ways."

"It's an interesting topic. Do you read a lot about it?"

"Yeah. I do a lot of research, too."

"That's really cool. How did you get into that?"

"I don't know. I think I read a book once and it made me want to read more about the character's condition. And other things that happened..." I stopped. I hoped he would guess I didn't really want to discuss that part of my life with him, yet.

He nodded. "I've always been interested in psychology, too."

Usually, I could never eat on a first date because I was so nervous, but the more we talked, the more comfortable I felt around him. There was never a moment of silence.

"So now that your best friend and brother are gone, what are you gonna do with all that free time?" He grinned, as if he were hinting at something.

"Um." I tried to keep from smiling. "Be bored? I don't know. Y'know they say when you're bored, that makes you a boring person."

"Well, you aren't boring to me. You've got much to say. I'm hooked on every word that comes out of your mouth. I find it so mesmerizing." He gazed into my eyes.

"What?" I blushed as my mouth fell open.

"I just find you so interesting, like I don't want this night to end." He sheepishly grinned and then looked away. "Sorry. That was cheesy, but true."

"It's okay. I feel the same way." He astounded me. *He* was too good to be true.

We finished our meal and headed to the lake. Along the way, we talked about music and kept switching out our mp3 players in his car to let each other listen to songs. I made him listen to a couple of Tori Amos songs, which he said he surprisingly liked, and he turned me onto a band that I had heard of, but had never heard their music. It was raw with beautiful emotional lyrics, and it wasn't the heavy metal I thought it was.

I loved having that musical connection because David was the only one I could really talk about music in length. It was great that we shared a lot of similar tastes. There weren't that many people who were as passionate about music as we were, which only made me like him even more.

When we got to the lake, there were other couples and groups, but we'd found a quiet spot.

"Why is it called Starlit Lake?" he asked, as he pulled the car into the lit parking lot.

"Because you can see the stars so bright that it lights up the lake. At least, that's what I've always heard."

We got out and walked down wooden stairs that emptied onto the sand. The water lapped against itself. We took off our shoes, and meandered along the shoreline. The sand was cool between my toes, and being around the water had a calming effect on me. Being with James had the same effect.

Crickets chirped while night birds sang in the trees above. The full moon's light glinted on the water. As we walked, we were quiet, but it was a comfortable quiet. Like we were just enjoying the sounds of the night.

I felt his hand brush against mine, and then his fingers laced through mine.

"So, do you like Birmingham?"

"I love it now."

"You didn't before?" The murmurs of the other people faded as we strolled toward the little playground for kids.

"Well, it's a new place. I still miss my friends, y'know. I hated the fact that we moved at the end of my junior year, but I like it here. It's nice and has a 'home' feeling to it."

"What made you move?"

"My dad got a job offer. He's originally from here so he is pretty familiar with the place. I will say, it's better than

Atlanta."

"Why's that?"

"Too much commotion there. One thing I've noticed is that it's so *green* here. It's so wooded and peaceful. Dad and I were driving around one day and we couldn't get over the vast trees, shrubberies. I mean, we saw one house literally hidden from the road because of the large trees."

"Hmm, I guess I've never had anything to compare it to. Is it not like that in Atlanta?"

"No. We lived in a suburb but it hardly had any trees. And every day they would be clearing trees for something."

"That's sad."

"The traffic here is nothing compared to there. You seriously have to give yourself a couple of hours to get anywhere. So, I definitely don't miss that."

"I can imagine. Do you have a lot of friends back home?"

"I wouldn't say a lot, but I had a few. We visited each other over the summer and we text and stuff," he said as we found our way to the merry-go-round.

"That must be hard," I said, and stepped up on the old merry-go-round. He slowly began to spin it. "Moving away from everything. From your friends and what you're familiar with. I'm not sure how I'd handle that. I'm close to my family. I mean, right now, it's been a few days without David and it's weird. I'm so afraid of growing apart."

"I have that same fear. I don't think you and your brother would grow apart though. Have you always been close?"

I gave a little laugh. "Not exactly. We used to fight like cats and dogs. He and Charles would create these stupid clubs and refused to let me be a part of them. But if anyone was ever mean to me, he'd stand up for me. We grew up and got over all that petty stuff and now we talk about almost everything. I'm closer to him than I am Abby. Which, by the way, they're dating."

"Is that weird?"

"At first. But I think they're perfect for each other."

"I assume you told David about me?"

"Of course. He still wants me to get his approval."

The merry-go-round sped up and I held on to the center bars behind me while the wind cooled my face. I closed my eyes and enjoyed the moment. Feeling like that was invigorating. It was like feeling free and really living in the moment. One that I always wanted to remember.

I felt the merry-go-round shake slightly and I opened my eyes to see James had gotten on and stood in front of me.

"How am I doing so far?" he whispered. His fingers softly stroked my cheek, and I laughed to myself as my heart was certainly getting a workout. Cardiovascular exercise was supposed to be the best for you, right? My clammy palms gripped the bars. Our eyes locked and I melted like a chocolate bunny under the sun.

He slowly leaned down, tilted his head, and tenderly kissed me. I closed my eyes and let his soft, warm lips mesh with mine. I released my hands from the bars and instinctively encircled them around his neck. I felt his arms wrap around me, holding me as if he never wanted to let me go.

For a moment, everything stopped, including the merry-go-round, the night birds. I heard nothing and it was the most peaceful silence. I didn't want to let go of my perfect night.

The memory brought tears as I wrote it all down in my notebook, with an accompanying poem. I'd never written poetry before.

> *I stare at your picture and you're always circling my mind*
> *How can I say I'm sorry for all the things I did*
> *This guilt weighs me down like an anchor tied to my feet*
> *I miss you and your memories keep me sane*
> *For I cannot bear to remember what I did*
> *I can only wish you have moved on*
> *But you're still on my mind*

I read some of my poems, nothing more, to Emma and even Dr. Meisner. Dr. Meisner described them as 'beautiful, but sad.' She said that I should continue with my 'beautiful gift'. Was it really beautiful? I just wrote what I felt. Was what I felt beautiful? If it was, then why was I in this place?

CHAPTER SEVEN

We held a little party for Scott when he left. It was rather bittersweet. Ginger was an absolute mess and wasn't faring well at all. Tracy was still gone and no one knew her whereabouts except for the staff. We gathered around in the common room where the staff had a cake and drinks on a table. Dr. Meisner had come, which surprised me since it was the weekend. Scott promised to visit us whenever he had therapy.

I thanked him for all his advice, and he said I could call or email him anytime. He told me I was a good listener and an honest friend.

When Scott left, it was rather odd. Like a small part of us didn't know what to do. But the days that ensued were just normal and somewhat frustrating. I was no longer on suicide watch so I got to take showers in peace. And each time Scott visited, it was the only time Ginger was ever happy. He really looked happy whenever he visited. And I wanted that.

Mom and Dad visited for the first time in June for my birthday, after a month of being there. *A month*. I thought I was ready, but I wasn't. I didn't want to see them. Why should I? They didn't care about me. They hid me away because they thought I was crazy. I didn't think I could ever face Mom's accusatory eyes or Dad's painful smile.

With my arms crossed, I entered the common room. Mom hesitantly stood from the couch and our eyes met. No bags hung under her blue eyes. I motioned for them to come outside. It seemed more private there.

"Happy birthday." Dad smiled and kissed my forehead. I didn't want to think about it.

"Happy birthday." Mom gave me a quick hug and then she and Dad sat on a bench, while I stood. "How are you?"

"I'm fantastic," I sarcastically said.

An exasperated sigh left Mom's mouth. "Why are you still like this? I thought maybe after a month, you would've calmed down."

"Did you come to see if I'm still crazy?" I asked.

"Corinne, we don't think you're crazy," Dad said. "But we want you to get better." His brown hair seemed grayer.

"Better? You think I'm supposed to be magically cured by being here?"

"You weren't any better at home," Mom said. "You'd been moping around the house for months, Corinne. We thought things got better once you started going out with Lisa more, but that just made it worse. It's time to move on."

"Move on? Is that what you've done?" My eyes blurred and I balled my hands into fists.

"I can't pretend it never happened. Nor can I ever be at peace with it. Forgiveness is a hard thing for me. But I've learned to forget it and move on."

Dad quickly glanced at Mom with hurt in his brown eyes. His face wrinkled in disbelief. "Carolyn," he said.

"I knew you could never forgive me," I told her. "I can't even forgive myself for what I did. Why do you think I tried to kill myself?" I threw my hands in the air.

"Do not talk that way," she demanded. Her voice was strong and full of conviction.

I shook my head. "I hurt everyone, Mom. James will probably never talk to me again. I just…" The tears took over.

"I did not send you here so you could think about some

boy," Mom said, in a calmer tone. "It's not good for you and him to be together, given your condition. Besides, you are young and you don't know what you want yet. And you're too young to be engaged."

"Whatever."

"Well, you were the one who pushed them all away. Maybe if you hadn't treated them so poorly you might have visitors."

That stung and I hated the constant battle with her. But then I stiffened. "You didn't tell them where I was, did you?"

"No. Look, I'm trying here, but I don't know how to act around you. It's like…" she hesitated. "It's like you died with him." Her chin quivered as tears trickled from her eyes.

"Carolyn, let me have a moment with Corinne," Dad softly told her.

She walked up to me, and I felt her critical eyes on me as I stared at the sidewalk, but when I looked up, her eyes were full of sorrow. She hugged me again, but it was unemotional and cold. Then, she left.

"Sweetie, your mom is very stressed out—."

"Making excuses?"

"Please, let me finish," he said sternly. "We want you to get better. We're trying to understand your condition. I'm sorry about her comment. She does not blame you, Corinne. She's also working on her own issues with her doctor and is getting better."

"Looks like it," I mumbled.

"I know for a fact your friends are not upset with you. And I know you miss them." He cleared his throat. "And David. We all do. It's still very hard for us as well, but we have to be strong for you. I know I should've been there more for you. I'm trying though. Dr. Meisner is helping us, but it may take a while longer for your mother."

Dad had never been the sentimental type. The words he spoke sank inside of me, and stung. The guilt was overwhelming.

"It's my fault, Dad. That all of this has happened. That

David—."

"No. That's not true."

"Dad, you can't protect me all the time."

"But you are not to blame. I don't blame you."

"I can't stop it." The tears came stronger now.

"I know, sweetie. That's why your mom and I decided to take you here. So you can learn to heal."

I nodded. We sat quietly for a moment. Mom mentioned my friends worrying about me. But who? I chewed on my upper lip. "Dad? Has—who's call—." I stopped myself.

"Every week he's written." He sighed. "We kept the letters at home until you're ready to read them. Amos is worried about you, as well, but we've told them nothing. We haven't heard from Lisa, though."

"He's writing me?" Why? After everything I said and did, why was he sending letters?

"I know your mom says you're too young for that kind of love, but I disagree. You are a strong, young woman, and very mature. He loves you very much and from what I can tell, he has no intention of letting go of you."

"He needs to. He deserves so much more. Perhaps I should write him a letter and tell him to move on," I said, more to myself.

"Look, right now isn't a good time to…I just think you should wait before you make such a big decision. You just need to work on yourself first. That's all. Now is the time to take that chance at helping yourself. Life is all about second chances."

I held up my hand. "Not now, Dad."

"I should take your mother home. We'll visit you again." He hugged me tightly.

My throat tightened. "You're leaving so soon? You could stay longer."

"Do you think you could try to be civil with your mom?"

I sighed. "I don't think she understands me anymore."

"We are trying to."

"I know *you* are. Anything I say around her, she has to

make a comment. Like what I'm feeling is wrong, as if I can just shrug it off. She doesn't get that no matter what I do or how I do it, the memory of him will always be there, haunting me. The nightmares are so real, Dad."

"I know, sweetie. I'm sorry. David's memory will always be there, but please try. Don't give up. I will be back." He kissed my forehead, and then left.

Today, I turned eighteen. What a day. I can't get Mom's face or Dad's words out of my head. They're so ashamed of me. Who would want such a crazy person for a daughter? James and Amos were the only ones who had contacted me. And James has been writing to me. Why hasn't he moved on? It's been months. What is he writing about? I'm nothing special. I've never understood his attraction for me. What am I supposed to do now? How am I supposed to take that chance and turn things around when they're such a mess? I'm so lost...

I closed my notebook and tossed it on the nightstand. My eyes felt so heavy, but I tried to keep them open, trying to fight off the sleep that would be inevitable because I knew the medication would kick in. But I didn't want to see the blood anymore. Or his twisted, mangled face.

My eyes betrayed me once they closed. I saw James's beautiful face. His azure eyes. I could feel his soft brown hair and smooth skin. His arms enfolding around me, protecting me. Holding me back like a seatbelt from the sudden jolt that pushed me forward. Sirens screamed in my head, forcing the hammer to awaken and pound. Nausea roared to life, but I swallowed the bile that lingered in my throat. A warm liquid dripped from my chin. A cloud of red obstructed my view. I heard voices. Lots of them. The seatbelt was cutting into me. I moaned as I tried lifting my arm to stop the trickle down my face but it wouldn't budge. My legs wouldn't move. Nothing did. "David." I'm not sure if I actually said it or thought it. I could barely move my head to see. My eyes and face stung. *David, talk to me. I'm scared.*

My eyes opened into a dark room as I sat up. Nightmare again. I sighed. My body was soaking from the sweat as it trembled violently. My heart pummeled against my chest as I gasped for air. Tightness filled inside my stomach and I doubled over. I grasped the blankets in my hand and waited for it to end. I placed my aching head in my hands until I could breathe normally, remembering what Dr. Meisner suggested. "David, I'm so scared." I cried. "How am I supposed to do this without you?"

CHAPTER EIGHT

Over the next couple of weeks, I went to therapy and did everything I was asked. It still didn't help. Only Dad came to visit. He said Mom was too afraid to come because she felt that she disrupted my healing, but I wondered if that were the real reason. I didn't request James's letters, but Dad mentioned they were piling up. I was afraid to read them because I feared to see his angry thoughts on paper.

"Corinne, why do you think James is so upset with you?" Dr. Meisner asked while we sat in her office during the thousandth session.

"Don't you listen? Because of the way I treated him."

"How did you treat him?"

"Badly." I turned my gaze toward the window at the trees in the bright sunlight.

"What are you thinking about?"

"I just keep thinking about how my life used to be. How everything was good. Just random memories pop in my head."

"Why do you think you're remembering that particular time of your life?"

I chewed the inside of my mouth. "Because I was happy."

"Would you like to share it with me?"

"What do you want to know?"

"What would you like to share?"

I thought for a moment. "Well…I remember hanging out with my friends before they left for college. It was a couple of days after I met James. I was going to miss them…

"Are you excited about starting college?" I asked David as he entered my room. I had just gotten off work from the glorious grocery store. (In no way was work glorious—it was awful). Mornings weren't too bad, since the only rush was the lunch crowd. I worked at customer service mostly, but on slow days, I stocked items. It was a nice interaction with the customers, something to break me out of my shyness more.

I tossed my purse onto the bed and went to the closet to find a shirt to wear instead of the hideous teal-green polo shirt we had to wear.

"Hell yeah," he said. "No offense, but it'll be great getting out of here."

"Lucky. Mom's probably going to hold me hostage since you'll be gone."

"Probably. Maybe she'll loosen the tether."

I shrugged. "Who knows?"

"Dude, do you know how awesome it's gonna be to go to every home game?" He stood in the doorway with his black t-shirt that hung a little over his khaki shorts. And of course, his Auburn hat molded to his head. And like always, he tossed a football in the air incessantly while he spoke.

Up. Down. Up. Down.

"Are you even gonna get anything done or is the football going to consume you even more?" I laughed.

"Funny."

I changed out of my work clothes and threw on some shorts and a tank. Then, he and I met up with Abby and Charles at our favorite Mexican restaurant. We ate there so much that they never asked what we wanted. They always knew.

It had always been the four of us, at least it had for several years, and it was like our last hurrah. I didn't know what I was going to do without them.

"If we have a good football year, I will love college," David said.

Abby tucked a few strands of her short dark blond hair behind her ear. She wore dark framed glasses and a tank top that showed off her broad shoulders and strong arms from working out all the time. "Are you sure you're even going to college to get an education? Or are you just going to be the most annoying football fan ever?"

Charles laughed. "It wouldn't surprise me. You've always been crazy."

"Whatever," David said. "I'm not that bad."

We all looked at him in disbelief.

"I don't know too many people that get so upset over a game they have to go take a shower and cry about it," I said.

Abby raised her eyebrows. "When was this?"

"A while ago."

Charles picked up a straw. "You almost broke my TV once."

I shook my head. "I'm sure you'll have some fellow complainers with you and they'll understand your need to scream at the TV about how Auburn's playing too conservatively. Or that when they're down by two touchdowns, the game is over."

We laughed and he agreed.

"So, what are you two gonna do without each other?" I asked David and Charles. Charles was going to be in New York for college. I couldn't imagine being that far away from my family.

David shrugged. "I don't know. I'm gonna miss him."

Charles sighed and took David's hand and squeezed it. "It's gonna be hard." They gazed into each other's eyes, but David's lips twitched like he couldn't hold back his laughter.

"Would you guys like a room?" Abby asked.

They broke down and laughed.

I took a sip of water. "I still find it amazing that you two remained friends through all of our moves."

I mentally counted the moves we had made throughout

the city of Birmingham. Changed schools four times. Which I guess compared to other people wasn't that bad. I just thought the reason we moved so much was because Mom couldn't stay in one place for a long time.

"Yeah. And we'll still be friends. Like, omigod, we'll be texting constantly," David said, his voice imitating a girl.

"I remember when you two used to sneak off into the woods with your pornos and once found beer," I said.

"Yeah, we actually stole that."

Abby's eyebrows furrowed. "Why would you steal beer?"

"The cooler was sitting in front of some dude's house. So we took it."

"You weren't a very nice person back then, were you?"

"I made things interesting. Kinda like you. I can't say I ever beat up on some guy. And then dated him."

She playfully punched his arm. "First of all, I'm glad you never dated a guy. Second, it was third grade. So we didn't date."

How my brother went from always getting into trouble to being such a decent mature person was beyond me.

"Remember when we threw water balloons at cars?" Charles asked.

"Ooh, or egged that girl's house." David said.

"Or TP'd this other house," I said.

Abby's eyes widened. "You guys were awful. I thought I was bad."

"Just those two," I corrected. "They were always doing stupid things and getting into trouble. They used to throw those stupid pop-its at me."

"At least it wasn't a sparkler," David said.

"I did that one time."

"Should I be worried?" Abby asked.

David leaned over and gave her a quick kiss on the lips. "I would never do anything like that to you."

"And if you did, you'd better run like hell because you know I could kick your ass." She smiled and batted her eyelashes.

"I'm just his sister. No biggie. Ugh, this sucks. I'm going to miss y'all."

"Please." Abby rolled her eyes. "You'll be so busy with James."

I looked away from her green eyes and felt my cheeks warm, but I was smiling.

"Aww, look, she's blushing," David said.

I threw a rolled-up straw wrapper at him. "Shut up."

"I can't wait until I hear about your first date." Abby grinned. "Are you excited?"

"Yes. Terrified actually."

"Don't be nervous," Charles said.

"I'm gonna try not to be. But I'm a little scared."

"Why?" David asked.

"Duh, Mike."

Everyone groaned at the mention of him.

Abby muttered something under her breath and then took a sip of her tea.

David leaned on the table. "Look, just because Mike was an asshole, doesn't mean all guys are like him. I know it's been hard to get over, but you can't live in the past."

"He's right." Abby squeezed my hand. "You're gonna have to let go of it eventually. I mean, James seems nice, right?"

"Yeah, but so did Mike. I want to go out with him, but work and just making good grades is gonna be enough."

David cocked an eyebrow. "Don't make excuses."

"I'm not. But I wonder if Mom and Dad will really let me do much without you. They don't trust me or believe I can take care of myself." For so many years, I wasn't allowed to go anywhere unless David was there. For the most part, I didn't mind, but anytime I was going to stay out late, he had to come with me.

"I don't think it was lack of trust for you, I think it was just everyone else they didn't trust," David said.

"So you think I should?"

Abby gave me a look that said 'are you kidding me?' "You

had better."

David shook his head. "Only you know the answer to that. We can't tell you what to do. You are the only one who knows when you're ready."

Charles placed a hand on my shoulder. "It could turn out to be the greatest thing or maybe not. But you'll never know until you try."

"Exactly," Abby said. "And I think you would regret this. I know you just met him like three days ago, but your face lights up when you talk about him."

"Life is too short not to take chances, you know?" David said.

"I know."

"Do you? Or are you just saying that?"

I chuckled. "Yes."

The next day, David left for Auburn. Mom and Dad took the day off while I left school early, though not without seeing James. Mom was a mess, but David kept telling her it wasn't like he was moving to a different state or a country.

The days in the week went by slowly. Having your best friend and brother move in one week was a bit much. James and I had lunch every day in the library and he called every night. I loved talking to him and hearing his gentle, soothing voice. He just gave me that feeling that I could tell him anything and he wasn't going to run away.

"That Friday, James and I went out on our first date," I told Dr. Meisner. I relived that memory once more for her. "After David left for college, James and I spent a lot of time together. After our date, I called David."

I dove right into my memories, reliving them, to where I was once a happy person. Dr. Meisner just listened. No note taking or anything…

"So how was your date?" David asked. I could hear him tossing around his football as we spoke over the phone. I'd rather hear that than the clicking of his mouse. Football meant he was paying attention. Mouse-clicking meant he was engrossed in his computer game.

I rested on my bed in my pajamas with the radio playing in the background and stared at the ceiling. The white lamp from my nightstand illuminated my room.

"It was really nice. We went out to eat and then walked around Starlit Lake."

"Aww. Did he behave?"

"Yes. He told me he's glad we met and then he kissed me."

"He did what?" I could just imagine his surprised face.

"Yeah, yeah. He kissed me."

"I'm glad you had a good time and took that chance. Are y'all going out again?"

"I don't know. I'll see him Monday."

"I hope this one works out for you. But you know I'd be there in seconds if he tries anything."

I rolled my eyes, but smiled in gratitude. "I know. But you don't always have to protect me."

"Cor, you're my sister. Of course I do."

Monday came way too quick, after a weekend chock-full of work, and late night calls from James. And then it was time for school. Usually David, Abby, Charles, and I met up in the commons area, which was a large hallway in front of the cafeteria, however, this was the first year without them. The principal didn't want any of the students going to their lockers or classes before the 10-minute bell rang. So they stuck about 1,600 kids in an area the size of a McDonald's.

As I walked into the crowded area, I felt like a new kid on the first day. I knew some people, but mostly just as acquaintances. I didn't hang out with any of them, though. A pang of fear crept its way into the pit of my stomach. I leaned against part of the concrete wall and waited for the bell to ring.

When it did, I filed in with the scrambling students to get to class, but then I looked up and saw James. A flood of happiness washed over me. It was the first time I was actually excited about school.

"Good morning." He smiled.

We moved out of the line of traffic. "Good morning."

"So, what's the first class?"

"U.S. History. On the second floor. You?"

"Chemistry on the fourth. Better get walking." He grinned, taking my hand.

"I don't want you to be late."

"We'll get it down to a science eventually." He winked. He opened the door to the stairwell and walked with me to the second floor. "I also took track at my old school, so I can run pretty fast."

"Even up all those flights of stairs?"

"It's nothing." He shrugged when we stopped outside my classroom.

I turned to him. "Thanks for walking me to class. Can't say that's ever happened to me."

"There's a first time for everything. See you in Precal?"

"Yeah."

He gave me a quick kiss, and then turned to go back to the stairwell. I squealed on the inside.

I walked inside my history class and took my seat. An average height girl with long blond hair that cascaded around her broad shoulders sat next to me. I didn't see her last week, but people's schedules were constantly being tweaked the first two weeks of school.

She pulled out a book and notebook and then let out an exasperated sigh. "You have got to be kidding me," she said with a raspy voice, and then turned to me. Her brown eyes looked annoyed. "I totally brought the wrong stupid book."

"You can share with me."

"Awesome." She scooted her desk right next to mine. "I'm Lisa, by the way."

"I'm Corinne."

"Cool. I'm new this year and I don't know a single person."

I gave a small laugh. "My brother and best friend left for college so I'm kinda in the same boat."

"Oh. That sucks. Who was that guy you were kissing out in the hall?"

I felt heat beneath my cheeks. "James."

"He's really cute. Ugh. I wish I had a boyfriend. There's this cute guy in my Spanish class though. He probably won't ever give me the time of day."

"I'm sure he would. Just talk to him."

"I'm working on it. So we should totally hang out. What's your number?" She pulled out her cell phone.

I thought it was odd that she just asked for it so quickly, but she seemed nice, so I gave it to her. She gave me hers and I put it in my phone.

"Awesome. I met this girl in my other class, Megan Trolley. She seems cool."

I personally didn't care for her. She was friends with Mike and they were all popular, but the entire time Mike and I were together, it was like I wasn't really their friend. Just some girl that Mike was with.

The bell rang and we took notes. When class was over, James and I had Precal and then we ate lunch in the library, like it was becoming a tradition. And then we had Technical Theatre. I couldn't believe how lucky I was to have two classes with him. But it was hard paying attention in class with him in it because I was so distracted. It was pathetic.

I loved the tech class because it never felt like we were in high school. It wasn't so strict. But how was I going to focus? It was such a hands-on class. What if I dropped a paintbrush and got paint on a prop? Or made a wall from a set fall down because he distracted me? I was being ridiculous.

I walked down the aisle of the auditorium and sat next to him. "Hey. How do you get to class so fast?"

"I'm secretly a ninja."

I rolled my eyes. "You're kind of a dork, aren't you?"

"And proud of it."

"Omigod, Corinne," I heard someone cry out. I turned my

head to see Lisa jogging toward us. She slid into the seat next to me. "I'm so glad you're in here." She reached over me and held out her hand. "Hey, I'm Lisa."

"James," he said and shook her hand.

"So what do we do in this class?"

"We work on sets, lighting, sound, costumes or whatever's needed for the plays," I said.

"I so want to work on costumes," she said. "Hey, there's a bonfire this Friday after the game. We should all so go."

"I have to work."

"Oh, that sucks. Well, maybe you and I could go," she told James and something inside of me arose. Jealousy, I quickly realized. Why was I jealous? James and I had only been out once and I wasn't going to get myself in too deep too soon.

"I'll think about it," James said.

Slight disappointment came over me. Ugh. Stupid jealousy.

"Cool. Megan Trolley and her gang will be there," Lisa said. "She invited me. It should be fun. I heard you're new like me."

"Yeah."

Was she trying to set him up with Megan? Or herself? Megan's gang. Which included Mike. I winced. My insides boiled but I stopped myself from getting bent out of shape. I didn't own James, so if he wanted to go he was more than welcome. I really hoped he wouldn't. I did have to work, but more or less, I stayed as far as possible as I could from Mike Malone. Or tried to.

After school, I went home and it was just like any other night off for me. I cooked dinner, then ate with Mom and Dad, which was weird without David, and avoided any sort of argument that might happen. I got to my room and saw that Lisa had texted a few times. I wanted to talk to Abby, but when I called it went to voicemail. I sent Lisa a message and she and I texted for a while, talking about how she really liked this guy at school and that she wished he'd ask her out.

I was still mildly upset about her asking James to the

bonfire. Maybe I was freaking out over nothing. I really didn't want to be associated with anyone who hung out in the same group as Mike Malone. I feared James would take Lisa up on that offer. I couldn't tell him what to do. Maybe he was like all the other guys. Just after one thing.

The next day started just like the day before. James walked me to my classes and then it was time for Theatre. Lisa always smiled when she saw me and seemed excited to talk to me. She was really nice.

Projects in tech were mostly to clean up the dressing rooms, the sound and light booth, and anything else that needed cleaning before we started working on plays. Lisa and I were assigned to the girl's dressing room.

I groaned once I saw the incredibly messy room. Costumes were strewn all over the white tiled floor while shoes cluttered underneath the vanity mirrors and counters.

"I can't believe we have to clean up after such disorganized people," she said. Her raspy voice reverberated in the small room. "Shouldn't this have been cleaned up already?"

"They had things going on over the summer. I don't know why we have to clean up after them."

"This is ridiculous. I should get paid for this."

I gave a small laugh. "No kidding." I picked up a makeup bag with pink lipstick smeared on the side of it and open mascara containers dried up inside. It was gross. "They're completely messy."

"Eww, that's disgusting." She pointed to the makeup bag.

After a few minutes of shuddering at the ungodly mess and complaining, we moved on to another subject. One that I dreaded.

"Okay, so I'll finally tell you my crush," she said. "But you can't tell anyone."

"Okay."

"It's Mike Malone."

What could I say to that?

"Omigod, he's so freaking hot. Do you know him?"

"Um, yeah." I hung a frilly blue dress in the closet.

"Yeah, I guess everyone knows him. That was a dumb question. I was talking to Megan and she said the last girl he dated had her brother attack him. She said it took a while for Mike to get over that. Poor guy." She hoisted herself on top of the counter.

Figures that Megan left out key parts in that story. It sickened me that Lisa felt sorry for him. I picked up more clothes to hang.

"She told me it was you."

I froze. "What?"

"Yeah. So did you and Mike date?"

"Unfortunately."

Her face twisted. "Why do you say that?"

"He's kind of an ass."

"Well, what happened?"

I took a deep breath and grabbed another dress from the floor. My hands trembled as I placed it on a plastic hanger. "I don't really want to talk about it."

"But we're friends."

"Maybe some other time."

"Okay." I could tell she was agitated. "So what about you and James? Are you guys serious? Because Megan seriously has her eye on him. She talks about him constantly and wonders why he's with you. She thinks you're crazy. I don't know why she says that."

The closet full of costumes quickly blurred. I cleared my throat as my face flushed.

"Corinne." I heard her right behind me. "Hey, I didn't mean to upset you. That's just what Megan says. I told her you two had gone out, but she doesn't seem to care."

"I'm not upset. We've only been out once. We're not serious."

"Oh. Well, then, should I talk to him about Megan?"

"It's up to you," my voice cracked.

"But you like him."

"Yes."

"Does he like you a lot?"

"I don't know."

She grinned. "Maybe I'll find out."

"It's okay."

"I wish you could go to the bonfire. It'll be fun."

"Yeah, sorry."

We finished cleaning the room and made it look presentable again. Lisa spoke the entire time, but I didn't say much. I was too lost in her wanting to get Megan and James together. Megan's comments. And Lisa obsessing over Mike.

I was more than relieved when the bell rang. I went out into the theatre, grabbed my backpack, and rushed out the back door to my car.

The afternoon sun wasn't the only thing melting in the heat, I noticed as I felt the perspiration on my skin. It sucked that my car didn't have air conditioning. I reached my car and dug into my bag for my keys. My hands shook uncontrollably as I fumbled around for the keys. What the hell *was* my problem? Was I really in that big of a hurry to get away from James before he could ask what was wrong? Or was it that Lisa brought back memories of Mike? Or was it just my hormones getting out of whack for their monthly ritual?

"Corinne." I heard his voice behind me.

"Yeah," I said, not looking up. I couldn't find my keys. Where were they?

"I think you dropped these." He held out the keys in his hand.

Without looking at him, I took the keys. I was afraid of what would happen if I saw his perfect face looking at mine. Lisa brought out so many insecurities suddenly. Did Lisa really know about what happened to me but refused to say? Was she taunting me?

"Thanks." I turned to unlock my car door.

"Are you okay?" He placed his hand on mine.

My whole body froze with his touch and I tried ignoring my sporadic heartbeat.

"Corinne."

I cleared my throat, trying to hold back the tears. I was not going to bust them out now. Not in front of James. I felt ashamed that I would even still consider crying over Mike Malone. Or even the jealousness.

"What happened?"

"It's nothing." Finally, I broke my rule, and looked up at him. Concern displayed across his face.

"Did I do something?"

"No. I don't exactly want you to see me like this."

"I'm just worried about you. You seem like you were hurt in there."

I leaned against my car with my keys tightly held in my hand. I was inches from falling apart at the seams. Good lord I was losing it. I didn't want to tell him for fear he'd just laugh. And think I was nuts. Maybe he needed to be with someone like Megan. "I gotta go."

"Okay. Can I call you later?"

"If you want." I opened the car door and slid in behind the wheel.

"Be careful." He walked away.

I pulled the door shut and then the shower of tears began. Why was I crying? This was ridiculous. Did I not think I deserved him?

I shook the tears away, started my car, and drove home. I grumbled the whole way because I had to work, but maybe it would keep my mind off things. I hoped for it to be busy.

Once I got home, I let my excited dog outside, and grabbed an apple for a snack. I played with Booger and that helped free my mind of the stupid thoughts.

I went to work and after the dinner rush, there were two buggies full of products that needed to be taken back to the shelf, so I worked on that with Amos. I liked being around him because he was funny. His head was full of curly reddish brown hair. He had a pudgy body and was from Ireland. I constantly teased him about some of the odd things he'd say.

"What's up, Corinne?" he asked.

"Just stupid stuff."

"Like what?"

I launched into my day with him as we put random things back on the shelves.

"Ah, you girls fret too much." He laughed. "I wouldn't worry about it."

"Easier said than done."

"True. But if James is smart, he won't even give any of that stuff a second thought. You're a great girl. Should give yourself more credit."

"Thanks."

"I mean, he obviously likes you if he's been walking you to your class." He nudged me with his elbow.

We talked the rest of the shift and then I went home and took a shower. Afterwards, I slipped into my tank top and shorts, crawled under the blankets and curled up. I closed my eyes.

Suddenly, he was there. His dark eyes peered into mine. A menacing grin displayed across his square face. Blond hair fell just above his eyes. His strong arm held both of mine above my head. His heavy body pinned against mine.

CHAPTER NINE

I heard a song playing, but it was muddled. It got louder, and then I opened my eyes. I realized it was my phone's ringtone and answered it.

"Corinne," James said.

I cleared my throat. "Hey."

"Did I wake you?"

"It's okay." I rubbed my eyes and the dream came back to me. "I'm just tired."

"I'll let you go. It's kinda late."

"No."

"Oh. Is everything okay?"

"Just had a bad dream."

"I'm sorry."

"Don't worry."

"Too late."

"Have you been worrying about me?"

"Kinda. You didn't seem all right this afternoon. I wanted to call earlier to see if you were, but I remembered you were at work."

"It was just a weird day. Lisa just brought up bad memories."

"Why did she do that?"

"She didn't do it on purpose." At least I didn't think she

did.

"Too bad I can't give you a hug right now. But we have tomorrow."

Instead of being excited, I hesitated. I didn't know how to act or what to say. "Yeah."

"You didn't have a bad dream about me did you?"

"No, it was about M—." I stopped myself. "Um...it—."

"You don't have to tell me if you don't want to. I don't like this phone thing."

"No?"

"Well, I love hearing your voice, but I can't see your beautiful face. Or your eyes."

My heart continued its irregular beating. It was hard listening to these words. It wasn't that I didn't think I deserved James, it was that I was scared of getting hurt. "I-I should go."

"Okay. Sweet dreams."

Not much else happened throughout the week, but I assured James I was okay and I appreciated his patience and not asking what was wrong. I guess he knew if I wanted to tell him I would.

Friday arrived, the night of the stupid bonfire. It never left my mind. I couldn't comprehend James being at the same event as Mike Malone. They were nothing alike, so I knew I didn't have problems with them becoming friends or anything. I shunned the thought of Megan Trolley flirting with James.

In theatre, James and I were assigned to change the gels for the light fixtures, which meant walking up to the catwalk above the theatre and working really high up. Not that I minded working so high, but showing James how to change the films, actually made me nervous for some reason. Perhaps it was just being that close in such a lowly lit area. The process was easy: Pull the colored gel from its place, and replace it with a fresh new one, so that when the lights are on, they display a richer color on stage. A color gel was simply a perfectly square, thin type of plastic that fit into a frame placed in the path of the beam of light. We'd have to change the gels since some of them would get old or crinkled.

"So have I done something?" James asked after I handed him a pile of gels. The dark blue gel he lifted did no justice to his stunning blue eyes.

"No, why?" I looked away from him.

"You just seem hesitant around me this week. Very different from last week."

I shrugged. "Oh. I don't know." I couldn't explain to him that I liked him so much and guarded myself. I knew I had put up a wall. "It's just been a rough week."

"Did Lisa say something about me?"

"No. We should finish."

"I'm sorry if I've said something."

"I should be the one who's sorry. I haven't been very nice to you, have I?"

"You've been fine. Just quiet. I know you've been busy working."

"Yeah."

"Guess I'll just have to visit you at work so I can see you."

"You don't have to if you don't want to."

"I know." He smiled.

That night, work slowed down around nine as usual on Fridays. I glanced at my wristwatch and sighed. Three more hours. I pulled several green bean cans to the front of the shelf. Then it was the green peas. Corn. Potatoes. James. I could've sworn I was going nuts. But it was like that all night.

"Excuse me, Miss, have you any Grey Poupon?" someone asked.

I turned my head. "It's aisle—. James." I smiled.

"That's me. How did you not know who it was?"

I shrugged. "I wasn't expecting you. Besides, I kinda go into zombie mode when working."

"Nice. Do you eat people?"

"No, I just kinda nibble."

"Great. The first girl I really like is gonna try to eat me."

I laughed and rolled my eyes. "What are you up to?"

"I was bored, so I came to visit you."

I stood frozen, though my heart could never stop when I was around James. "Bored? Bonfire wasn't any fun?"

"Bonfire? I didn't go to that."

"You didn't?" I tried not to sound like I was ecstatic by the news.

"No. I was never really planning on it. Since you weren't gonna be there, what's the fun in that?"

I hid my smile as I turned back to the cans.

"This is fun though."

"What?"

"Watching you work."

"You've got to get a life if you think watching *me* work is fun." I shook my head.

"I do have a life, thank you very much."

"Oh?"

"She's working right now."

My heart skipped and a can of tomatoes fell out of my trembling hand. He bent down, picked it up, and handed it to me. I felt like a girl in a movie or a book. How could I have ever been so fortunate?

"Um, thanks," I muttered.

"Corinne, how are those cans coming along?" Brandon, my supervisor, made his way toward us. He was a tall, extremely thin, black man. He had no hair to cover his shiny head and he was only twenty-two. His glasses shielded his brown eyes, but nothing could cover his bright, white smile.

"They're coming," I said.

"Excellent. We'll need you to hustle so we can get that done. I'll need you back on the floor at ten, since Sheila's going home."

"You got it."

"Is he being a distraction?" He teased, nodding toward James.

"You have no idea," I mumbled so quietly that neither heard me. "This is James."

"Nice to meet you, man." Brandon held out his hand and

they shook. "Have a good night," he quickly said after his name was being called over the intercom.

"You too," James called after him and then turned to me. "A distraction, eh?"

I blushed. "You weren't supposed to hear that."

"I'll leave you alone, then. I'll see you when you get off." He hugged me.

"What?" I didn't recall us making any plans. Not that there was anything we could do since it would be midnight.

He grinned. "Yeah."

Work finally ended and I was exhausted. School and work definitely made my days seem twice as long.

Brandon accompanied me outside the cool September night and watched me walk to my car, like every night.

"I can take it from here," I heard James tell Brandon.

I saw James walking toward me with my favorite smile on his face.

"Good deal." Brandon smiled, and then walked back inside.

"Did you seriously sit out here and wait for me to get off work?"

"Maybe. I went to the bookstore."

We reached my car and I leaned against it, facing him.

"Is that bad?" he asked.

"No." I crossed my arms in front of my chest. "I guess I don't get why you're so interested in me. I mean, you could have anyone and yet here you are talking to me." I wondered if he could tell I was blushing under the fluorescent parking lot lights.

He lifted my chin slightly and our eyes met. "I'm completely drawn to you, Corinne. You make me feel like I can just be myself around you. I'm happy with you."

I sighed—not meaning to sound so disappointed. But it just made no sense. He barely knew me. I bit my lip hoping he wouldn't bring out the 'l' word. Too many times boys pulled that out, way too soon, but only from wanting one thing. I immediately felt guilty for not even giving him a chance."

He frowned and removed his hand. "I'm sorry."

I felt awful, knowing I had just hurt his feelings. "Don't be. I'm being difficult aren't I?"

"No. I'm getting afraid to speak my mind though." He gave a sheepish grin.

"I don't want that." I grabbed his warm hand and our fingers intertwined. "I just have a hard time expressing myself sometimes. You're the first guy I've dated since…" I dropped the thought.

Concern flashed in his blue eyes, and then his gaze was intense. I could feel myself slipping, but I forced myself not to.

"I'm not here to hurt you or play games. I really mean what I say."

"It's just hard for me. I haven't exactly had the best luck with this."

"If you'd rather not do this, we don't have to. I'll understand if you're not ready. It won't be easy, but I'll walk away."

I shook my head. "No, I do want this." I chewed on my lip, probably biting several holes in it. "I'm not making this easy, am I?"

"It wouldn't be called a relationship if it was."

I nodded. I was afraid to be vulnerable or taken advantage of. But, there was something about James that made me believe him. Then, I heard David's encouraging words. *Take the chance while it's still there. You may regret this.*

"Corinne."

"I feel myself gravitating toward you. I'm scared, but there's something about you. I feel like I can tell you anything. But there are some things that I can't talk about yet."

He pulled me closer and I laid my head on his chest. He kissed my forehead, sending my heart into a frenzy, as usual. He made me feel safe. Being in his arms felt natural. Like it was meant to be.

"Did you ever finish your book?" he asked after a few minutes.

"Yeah. I've read it a million times, but it still makes me cry."

"But they find their way back to each other."

I looked up at him, wondering how he knew that.

"I've seen the movie."

I rested my head against him. "I don't know what I'd do if I got Alzheimer's. I'm so afraid of losing my memories."

"Well, I suppose I could write our story and I could read it to you."

"You would? What would you write?"

"Well, I've never written romance, but I'd start out with how I met this amazing girl who made me smile and how I couldn't stop thinking about her."

He lifted my chin, and pressed his lips against mine. I ran my hand through his short hair, pulling him closer. Electricity ignited just like the first time we kissed. I could feel his heart beating fast with my other hand. I smiled inside, knowing my touch, and my kiss, made his heart go into hyper-drive.

CHAPTER TEN

A few weeks later, James wanted me to meet his family. Of course, I was nervous. I didn't even know what to wear. Or what to say.

"I don't know why you're so nervous," Lisa said. I took the day off from work and she came over, since she was complaining about being bored. I liked hanging out with her, but she could be kind of demanding at times.

"What if they don't like me?" I changed sweaters for about the hundredth time while Lisa lay on her stomach on my bed playing with her phone.

She let out an exasperated sigh and rolled onto her back. "Then they don't like you. But you know they will. Everyone likes you."

"That's not true."

"You have nothing to worry about. I'm surprised he's just now bringing you home. How long have y'all been going out?"

"It doesn't matter."

"If I were dating a guy and he waited so long for me to meet his family, I would think something's up."

"Like what?"

She shrugged. "I don't know. Maybe he's seeing someone on the side. I mean, it would be easy for him to."

"He wouldn't do that." My stomach clenched.

"Maybe not. He flirts a lot though."

"With who?"

"I don't know. I just see it in the hallways and sometimes in tech."

"But he's with me between classes."

"Okay. Fine. I don't know what I'm talking about," she snapped.

"I didn't say that. I just—."

"Just drop it. What am I going to do tonight?"

"I don't know." I wasn't sure why she didn't seem to like James. She never really liked it when I went out with him. And she would get agitated sometimes that I was with him and not her.

"Can't you cancel and hang out with me? We could go shopping."

"I can't. But we can go Tuesday. I'm off."

She sat up and smiled. "Okay. Well, have fun and call me later." She gave me a hug and then left.

I grabbed my keys, and then drove to James's house, still nervous, and trying to block out the things Lisa said. It was like she knew every single one of my insecurities and plucked at them like guitar strings. I wondered if she even realized that.

When I got there, James opened the door and like usual, I could tell he was happy to see me by the look in his eyes.

"Mom, Dad, this is Corinne," James said. Their faces lit in excitement as they shook my hand. His mother had such a bright smile that was contagious.

"Well, it's about time we met her," she said with a hint of a Southern accent. Her dark chestnut curly hair surrounded her round face. She looked adorable in the red apron that wrapped around her large waist. She wore a long sleeved, black shirt with jeans, and stood the same height as me. I saw where James got his gorgeous eyes. "We've heard so much about you, dear and you are just precious."

"Good things, I hope."

"It's always good things with you," James said.

I glanced at him, and tried not to blush.

"Are you hungry?" Mr. Arion asked. It was uncanny how much James looked like him.

"Yes."

"Good. Dinner's ready."

I looked around their cozy home. Family pictures filled the light green walls of the living room. A hardwood staircase descended in front of the door. I inhaled aromas from the kitchen and my stomach growled.

"So this is my house," James said.

"It's really pretty."

"Thanks."

"So, you must be the infamous Corinne," someone said. I turned and saw a younger version of James clamber down the stairs.

"This is Tony, my brother," James said.

"Nice meeting you," I said. He had dyed his short, spiked hair blond. His khaki shorts came to his knees and were held up by a black belt with silver squares on it. He reminded me of a young punk rocker.

"Yeah, you too," he said. "I've heard quite a bit about you."

I looked at James. "Seems like you talk about me a lot."

"You have no idea," Tony said. "It's like he's teetering on obsession."

James rolled his eyes. "Watch it."

He shrugged and smirked. "I'm just telling her the truth. You should read the songs he writes about you."

"And we should eat now." James put his hands on my shoulders and steered me into the dining room.

His dad sat at the head of the oval table, and Mrs. Arion came out of the kitchen and placed a casserole dish in the middle. There was a large salad bowl and bread on either side. The sweet aroma of the lasagna made my stomach growl again.

"Smells good," I said.

"Well, thank you," Mrs. Arion said.

"My mom's the best cook," James said.

"Suck up." Tony teased.

As we ate dinner, I must have heard over a hundred stories. Mrs. Arion was a great storyteller, and I guessed that was how James and Tony became writers. She told stories about how she and Mr. Arion met in an ice cream shop and how James and Tony were always in trouble as kids.

"Don't let his 'perfect' attitude fool you," she said. "He wasn't always so perfect." Mrs. Arion, laughed, though it was more of a small giggle.

James leaned closer to me. "I have no idea what she's talking about. She's lost her mind."

I smiled. "Uh-huh. I bet."

"You know when he was little he was such a ladies' man. He would have fifteen different girls knockin' on the door. 'Can James come out and play?' they'd ask. He sweet-talked them and showed off. So this one time, James thought he'd be cute for the ladies and macho-."

James groaned, and I actually saw his face flush. "Oh please don't tell this one."

"Yeah, I'm so not bringing any girls home," Tony said.

"Your time will come," Mr. Arion said.

"Anyway, one day after school, these girls followed him home," Mrs. Arion continued. "At that time, we had a pool. So a few of his guy friends placed a bet on him to strip and go swimmin' in front of the ladies."

"How old was he?" I pressed my lips together to hold my laughter.

"Oh about seven or eight. James was adamant about gettin' a couple of bucks and agreed. So this little doofus actually stripped in front of these ladies and started dancin'." She brought her hand to her chest. "Thank God, he left his underwear on. I yelled at him and he was not amused with me. Lord knows what the neighbors thought."

I couldn't hold it any longer. She had me laughing so hard I cried.

"Hey, at least I got my money," James said. "Sorry to say my stripping days are over."

"Thank you," Tony said.

After we helped clear the table, and they refused to let me help with the dishes, James led me upstairs. Going into a guy's bedroom wasn't exactly a favorite of mine, but then I reminded myself that his parents were there.

"I'll warn you, my room is kinda messy."

"Whose isn't?"

"True."

As we got to the top of the stairs, Tony came up behind us. "Hey I gotta song for you to look at later."

"Cool," James said, and then Tony went to his room.

James led me down the hall.

"So, he writes songs, does he sing or anything?" I asked.

"He plays a guitar. He wants to be a rock star."

"Wow. How do your parents feel about that?"

"Uh, Dad's not too crazy about the idea but Mom's just glad he's a happy teen, I guess."

"I could see that. What about you? What do you wanna be?"

"I don't know. Maybe an English professor. I think I would look good in a sweater vest and a pipe."

I rolled my eyes. "You really are a dork."

He stopped in front of his closed bedroom door. "What about you?"

I shrugged and then reached behind him and turned the knob and opened the door. "I don't know."

"You have to know something. What about something in theatre? Or psychology."

"I've thought about something in psychology. I really want to help people."

"I think you'd be great at it. You're selfless and genuine."

"Thanks."

I looked around his room. The beige walls were covered with two copies of Van Gogh paintings, something I never would expect in a boy's room. There was a poster of Pink

Floyd's The Wall, a group photo of the Red Hot Chili Peppers and an Auburn pennant. He had a built-in bookshelf that was overfilled with books and DVDs. He had a couple of family pictures on his dresser and then one of us on his nightstand next to his enormous sleigh bed.

"Nice bed," I said.

He smiled. "I know."

"What's with the big grin?"

"Nothing. I think it's funny you mentioned that first."

Heat dashed to my cheeks. "Oh, I didn't mean anything by that."

"I know. I was kidding."

Papers and books cluttered his desk. I walked over to his bookshelf and read some of the authors. John Knowles, Shakespeare, Poe, Dean Koontz, Robert Jordan, and Stephen King, to name a few.

"You have quite a collection here," I said.

"Thanks. I love reading. But more than that, I love spending time with you." I felt his hands around my waist, and then he pulled me onto his bed. He slowly rested my head onto his pillow. He brushed a few strands of hair from my face and as he looked into my eyes, I saw a peace, contentment, and maybe a little bit of love. I had to guard myself, though. I couldn't let myself fall so easily. Not again. I couldn't get hurt again.

A soft sigh escaped his mouth as his fingers gently brushed my jawline. He kissed my cheek and then I felt his breath just below my ear. "I'm so glad we met," he whispered.

My pulse climbed higher. "Me, too."

I felt his lips on my neck, and my body wanted more. His mouth moved to mine. His lips were warm and firm, his tongue pressed inside until it found mine. I reached around his neck and then I felt his hand on my stomach, slowly reaching upward.

I stopped his hand, and he immediately removed it.

"Sorry," he said, and then pulled away.

I sat upright, silently cursing Mike. I gripped the edge of the mattress and stared at the carpet. "Don't be."

"I'll make a promise to you," he said, sitting next to me. He took my hand in his.

"What?"

"I know you're hesitant and skeptical, which is completely understandable. I can tell you've had a bad experience. I promise that I will never hurt you and that I will always be there for you. I know you've probably heard those words in the past, but I truly and utterly mean them with all my heart. I'll prove it to you."

"I appreciate that, but you can't promise something like that. That's like predicting the future."

"Maybe. But I still promise it to you."

"James, I just can't let myself get wrapped up in this too quickly." But I wanted to.

"Can I ask what happened to you? I just feel like it will help me understand better." His voice was soft.

I bit my lip and could feel the sweat forming in the palms of my hands. "The last guy I dated…tried to…do things with me. I kept saying no but it was like he didn't want to listen. He always kept trying. I broke up with him, but he wouldn't accept it. I told David about it, and he pretty much saved me one night at a party. I honestly believed David would kill him," I explained staring at the floor, but not exactly seeing it. My mind was back at the party.

He squeezed my hand. "Corinne, you——."

"We went to a party and he found a room and was a little drunk so his pressuring was so much more. He kept kissing and grabbing me. I slapped him, but it just made him angrier. He hit me and then I was flat on my stomach with him on top." I was sobbing now, and I felt James's arm around me, holding me tightly.

"Jesus, Corinne."

"David had gone to the same party and was looking for me," I said, once my tears subsided. "When he saw blood on my face and my clothes ripped, that's when he went nuts."

"I don't blame him."

"David punched him a couple of times but, I stopped him."

"It was Mike, wasn't it?"

"How'd you know?"

"Just the way he treated you that day in class. It's gonna be hard not saying anything to him."

"Please don't. I just want to let it go."

"I won't. How long were you two together?"

"We started dating freshman year and things were great. We had a great summer, but then after a year of being together, things just changed. I guess it was probably his hormones or the fact that all of his friends were having sex. I don't know. I broke up with him halfway through tenth grade, but then a few months later, he wanted to try again. He was sweet again, so I agreed. And then that happened."

He shook his head. "Did you guys report him or anything?"

"No. He was afraid to come near me after what David did. I just remember the hatred in David's eyes that night."

"Your brother cares about you a lot. I know what that's like to look after a younger sibling."

"I'm very grateful to David. He's always looking out for me. I hope you don't think I'm telling you this to scare you."

"No. I am sorry, Corinne. I can't imagine what I'd do if someone did that to you now. I think I'd go nuts on them, too."

"I really like you, James. But I'm just not ready for the physical stuff."

"Hey." He lifted my chin and our eyes met. "We're in no hurry. We can take as much time as you need. But I promise I will never hurt you."

"Please don't promise that."

"Well, I promise you I will try to never hurt you. And to always be there for you. I do swear I will never treat you the way Mike did. I could never do that, to anyone, but especially you. I care about you so much."

His eyes were so sincere, and I believed him. James pulled my face closer, and kissed me softly. He started to pull away, but I kept him there. Our mouths moved liked harmony and I wondered if our hearts did the same. My whole body buzzed with excitement. It felt right. Like nothing I had felt before and I never wanted it to end.

I left his house, though he didn't want me to. I checked my phone and saw that Lisa called and texted several times. She basically gave me a rundown of what we'd be doing Tuesday night when we hung out. I thought it was strange, but I guess being new and meeting someone will make you excited.

I called David once I got home and he was upset because Auburn lost to Florida. He wasn't in the best of moods, and I could just imagine the whole city of Auburn wearing black.

"I'm sorry we lost." I swiveled in my desk chair. Booger rested beside me on the gray-carpeted floor, though it would soon turn black from his fuzzy hair left behind. I had some music playing in the background.

"It's all right. How was meeting the parents?"

"They're very sweet. They seem to like me. His mom made some really good lasagna."

"What I would do for a home-cooked meal."

"Tired of Taco Bell already?"

"Never. So, are you gonna bring James here one weekend? It would be fun."

"I could. I'll have to ask him."

"You should. He could stay here and you could stay with Abby. What else did y'all do?"

"Not much, just talked. You'd like his brother. He plays the guitar."

"How come you're just now meeting this guy?"

"I don't know. I also told him about Mike."

"Does he think I'm a crazy loon now?"

"No. He understood and said he'd probably do the same thing if it happened now. It was weird though because he promised me he would never hurt me and that he would always be there for me."

"Why is that weird?"

"You can't promise that."

"Why not?"

"Because. You can't predict the future."

"Do you think he's gonna hurt you?"

I sighed in exasperation. "No, but you can't just say you'll never hurt someone. He may not ever lay a hand on me, but he could break my heart other ways."

"True. Did he sound like he meant it?"

"Yes."

"Well, I don't know the guy, but from what you've told me, he sounds like a stand up guy. Still needs my approval."

"Yes, yes I know. You know, you could come and visit"

"I know, but I'm buried in school. Too much busy work."

"And football."

"Shut it."

"That's what I thought." I chuckled.

"Seriously though, what does your gut tell you? Can you trust him?"

I didn't like answering questions like this. I didn't want to face it. Maybe I was just stubborn because the only guy I had trusted completely lost my trust. I thought about how James always seemed concerned about my feelings and respected me. He cared about me.

"Yes," I finally answered.

"Trust your instincts. And if that doesn't work, all it takes is one phone call and I'm there."

"Thanks, David."

"You're welcome. You're my only sister, of course I'm gonna watch out for you and take care of you. But since I can't be there, it's nice to know someone has taken that role."

"I *can* take care of myself, you know."

"Yeah, but you know what I mean."

"I do. I love you."

"Love you, too, Cor."

CHAPTER ELEVEN

I closed my eyes and the tears sped down my cheeks. I would give anything to hear my brother say he loved me once more. I needed him and I wanted to be with him. I opened my eyes to see Dr. Meisner handing me a box of tissues.

"Oh, god," I sobbed. "All he ever wanted was for me to be safe. I couldn't even do that for him."

"It wasn't your fault."

"He was my brother. How could I have done this to him?"

"You didn't do anything."

"Stop saying that," I yelled. "Everyone says that, but they're just being nice. I killed my brother." My body trembled and I couldn't stop crying.

"Do you feel like hurting yourself right now?"

"I just want the pain to end."

"I know. You are getting better, though."

I didn't feel it. I was trying so hard to do everything that was asked of me, but I felt no different.

I left her office, wiping my tears. When I made it back to my room, I finished crying. I wanted to feel anything but this. This constant nothingness.

The door opened and Emma burst through. She looked as

if she were going to slam it but thought better of it. She closed it quietly and let out a frustrated groan.

"What happened?" I asked.

She shook her head. "Why do they allow Tracy to just speak her mind? All I was doing was watching TV and she just won't shut up. I mean, it's like she doesn't even try to be a better person."

"What did she say?"

"She kept telling me I need to lose weight. Doesn't she know that doesn't help? Why did they even let her out of seclusion?" She took an uneven breath.

I got up and hugged her.

"Let's go outside," she said. "It's nice out there."

"Good idea. Maybe I can thaw out." I swear they acted like this place was an igloo or something.

We walked outside, and my body immediately warmed. It was hot and felt like walking into a damp oven. But this was expected during the summer in the South. I didn't mind though. I hated being cold.

"How was therapy today?" she asked.

"Okay. I cried again."

Emma frowned. "Sorry. If it helps, I really like hearing about James and your brother."

I had been telling her the same memories as Dr. Meisner. Emma listened, like Dr. Meisner, and always wanted more.

"Thanks," I said. "How was yours?"

"Good. I've gained five pounds since last month. So that's something."

"You don't deserve to be here, Emma."

She glanced at me. "Neither do you."

I looked away. If only she knew.

CHAPTER TWELVE

I followed Lisa to her house after school and then we rode together to grab some food. We'd planned on shopping, since she wanted to find a dress to wear to the school dance. We stopped off at the store first since she had to get something. I didn't really like being there on my off day, but it wasn't that big of a deal. We walked inside and I saw Amos.

"Who's the Betty?" he asked.

Lisa furrowed her eyebrows. "What?"

"Sorry. Who's the girl?"

"I'm Lisa. And you are?" She was definitely checking him out.

"Amos. What brings you two here?"

"I just have to pick up something for my mom," Lisa said.

"Is that an accent I detect?"

"Yeah. I'm from Ireland."

"Omigod. What made you move here?"

"Me Da is originally from here. Married me Ma, whose Irish, and moved to Ireland. I grew up there but moved here because me Da wanted to live in the States again."

"Do you like it here?"

"Yeah."

"How late are you working?"

"Until ten."

"Aww. Well maybe you can hang out with us sometime."

Amos smiled. "Yeah, maybe." He looked to me. "Where does this go?" He held up a tapioca loaf. "I have been all over this store searching for where it goes."

I shrugged. "I don't know."

"It's damaged now," he said and tore open a part of the box.

Lisa laughed. "Omigod."

I rolled my eyes. "I can't believe you did that."

"What, like you've never done that before?"

I playfully hit his arm. "Shut up."

"I gotta get back to it. See ya later."

"See ya tomorrow," I said.

"What was that?" Lisa turned to me.

"What?"

Her eyes narrowed. "You were flirting with him. I wish I could be like you. You have a boyfriend and then have another guy who likes you."

"I think Amos was more interested in you."

"Really?"

"He couldn't stop looking at you."

Lisa hooked her arm around my neck. "He is adorable."

"He's single. And really nice."

"You have to hook us up."

"Oh no. You guys can talk amongst yourselves."

"Maybe I'll get a job here."

"Over Mike? I thought that's why you were looking for a dress tonight."

She sighed. "He won't ask me out. We talk all the time in class, but I just don't get it."

"I wouldn't worry about it."

"Why?"

"Because he's an asshole."

"Maybe you just don't get him like I do."

"Let's just go look for a dress." I didn't want to argue with her. We made it to the mall and went to just about every shop that had dresses, but she couldn't find one.

"This is ridiculous," she said.

"We can go to a different mall later."

"The dance is this Saturday, Corinne," she snapped.

"Okay. You still have four days."

"You don't get it. I have no date. No dress." Her brown eyes watered. "I just want to go home."

"Lisa, it's okay. It's just a dance. There'll be plenty more."

"I said I want to go home."

I didn't know what to think. I took her home, and by then, she had calmed down and acted like she hadn't just flipped out over nothing.

Over the next few months, Amos and Lisa started hanging out with James and me. We went to movies, dinner, or hung out at one of our houses. When we were at James's, Tony would join us sometimes and play his guitar, and I could tell he was developing a crush for Lisa. She and I worked together, but I couldn't decide if that was so she could spend more time with Amos or so she could keep an eye on us.

One night we were at James's watching a scary movie in the dark. James and I were cuddled on one end of the L-shaped couch, while Amos and Lisa were on the other end intertwined.

At one point, I got bored with the movie and turned over to face James. He smiled and pulled the blanket over us like it was our own private bubble.

"I like this movie better," he whispered and drew me closer. He pressed his lips to mine and I slid my hand under his shirt. I traced over his taut muscles and smooth skin, and he quivered. I jumped a little when I felt his hand on my bare stomach.

"Would you stop?" I heard Lisa snap.

Heat rushed to my cheeks and I removed the blanket from our faces. I couldn't believe we were making out in front of them. "I'm sorry," I said but she didn't hear me.

"I was just trying to kiss you," Amos said, and I realized she wasn't telling us to stop.

"I don't want you to, okay?"
"Why?"
"I know you're cheating on me," she said.
"What?"
"I saw you flirting with Amber last night at work."
Amos sighed. "I'm not dealing with this again."
James and I sat up and he turned on a light.
"I want to go home." She stood and grabbed her jacket. "Corinne, can you please take me?"
"I don't have my car."
"I'll take you," Amos said.
"I don't even want to look at you right now."
"I can't do this anymore, Lisa."
"Fine. Whatever." She turned to me. "Can we go now?"
"Here." James handed me his car keys. "Just take her home and I'll get my car tomorrow."

I didn't want to leave, but I gave him a quick kiss, and left with Lisa. "What happened?" I asked her.
"He's dating Amber behind my back," she sobbed.
"Why do you say that?"
"Because they constantly flirt at work. He's never told me he loves me."
"James and I haven't said that to each other. And we've been dating for a while." I was hoping to cheer her up.
"You know, not everything revolves around you and your perfect relationship. Ugh. You people annoy me."
"Lisa, what's wrong?" I pulled into her driveway.
"I just wanna be left alone." She opened the door and slammed it. I didn't know what was up with her. But it was getting worse the more we hung out with other people. I felt bad for both of them, but especially Amos. He seemed pretty broken up about them. Lisa started cancelling on me anytime we made plans for random reasons. She was sick. She fell asleep and forgot. That lasted for about a month, and anytime I'd see her in school she just seemed really depressed. I guessed it was because of Amos.

In the meantime, James and I spent more and more time

together. David finally met him over Thanksgiving weekend, and approved. Just being with James enlivened me. Made me come out of my shell even more and have more confidence in myself. I was falling for him. Hard.

That Christmas, David came home, and it was nice having him home again. School was out for all of us and I was excited. Not only because I didn't have to go, but because I got to spend time with my family more. I loved the holiday time because of that, and James felt that way, too.

"Did ya miss us?" Mom hugged David tight.

"Of course I did."

Booger couldn't contain his happiness as he jumped on David for attention, almost shredding his brown t-shirt and khaki pants. He then ran and grabbed his new hedgehog and threw it around.

"I see you've already taken the stuffing and squeaker out." David bent down to pet Booger. "This is a new toy, right?" he asked me.

"Yeah. The stuffing and squeaker didn't last long." He stood and hugged me.

We had a small dinner with James and Abby. I was glad to see her, since we hadn't talked much during the semester but I guess both of us had been busy. I had invited Lisa, but she declined saying she would be too uncomfortable around a lot of people she didn't know.

After we had eaten the pot roast Mom had prepared and cleared the plates, she brought out her homemade apple pie, my favorite, and pecan pie, David's favorite.

"Corinne, have you heard some stories about James from his mom yet?" Mom asked.

"Yeah, I've heard a few." I smiled at James.

"Ooh, is it my turn to hear some stories?" he asked as Mom scooped him a slice of the pecan pie.

"Uh uh." Abby waved her hand. "I've been waiting for a story on David, so you'll just have to wait your turn."

"Lord, honey, we'll be here till next week if you want us to tell David stories." Mom rolled her eyes.

"Well, did he ever tell you he was afraid of the dark and had to get his little sister to hold his hand to turn on the light?" I asked.

"Y'know, Maw and Paw's house is very dark," David said. "I couldn't see."

"Uh huh. Or my personal favorite, when he had just finished watching Indiana Jones and got the bright idea of wanting to swing around on a rope like Indiana did. So he gets this rope, ties one end of it to his wrist." I giggled and continued explaining through my laughing. "And attaches the other end to a tree branch and proceeds to swing across this ditch. I came up and asked if he needed help since he was just hanging there over the middle of the ditch by this rope that was strangling his hand."

A round of laughter was heard from the table.

"You weren't a bright kid, were you?" Abby asked him.

"We playing that game, are we?" David raised his eyebrows.

"I never did anything stupid, so I don't have any stories." I raised my head high.

"You may not have done anything stupid, but you've said some dumb things," he quipped. "We were driving up to Mentone right?" David leaned on the table and looked at James. "Now, there are tons of rocks up there, 'cause you're going through the mountains and whatnot. All of a sudden, you hear this small voice ask, 'How'd they get those rocks up here?'"

Laughter bellowed in the dining room. I closed my eyes and buried my face into my hands. "Okay, I was like five years old."

"Ha! Try fifth grade."

"I have no idea why I asked that." I shook my head. "I mean, as soon as I said it I knew the answer. It wasn't one of my proudest moments." I rolled my eyes as James continued laughing.

Once we all settled down, we helped Mom clean the table and the dishes. Abby, David, James, and I went into the living room and played charades. David and I had an inexplicable link to our charades guessing, and Abby refused to let us team up together. So, it was James and I versus David and Abby. James and I realized we made a good team, which frustrated Abby.

A few nights later, when I was off work, a rarity working in a grocery store during the holidays, James, Abby, Lisa, and Tony came over. Tony brought his guitar and played a song after I let him listen to it.

"Wait," I said. "You said you'd never heard that song before just now."

"Right," Tony said.

"But you just played it. I mean, how is that even possible? That was amazing."

"Thanks. I don't know, I just hear it and can pick up on it."

"That was seriously amazing. What did you think, Lisa?"

She'd found a magazine and was flipping through it on the couch. She shrugged.

"You gotta play 'Stairway to Heaven,'" Abby said.

David groaned. "Seriously? Of all the Zeppelin songs I let you listen to, that's the one? Play 'Thank You.' Or 'Ramble On.'"

"I don't know those."

"You don't listen to Zeppelin?" David asked, disbelieving. He felt that everyone should like Led Zeppelin.

"No. It's not really my style."

David shook his head and I laughed. Here came the tangent. "Okay, no, I'm not buying that. You wanna be in a rock band, right?"

"Yeah."

"I don't care what music you play, but you have to have listened to Zeppelin. You can't start a band without doing so. That's like eating cobbler without ice cream. It's sacrilegious."

"I think someone's getting cranky because he's been away from the computer too long," Abby teased.

I smiled. "Is he starting to get the shakes?"

Lisa sighed and tossed the magazine aside. "Can't we watch a movie? Or go out? This is boring."

"Lisa," I said, not hiding the dismay in my voice.

"What? I don't necessarily wanna come over here all the time and listen to Tony play. Can we please do something else?"

Tony blushed. "Sure."

"No, you don't have to stop."

"It's cool. I should take a break anyway," Tony said.

I felt bad because Lisa wasn't having a good time and no one seemed to enjoy her company. I couldn't understand why she was like this with other people, but not with me. At least not all the time. It annoyed me that we had to do what she wanted to do, but I didn't want her to go off on anyone.

"What would you like to watch?" I asked.

She shrugged. "Let's watch a stupid horror flick."

David gave her the remote and she flipped through the movies online. She landed on an older movie that was pretty cheesy. We all laughed at how ridiculous it was, but at least it seemed like Lisa was enjoying herself.

"Okay, if you were to go on a killing spree, would you really use a fisherman's hook?" I asked.

"I'd use an ice pick." Tony said.

Lisa laughed. "An ice pick? What kind of killer are you?"

"Well, think about it. A knife is too overrated, and a gun just isn't gory enough. And with an ice pick, you could do lobotomies."

Lisa grimaced. "That's disgusting."

"Tony, you watch way too much of that serial killer stuff," James said.

"Does anyone want anything to drink?" I stood. A few of them nodded and told me what they wanted.

"I'll help," James said and met me upstairs in the kitchen. "Hey, is she okay tonight?" He lowered his voice.

"I don't know. I don't get it. I'm sorry, is she ruining your night?"

"No."

"I just feel bad for her. She has no friends and I can tell none of y'all want her here."

A hint of a smile played at his lips. "This is your house. You can have whoever you want. I'll admit, she can be a little difficult at times. Especially when she tells you I'm probably cheating on you."

I sighed. "I don't know why she does that."

"You want my opinion?"

"Sure."

"I think she's jealous of me. And I don't mean she's into you like that, I just mean, I don't think she likes sharing you."

"I guess I never noticed that. But she does always get upset when I'm with you. I think she might have something going on."

"Like what?"

"I don't know, but she's very clingy. She's different with me, for the most part. I can't just unfriend her."

"No one's saying you do. You have such a huge heart."

"Thanks," I said as he grabbed some glasses from the cabinet. I reached inside the freezer for some ice and started putting them in the glasses, but I kept one in my hand. "And thanks for being so awesome."

He gave a warm smile and wrapped his arms around me. "Of course. Mmm…I wish we could have every night together."

"Me, too." I pressed my lips tightly together to keep from laughing, and then quickly placed the ice cube down his shirt.

He squirmed to get his shirt untucked as I laughed. Relief came over his face as the ice fell to the floor. "You're so gonna get it." He tossed the ice in the sink.

I darted from the kitchen and into the empty dining room, and then I felt his strong arms swiftly wrap around me. He wrestled me to the floor and held me down. But as soon as I looked into his eyes, I felt like the ice cube melting in my hand.

"I've got you now." He leaned down and kissed me. He released my hands and I ran them through his hair. His warm lips grazed my neck, sending a current throughout my body. My breath caught and I wanted to be alone with him.

"James," I whispered and he stopped. "My heart is beating so fast."

He gave a lopsided grin and brought my hand to his heart. It was going just as fast as mine. "You're too good to be true."

"I don't know about that."

"You're so wonderful in every way. And so very ticklish." He tickled me until I called a truce through my laughter. He helped me up and we walked back into the kitchen and finished getting the drinks. James helped me carry them back to the TV room.

"Bout time," David teased. "I'm a little parched thank you."

"Whatever."

Lisa turned to Tony. "Anyway, you're right about people never forgetting that special person. It's like Heaven. When you die, there's a place reserved for you. You'll never lose that place. And no one could ever replace you."

James leaned against the couch, and I sat in between his legs with his arms loosely around me.

"What are we talking about?" I asked and poured Coke into my glass. I waited for the fizz to go down and then took a sip.

"We're talking about going to college and how people drift apart," Abby said. "Lisa was just saying that if you're meant to be friends or whatever kind of relationship, you'll always have that place for that person."

"What started this conversation?" James asked.

"David and I were talking about how we don't really talk to our old friends since college," Abby said. "Even though half of them go there."

"I'm sure we all fear that loss of friendship," I said. "I know I do. I was scared that when you and David left, you'd be too busy for everyone."

David popped his knuckles. "You know that wouldn't

have happened." I turned to him and noticed his fingernails were almost nonexistent. Probably from biting them during the Auburn games.

"And you know I would never forget my little Corinne." Abby batted her eyelashes and smiled.

James held me tighter. "Hey now, I might get jealous."

"I should probably not mention last night then, huh." I joked. Abby and I always played like that.

"Eww, please don't say that." Lisa's face twisted in disgust.

"You know we're joking right?"

"That's not even funny. Gay people are disgusting and should be put in a hospital."

I felt my jaw drop. "That's a horrible thing to say."

"Whatever. It's true."

I felt the mood in the room getting tenser. I turned my attention back to the movie, but I was upset with her. How could I have been friends with someone so close-minded? I chastised myself. Of course anyone could feel or say whatever they wanted without being judged. But it made me see her in a different light. How much more was there of her that I didn't know?

"What do you suppose happens when you die?" Tony asked.

"Uh…that was random," James said.

"I was just thinking of the earlier conversation about losing someone. I mean, when you die, that can't just be it. There has to be some sort of life after death."

"I think when you die, there's total blackness," I said. "And then you see memories that replay from your life. At least, that's what I hope. If that's such a thing to hope for."

"I've just always wanted to know," Tony said. "I mean, I've read so much about it, but no one knows for sure until they die, obviously. It's insane the things I've read. Like out of body experiences. People will die for a few seconds and drift from their bodies and see everything from above."

"You sound like you want to kill yourself just to experience death," Lisa spat. "That's pretty selfish y'know?"

James sighed. "He's not going to kill himself, okay? Why do you have to bring this stuff up, Tony?" I could hear his frustration and could tell this wasn't the first time he talked about this.

"Sorry. I was just curious."

"Curious about death?" Lisa stood, her face reddening. She snatched her coat, scarf, and purse. "You are a sick psycho. Killing yourself is not something to be curious about." Her brown eyes watered. "You're a fucking loser if you think that." She stormed out of the room.

"Lisa," I yelled and got to my feet. I really hoped she didn't wake my parents.

"I'm sorry, I didn't mean to make you mad," Tony called behind me. I stopped him from going after her.

I found her upstairs in the living room. "Lisa, what is the matter?" I asked.

"I don't appreciate people talking about death and suicide."

"I'm sorry. He won't do it again."

"Why is he always hanging out with us? I mean, do you have a secret crush on him or something?"

"Stop. What is with you? You're up one minute and down the other. And I'm afraid to say anything to you because you'll get upset."

"You really want to know?"

"Yes."

"My father killed himself. Are you happy now?"

I was shocked, but I couldn't decide which part was more shocking. The news or how she presented it. "I'm sorry."

"Whatever. I gotta go. Have a good night." She opened the door and a burst of cold air hit me, and then she slammed it behind her.

Stunned, I made my way back to the TV room.

"Are you okay?" James asked as I sat next to him.

"I guess."

"I'm so sorry." Tony covered his face. "I didn't know."

I guess that confirmed that everyone had heard her. I was

surprised my parents hadn't come down.

"Does she have a disorder?" David asked.

"I don't know." I was embarrassed, yet I still worried about her.

"I wonder if she's off her meds," Abby said. "Did she say when all this happened?"

"No. I need to go talk to her."

"If I were you, I'd let her cool off first," David said.

Abby removed her large hoop earrings and rubbed her ears. "Always the worry wart."

I twisted behind me to face James. "Would you hate me if I cut tonight short to go talk to her?"

"No. I understand."

After saying goodbye, I made my way to Lisa's house. I'd sent a text letting her know I was on my way and she said okay. When I got there, she was already in her bright pink pajamas. I hoped she had calmed down enough to talk. Her eyes were red from crying.

"I'm so sorry," she said. "I feel awful for the way I acted."

I followed her to her room, which was very girlie with light pink walls and makeup strewn across her white dresser. Pictures of flowers and butterflies hung on her walls and a picture of her and her parents was in a small frame on her nightstand. She looked to be about twelve years old in the picture.

"Tony really feels bad." I didn't know what to say.

"It just creeped me out."

"I understand."

"But I shouldn't have reacted that way. My medication isn't working. They might bump me up to some Lithium. Help stabilize my mood, so they say."

Lithium. Treated for Bipolar Disorder. I remembered reading that. "Lisa, I—."

"You've been such a good friend," she said. "I've been trying to hide this from you because I didn't want you thinking I'm crazy. You're my best friend and I'm so sorry." Her eyes watered.

"I'm not going to judge you."

She nodded and wiped her cheek. "I was eleven that day I came home from school. There was an ambulance in the driveway and two police cars. Everyone on the bus just stared. I didn't want to get off the bus because I knew what had happened. I didn't want to talk to the police officer or my mom. But when I saw them wheel my dad out on a stretcher, I lost it."

"That's awful."

"He told me the night before that I was the best little girl anyone could ask for and that he loved me. Then he hung himself in the basement. From then on, I promised myself I would never be so selfish like him. I would never leave my mom or if I ever had kids, I wouldn't leave them." She shook her head. "How could he just abandon us? I have no respect for him. I needed a father and he deprived me of that."

"Did he ever try to get help?"

"Yeah. Mom sent him to doctors, but I don't think he ever took his medication. And thanks to him, I'm a mess."

"Do you see anyone?"

"Yeah, but my doctor's a complete douchebag. I keep asking my mom to change, but she won't. She said I needed to stay with him because I've been to so many."

"I'm sorry." I leaned over and we hugged.

She shrugged. "Don't be. I'm sorry that I ruined your night. I bet your friends hate me."

"They don't."

"Well, all that matters is that you don't hate me." She gave a wide grin. "Let's watch a movie. I'll make popcorn."

I knew I was past my curfew, but my parents were asleep. I sent a text to David explaining that I'd be home later. Luckily, I got home without getting into trouble. I went into David's room and plopped down on his bed. He was clicking about ninety miles an hour at some computer game. I wondered if he ever got carpel tunnel. I told him everything I learned about Lisa. We had no secrets and I talked to him about everything.

"Damn. Would she ever forgive her father?"

I shrugged, absentmindedly playing with the loose strands that fell from my ponytail. "I don't know. It's kinda scary though. Could you imagine being in that much pain you would end your own life? I've read about it. It's terrible."

"If any of my friends or family were ever in that situation, I would do anything and everything I could to save them. Not saying they didn't try to save her father. But I'm sure you know that men hide their depression a lot better than women."

"Yeah. I know I'm not in her situation, but I just don't see how you could disrespect someone who attempts suicide or even actually does it. There's a reason they're in pain right? A depressed person isn't going to ask for help. But I don't get how you can just hate that person or whatever."

"She's been hurting for years. I can see why she'd be upset after all these years. She should come to terms with it eventually or it will stick with her forever."

"I don't get how people think it's selfish. I mean, I kinda do."

"Because they look at it as you only thinking about yourself. Your pain or your misery. You're not thinking about how it affects others."

"True, but if you're in a lot of pain you probably can't help but constantly think about it. Or think about ending it. Can't people see you need help?"

"Some people ignore the signs." After a few seconds, he chuckled. "You should be a psychologist. You'd make a good one. Or at least a person to help others understand mental illnesses."

"I should."

A few nights later, we had our traditional Christmas Eve dinner, and James and Abby came over. After dinner and talking with my family, James and I retreated to my room. My parents didn't say anything, but I guessed they trusted me, and my grandparents were there for them to entertain.

I turned the radio on and then sat on the bed next to James. He reached behind his neck. He did that when he was nervous.

"Are you okay?" I asked.

"Yeah." He handed me a wrapped present about the size of a DVD. "Merry Christmas. I hope you like it."

I tore the shiny red paper and found a journal. I opened it and found that he'd written in it. *To my Corinne. You wanted to read my poems, so I compiled the ones I wrote about you. I just want you to know how much you mean to me. Love, James.*

I couldn't speak. I was so moved by such a personal gift. Every single page was filled with his thoughts and words for me. It brought tears to my eyes. I looked up and our eyes met.

"You wrote all these?" I asked.

"Yeah."

"Were you afraid I wouldn't like it or something?"

His lips turned up slightly. "A little. I hope it's not corny or anything."

"You are such a fool."

I pounced on him, crushing my mouth to his. He fell backward on the bed with me on top. I felt his hand through my hair, holding me by the nape. We rolled over and our legs tangled. My breath hitched as his lips traveled from my jawline to the hollow of my neck. He tugged at my sweater, pushing it over my shoulder and then brushed his lips along my collarbone.

I trembled as I unzipped his jeans and slipped my hand inside. He let out a low moan and kissed me harder. His breathing labored and his body shuddered before it tensed and then he relaxed.

"Wow," he said.

I felt a sense of power because I could make someone feel that way. It was strange, yet invigorating.

"Your turn." He kissed just below my earlobe. His lips then gently tugged on my lower lip. His tongue grazed mine. He slid his hand up my skirt, and my body jerked. I couldn't calm my breathing and my heart was beating about two-hundred miles an hour. I gasped once he found the place he was searching for.

My body warmed and I felt this incredible surge of love and lust. Feeling his touch always made my body ignite.

We lay there, holding each other, our foreheads touching, breathless.

"Does this mean you like my present?"

I gave a soft laugh. "Of course I do."

"Are you okay?" His lips grazed my cheek.

"Yes." I was always okay when I was with him. He was everything I could have ever asked for. It was as if we were connected and fit perfectly together. I knew he was the one I wanted forever. There was no denying it. I was in love with James.

When he left, I was still in a daze, and glad everyone had gone to bed because I didn't want them to see the goofy grin that was probably on my face. I went to the living room to stare at our Christmas tree.

"Hey," David said, and I jumped.

"I didn't know you were still up."

"You kidding me? It's Christmas Eve. I'm waiting on Santa."

I rolled my eyes and sat next to him on the couch. "Dork. Did you make Santa some milk and cookies?"

"No, I tried getting Abby to, but she wouldn't. So, what did James give you?"

"He made me a book of poems." And left me wanting more of him.

"Are you serious? Man, I need to take lessons."

I laughed. "I'm sure you're doing just fine."

"Thanks." He hooked his arm around my neck and proceeded to give me a noogie.

"Ow!" I cried. "Stop it." I fought with him and finally broke free, trying to straighten my hair. Some things will never change, I suppose, between siblings. I playfully pushed him. "Jerk."

"I prefer to be called 'best brother in the world' thank you."

"Maybe when pigs fly," I teased.

We stayed up pretty late talking that night about how he missed home and random memories from our childhood. We were always nostalgic.

I watched the colored lights on the tree doing their blinking dance and the way they shadowed the branches on the wall.

I loved Christmas trees and I'm not sure if they just symbolized the time or what it was but looking at them always brought peace. And I thought about how lucky I was to belong to my family and to have such an amazing guy. It was never about the presents. It was just about being with them and really cherishing the moment. And I didn't think people realized that until they lost someone. At least, I didn't.

CHAPTER THIRTEEN

"It'll be awesome," Lisa said in a sing-song voice. "Oh come on, Corinne. You can bring James and Tony. The more the merrier."

I groaned. I hated parties.

"What if no one comes?" She pouted. She knew exactly how to make me feel guilty.

"Fine." I really just wanted to spend New Year's with my brother because he was going back to school soon. And of course James.

"Yay," she yelped and hugged me. "It's going to be amazing. I promise."

It was not amazing by any means.

It seemed like everyone from our school was there, bumping and grinding to some really awful music. I told Lisa we'd make an appearance and that was it.

"Damn, I didn't think she knew so many people," James said as we all walked inside.

"Neither did I," I said. I was shocked so many people could be squeezed in such a small house.

"Eh, you send out an invite for a party and have alcohol and people will swarm," Tony said.

Lisa stumbled a little as she made her way to us in her red stiletto heels and hugged me. "You made it," she shouted over the music. She had somehow slid her stocky body into a flaming red, satin, strapless dress. I wasn't sure it was the right size for her, but she didn't seem to care. Her blonde hair was pulled back with a clip and she wore red lipstick to match the dress. I could sense she was on the prowl tonight with her daring brown eyes. "Isn't this amazing?"

I smiled. "Yeah."

"Hey, Tony." She hugged him. He was nervous because he was planning on asking Lisa out and kissing her at midnight. James worried because of the whole movie night incident. He didn't think it was such a good idea. I kinda wanted them together so that maybe she would stop thinking of Mike, since he was all she talked about after she broke up with Amos.

"I'm so glad you guys came. I wanna dance. James, will you?" She grabbed his hand.

"I'm good, thanks."

She frowned, but then Tony grabbed her hand and she happily followed him to what was now the dance floor instead of the living room. With her high heels, she surpassed his height by a couple of inches.

The music reverberated throughout the house and I feared cops being called for noise disturbances. I couldn't dance to save my life, but James convinced me to join him. He laughed at my absolutely goofy dance moves.

After a while, Tony made his way over to us. Lisa had gone and gotten a drink. I thought it was cool that she'd been dancing with Tony the whole time. Maybe she had grown to like him. "It's almost time," Tony said. "I-I don't think I can do it." He looked as if he was going to be sick.

"Do you like Lisa?" I asked him.

"Well, yeah."

"Then go for it. You can't do any harm in trying."

Tony took a deep breath, and then made his way over to Lisa. I watched them as they talked. I saw her warm smile and I felt that everything would be all right.

"I wish you wouldn't encourage him," James said.

"Why?"

"I don't want him to get hurt."

"I don't either, but she's been spending the whole night with him."

He nodded, but I knew he still wasn't keen about the whole thing. "I'll be right back."

I looked at him wondering where he was going and he mouthed 'restroom.' I nodded.

Seconds later, I felt a tap on my shoulder, and I whirled around and froze. Dark eyes peered into mine, as if expecting something.

Mike smiled. "Hey, Corinne."

Why was he talking to me? My stomach curled from the uneasy feeling forming inside. "What do you want?"

"How are you doing?"

"Leave me alone." I took a step to the left, but he moved in front of me and grabbed my arm. I snatched it away. "Don't touch me."

"You need to learn to chill out."

My teeth clenched. "Get out of my way."

He held his hands up as if surrendering. "Your friend is looking really hot tonight."

"Stay away from her."

He raised his eyebrows. "Are you jealous?" He raised his hand to my cheek, but I batted it away. "You're a lot more vivacious than I remember."

I scanned the room for James. I wanted to leave. Why did we come to this party? Did I feel that bad for Lisa? And then I met her eyes. They were cold and calculating. I couldn't believe she was glaring at me for talking to Mike. "Please leave me alone." I tried to walk away again, but he grabbed my arm and pulled me to him.

"Let's dance. For old time's sake?"

He gripped my wrist and I slapped him hard across the face.

"Hey!" I heard James yell behind me. He pushed Mike away from me and stood between us. "Don't touch her ever again or I'll handle you worse than her brother did."

Mike laughed and rolled his eyes. "Always got someone protecting you," he said to me and then walked away.

Everyone seemed oblivious as to what was going on. They carried on their drunk dancing and laughter. The countdown started, but I just wanted out of there. But I didn't want that incident ruining my night.

"Are you okay?" James asked, holding me close. I breathed in his warmth.

Our eyes locked, and I pulled his face down to mine and kissed him. I wanted to tell him that I loved him and that I appreciated him more than he ever knew. I hoped my kiss would be enough for now.

People shouted and cheered as the New Year started. But I ignored them, still kissing James. It almost felt like we were the only ones there. His arms were around me so tight, as if he didn't want to let me go.

"Get the fuck away from me," someone yelled nearby.

I turned just in time to see Lisa shove Tony. I gasped as he fell backward onto the table with snacks and drinks. It buckled under his weight and all the beer bottles, chips, and punch crashed to the floor and onto Tony.

"You are such a freak," Lisa shouted.

People laughed, and as James and I rushed to Tony's side, everyone went back to their own worlds. Tony's face was red, but not from the punch. James helped him to his feet, but he pushed him away and went outside.

I turned to find Lisa walking toward her room. What had happened? I pushed my way through the drunk, sweaty bodies and grabbed her hand. "What happened?"

"Let go of me." She pushed me, causing me to stumble backwards.

I followed her to her room. "What did he do?"

"Get out!" she screamed.

"I'm so sick of this, Lisa. Would you just tell me?"

"He kissed me. He put his grubby little hands on me."

"Did you have to push him like that and embarrass him?"

"He embarrassed me. He freaks me out with all his death and gloom talk. Like all he wants to do is kill himself just for experience sake."

"He doesn't want to do that, okay? You're freaking out over nothing."

She narrowed her eyes and crossed her arms in front of her chest. "Like you did with Mike?"

I rolled my eyes.

"I saw you dancing with him." Tears poured down her face. "How could you? You know I like him. I swear, it's like you were pushing Tony on me so you could have Mike all to yourself."

"I have James," I yelled. "Yes, Mike and I dated, but he tried to rape me, Lisa."

There was a knock at the door, and then it slowly opened. And wouldn't you know, Mike Malone walked in.

"I saw you crying, Lisa," he said. The same voice he used whenever he was trying to make up with me. "I came to see if you were okay."

She looked from me to him, and then smiled. "That's so sweet." She looked at him like he was some savior. It sickened me.

"We're fine, okay?" I told him and then crossed my arms.

"Mike, did you ever try to rape Corinne?" she asked.

"What?" His face twisted in confusion. "I would never do that to anyone."

Then, she turned back to me. "You're such a liar. Why don't you and your little freak friends leave?"

"I'm not lying."

Mike sauntered closer and my body stiffened. "Why don't you give us some privacy? Unless you want to join us."

"Lisa, you don't want to do this."

"I told you to leave."

I left her room, grabbed my coat, and stormed outside. It was so cold and the wind just ripped through like I wore nothing. I was so mad that my body shook and my jaw ached.

"Corinne," James called and I went to him. A look of

concern in his eyes. "What happened? You're tense."

I couldn't stop the tears. "He's in there with her. I told her what he did to me, but he denied it and she called me a liar." I hated hearing what she said to me and I hated seeing her welcome Mike into her room.

"Come on." He tried to get me to walk, but I stood still. "Let's go home."

I shook my head. "I can't just leave her here with him."

"She made her decision."

"She's drunk. She doesn't know what she's doing."

"Don't make excuses for her."

"James, if anything goes wrong, there's no one in there that will help her. They don't care about her."

"Why should you?" His voice raised. "She doesn't care about you or your feelings. I hate the way she treats you. And I hate seeing you hurt. You can't save everyone, Corinne."

"If anything happens to her, it's on me."

"No, it isn't. You warned her and she kicked you out. You've given her more than she deserves."

I didn't know why I was still protecting her after the things she said to me. I felt my shoulders slump, and James drew me into an embrace. We stood there shivering in the cold while I cried. I didn't want to leave her, but I did. And I felt like such an awful friend. But I couldn't handle her anymore. I mean, I had never experienced so much drama in one night. I couldn't believe I had argued with James over Lisa. So I cut her from my life. Sort of.

CHAPTER FOURTEEN

I didn't really spend much time with Lisa after that. She and Mike started dating, and I saw her at work on occasion. I started hanging out with Amos more, which upset Lisa because apparently I had chosen him over her. I tried my best to ignore the stupid drama she always tried to create. I wondered why she even still worked there.

Spring break finally arrived, and while I was excited to have an entire week off from school, not to mention a whole week with James, David, and Abby at the beach, in the back of my mind there was a an annoying reminder that James was graduating soon. I hated thinking about it.

The day before our beach trip, Mom had cooked lunch, which was odd since we never had lunch like that. But she claimed she just wanted to enjoy a meal with the family before we left her for a week.

Dad sighed and pushed away from the table, the way he always did when he ate too much. He groaned like he was in pain.

"Why'd you eat so much?" Mom asked.

He shrugged. "It was good."

She rolled her eyes. "What time are y'all leaving tomorrow?" She had already gotten all the particulars of our trip, but I guess she wanted to hear them again.

"In the morning," David said.

"And you are to share a room with James and Abby and Corinne are to room together." She wasn't asking.

"Yes, I know," he said, but I knew that wasn't how it was going to be, unless I really wanted to share a room with Abby, Mom and Dad certainly didn't need to know the truth.

"Well, I gotta get ready for work," I said, and David and I both pushed our chairs from the table in an attempt to escape the interrogation.

"Corinne, hold on," she said.

"Busted," David said, and then went upstairs. Dad cleared the table and then left.

"What?"

"Sit down."

I silently groaned. I didn't know where she was going with this, but I knew I wouldn't like it by the tone in her voice.

She leaned forward on the table. "I'm concerned about you and James."

"What do you mean?"

"Well, he's graduating this May."

A pang of sadness hit my stomach. Like I wasn't aware of that fact. Thanks for reminding me, Mom. "Okay?"

"Has he heard back from any colleges?"

"A couple. But he's waiting for Emory."

"That's three hours from here."

I sighed, and tried not to let the tears come out. "I know."

"So, what are you going to do?"

"I don't know. We'll work it out." I hated that my voice shook. I felt sick.

"I just want to warn you that the distance will make you two grow apart. He's going to be off doing all kinds of things. How can you be sure he'll be faithful?"

"Because I trust him. I love him." It was the first time I'd said it aloud to anyone, but I felt it.

She looked at me like she didn't know what I was talking about. "You're too young to know what love is. I just hope his going on this trip isn't some attempt to go further with you."

I was shocked. "You think he's been going out with me for seven months just so he can get me in the sack?" I was hurt by her words. Did she not trust James? Did she not like him?

"That's what happened with you and Mike. I'm not telling you all this to hurt you. But James just seems a little too perfect. I'm just warning you not to lose yourself in him. I've done that before and it didn't end well."

I knew she was referring to a guy she'd married right out of high school, but he had left her for some other girl. But James wasn't like that. "What if your warning isn't necessary?"

"It always is at your age. I just don't want to see you get hurt when he leaves for college and decides he doesn't want to continue this."

"I have to go to work." I got up from the table and went to my room to change.

While I drove, I wanted to release the tears, but I held them back. I didn't want my coworkers asking what was wrong. Of course, all the things I'd previously thought about came to mind. I thought about him going to college and meeting people and getting bored with his high school girlfriend. I thought about us drifting apart. And it tore me up. It made me so anxious that I wanted to throw up.

I got to work and it was busy, which I welcomed. It helped take my mind off things. But when my break arrived, I was back to my thoughts, until Amos joined me.

"What's wrong?" Amos asked.

"Nothing."

"It doesn't seem like nothing. It's eating you up."

"It's my mom. She thinks James only wants one thing and that when he leaves for college he'll forget about me." I covered my face.

Amos brought my hands down and squeezed them. "Mothers always worry. Have you talked to James yet about college and such?"

"No. I'm scared."

"I've seen you two, though. You're strong, and you guys will make it. Try not to let it bother you. Besides, the distance is so close, I'm sure he'll be here every weekend."

"Thanks." I felt better. Until I got off work and those same thoughts nagged at me. I had to put all of it on hold. There was no way I was going to let it ruin my week. I couldn't wait to get home so I could cry in the shower where no one could hear me.

But then I saw James leaning against my car. He had a big smile that was contagious. He greeted me with a kiss.

"Here, read this." He handed me a piece of paper. I didn't want to read it, especially when I saw the Emory logo. He'd been accepted.

I smiled. "Congratulations. I'm so proud of you." I hugged him and tried so hard to be excited for him. I was, but I was torn between that and the sadness I'd been feeling all day.

"What's wrong?" he asked. He wasn't even looking at my face. I guess I wasn't good at hiding my feelings.

"I'm just tired. It was a busy day." I hoped he bought that because I didn't want to ruin his moment. "We should celebrate the good news this week."

"I've thought about it, too." His voice was low and I knew he wasn't talking about celebrating Emory.

He held me at arm's length. I couldn't stop the tears. "My mom said we'd grow apart and that you were too perfect. You were just going this week to take advantage of me." I wasn't sure he could really understand everything I said through my sobbing. I sounded pathetic, but he just drew me closer.

"Do you believe her?" I could hear a strain in his voice.

"No. I mean, I've had thoughts about what could happen when you leave."

He tilted my chin up, and our eyes locked. "I love you so much, Corinne. I'm scared, too. I don't want to lose you because I honestly don't know what I'd do if I did."

It was the first time he said he loved me. I never thought he could ever be scared of losing *me*. It was like he took the thoughts out of my head and used them for himself. Because I didn't know what I would do if I lost him.

I wrapped my arms around his neck and kissed him like it was our last time. I was never good at words, so I hoped I could show him how much he meant to me. I pressed my lips firmly to his, not withholding any restraint. I wanted him right then, but it wasn't the right place.

Our foreheads rested against one another. "I love you," I whispered.

CHAPTER FIFTEEN

The seven-hour drive to the beach was uneventful since we left in the morning. When I got out of the car, I stretched and inhaled the salty air. I loved the beach, and I was fortunate enough to come every year with Abby, since it was her parents' condo.

We got inside the three-bedroom house and Abby and David claimed their room and James and I claimed ours. My stomach felt like I had swallowed a bowling ball. I wanted to take our relationship to the next level, but I didn't even know where to start. Or how. He collapsed on the bed, tired from the long ride. I grabbed my swimsuit out of my bag, since we all decided to go swimming. I hoped it would calm my nerves.

I slipped on my swimsuit and wrapped a towel around myself. I walked out into the bedroom and found James sitting on the edge of the bed in just his swim trunks.

Seeing his taut muscles made me blush. He was hot, and my heart reacted frantically. When I met his striking blue eyes, he smiled. I wanted to run my hands through his unkempt hair and ravish him. I wasn't sure where these thoughts had come from, but I had to think about something else.

"Don't I get to see the suit?" He grinned as I walked closer to him.

"It's really cold in here." Which was a complete lie. It was hotter than hell in here.

"I'll keep you warm." He yanked me closer, the towel dropping to the floor, and I sat on his thigh. His arms wrapped around me and I lay my head on his shoulder.

He bent his head closer and I reached up and pulled his mouth to mine. His hand rested on my thigh and my pulse raced. I broke the kiss, trying to catch my breath. I didn't want to stop, but I had to wait until later. That is if I could bring up my courage.

"What's wrong?"

"You're kinda driving me crazy."

"Hmm. Good?" He nibbled on my ear. "Or bad?" I felt his hand at the edge of the waistband of my swimsuit.

I practically leapt from his lap. "We should go swimming. Swimming is good."

He chuckled. "You're driving me crazy, too, you know. Especially wearing that."

We met Abby and David out on the beach. The soft gritty sand was cool between my toes. And the beautiful bluish green water crashed against itself and lapped over the sand.

"It's kinda late to be swimming, y'know?" David said.

I smiled. "I just want to dip -y feet in." I walked closer to the shoreline.

"Ha! I know what that means."

"What?" James asked.

"Means, she'll grab your hand and pull you in with her."

"I would never do that." I elbowed David.

I moved into the water until it came up to my knees while the rest of them stayed behind. Suddenly, I felt my body being lifted. I let out a yelp and then was dropped into the water. As I came up for air, David was right next to me.

"I finally got you." He laughed. "After all these years." He helped me up and out of the water.

"Just wait. I'll have my revenge." I wiped the water from my face. "Why didn't you come save me?" I teased James, and then looked to Abby. "And you. I can't believe you let him do that."

She laughed along with James. "Hey, it was not my fight."

We went to dinner, and then took a walk on the beach. That night was the first time James and I slept in the same bed. We made out a little, but didn't go any further. I wondered if I was really ready to move further, or maybe I was just so scared.

We fell asleep in each other's arms, and the feeling was amazing. I wished I could have him sleep by me every night.

The next morning I woke up, but James was still asleep. I came out of the room and saw David and Abby sipping coffee out on the balcony. I opened the sliding door and joined them. The morning was cool, and very bright. Off in the distance, I could see dolphins jumping.

"Morning," Abby said.

"Hey." I sat in the chair next to her and hugged my knees, staring out into the ocean.

"Ready to go sailing today?" David asked.

"Yeah. It should be fun."

"So what did Mom talk to you about the other night?"

I sighed. "James and me."

"What about it?"

"She thinks he's only been with me to get me in the bed. And she also brought up the fact that he's going to college and that he'll forget about me."

"Wow. Go Mom for the pep talk."

Abby shook her head. "Does she not like James or something? Or is all this because of Mike?"

"I don't know. She says I'm too young to be in love."

"She's probably just looking out for you," David said. "But you seem really happy with him. I'm sure if you two really want it to work, you'll make it happen."

Abby sipped her coffee. "I like him. He takes care of you. I mean, he hasn't tried to do anything you didn't want to do."

"Don't be afraid, Cor. Don't listen to Mom—about certain things. I see that he cares deeply for you."

"I think he's in love," Abby said.

"He told me last night. I just hate that he's going to be gone."

"I know. But you'll make it work. And you can always visit each other on weekends."

"If Mom will let me."

"If she doesn't, do it anyway. What's she gonna do? Ground you? Live a little. I know she sheltered you a lot, but now's your chance to change all that."

The door to the balcony slid open and James appeared, sleepily. "Good morning," he said. He looked like he hadn't slept at all.

"Hey, you okay?" I asked as he sat next to me.

He rubbed his face. "Yeah, just need some coffee."

"I'll get you some." David stood. "I need a refill anyway." He and Abby went inside.

"It's beautiful out here," James said, but then held his head in his hands.

I massaged his back. "What's wrong?"

He groaned. "I think I'm going to be sick." He got to his feet and rushed inside. I came inside and closed the door behind me.

"What's wrong with him?" David asked.

"I think he's sick. Is there any medicine?"

"Yeah, there's some in the kitchen," Abby said. "We could skip out on the sailing today and just stay in."

"No, you guys go ahead." I sifted through the medicine cabinet and found some anti-nausea medicine. I took it and grabbed a towel and wet it with cool water. "I'll stay here with him."

"Okay."

I went into the room and found James in the bed moaning. It was a pitiful sight, but I was able to get him to take some medicine. I pulled the covers up to his chin and placed the cold, wet towel to his forehead.

He opened his eyes and smiled.

"What?" I stopped dabbing his face.

"God, I love you. How did I get so lucky to have such an

amazing woman?"

My heart skipped a beat. We stayed in the whole day and I took care of him. By morning, he was fine and we swam and spent most of the evening on the beach talking. Lying in the sand, listening to the waves, and having his arms around me was the best feeling.

"This is amazing," I said, gazing at the stars. It was like I could see every one of them it was so clear.

"I know. I'm pretty awesome."

"I meant the stars."

"Ouch. Don't make me toss you in the water."

"You wouldn't do that."

He drew me closer and kissed my forehead. "No. I wouldn't."

We stayed like that for a while.

"You know, Emory has a good psychology program," he said.

"Yeah, I'm sure you don't want your girlfriend following you to school."

"Why wouldn't I?"

"Because. What if something happened? I can't just go where you go."

"Georgia State has a good psych program, too."

I rolled my eyes and playfully shoved him.

"Just something to think about." He sounded serious and I actually started thinking about us living in the same city, but being in college.

"I wish every night could be like this," he said.

"Me, too."

"Just always remember this night. Whenever we're apart, you have this. At least, it'll help me. I'm going to miss you so much."

I didn't want to cry. But we still had several months before he left.

We made our way back to the condo and said goodnight to Abby and David. James walked in the room first and I stopped him from turning on the light. I closed the door and let the moon be our light.

I hoped he didn't see my hand shake as I reached up and pulled his mouth to mine. I walked us to the bed as we continued kissing. I lifted his shirt and kissed his chest. Then, he helped me remove his shirt. I backed him into the bed and he sank down.

Taking a deep breath, I straddled his lap and kissed him. I softly tugged at his bottom lip and I felt his hands reach around my neck and untie my halter knot. The top fell, and he unhooked my bra. His warm lips traced my jaw line and then down to my neck. I tilted my head back, letting the rapture take over.

He lay back and I kissed his neck, his chest, and nibbled on his ears. He rolled on top of me, holding himself up and I slid off my dress. I wanted him. I was ready. My mouth was all over his and I nervously fumbled with the button on his shorts. As my hand brushed against him, it was obvious that he wanted me too.

"Corinne." The way he said my name, with such desire, made me yearn for him even more.

I finally unbuttoned his shorts and unzipped them. He helped me remove them, and then I wasted no time in taking off his boxers. I touched him and he moaned.

"Wait." James tried to pull away but I held him tightly.

"No, I'm ready."

"Let me get something." He got up and I didn't realize how much I had been trembling. He came back, and gazed at me in the moonlight that poured into the room. "You are so beautiful." He kissed me, and then left a trail of kisses all the way down to my stomach.

I was on fire. I didn't know how much longer I could last, but I guessed he was trying to slow things down. His touch was warm and soft and I tried to calm my breathing.

"Are you sure?" he asked.

"Yes."

"Please tell me if I hurt you."

"Stop talking," I said, and then I grazed my lips just under his chin. Then, to the hollow part of his neck.

Finally, he slid off my underwear, and then pulled the covers over us.

CHAPTER SIXTEEN

I would always have that night to remember. After that night, I loved him even more, if that was possible. I wanted to stay like that forever. The months that followed went by fast. Too fast for me. James graduated and I turned seventeen that summer. We spent every minute of our summer that we could together. We spent time with Abby, David, Charles, and even Amos. I couldn't have asked for a better summer, but all too soon, one by one, my friends left for college, except Amos.

James and I wanted to do something special on our last night, but it really ended up being just us in his room not watching movies. We talked, we made love, we lay quietly in each other's arms, neither one of us wanting it to end. I tried not to cry, but that didn't work.

"You know in a couple of days will be a year since we started going out." He nuzzled my neck.

"Yes."

He turned over, pulled the drawer from his nightstand out, and then faced me again. "Which is why I want to give this to you now." He handed me a little black box.

My heart stopped for a moment. I sat up and took the

box. "What is this?"

"I love you with all my heart and always will. I want you to know that you're the only one for me. I'm forever yours, Corinne."

I met his gaze. "Why are you saying this?"

"Because it's what I feel, and I've never felt like this. And I'm going to keep my promise no matter what it takes. I won't lose you."

My vision blurred and he opened the box. I looked down and inside was a silver ring with a round blue sapphire in the center and round diamonds on either side. "James."

"I promise to love you for the rest of our lives. Will you marry me?"

I wasn't sure I heard him right. Our eyes locked and I couldn't speak. This was crazy. We were young. But then, why did it feel so right? "Yes."

He exhaled and then smiled. He carefully took the ring and slid it on my left finger. "I love you." He kissed me.

"I love you, too. You make me so happy."

"You do the same for me."

We lay back down, his arms around me, and me staring at the ring. "H-how did you afford this?"

"It wasn't easy." He sighed. "I had to do a lot of bachelorette parties."

I playfully punched him.

"I had a lot of money saved up for college in case I didn't get a scholarship."

But one question burned at the back of my throat. "Can we wait a while though? I mean, before actually getting married?" My voice was barely above a whisper. I didn't want to hurt his feelings.

He kissed my forehead. "We could get married tomorrow, or ten years from now. I just want to be with you. Now, if only I could just squeeze you in my suitcase, I'd have everything."

I pulled him tighter and pushed back the tears. "This is going to be so hard."

"We'll get through this. I love you too much to ever let you go."

"Absolutely not." Mom put her hands on her hips and raised her eyebrows.

I couldn't hide my ring anymore, so I finally confessed to my parents. And now I was regretting it.

"You are still in high school," she yelled.

"Mom, it's not like we're getting married tomorrow."

She shook her head. "You're too young. You still have college to worry about."

I groaned. "You got married young."

Her blue eyes sliced to mine. I'd just hit a nerve. "And you know how that turned out," she said.

It wasn't a good tactic on my part, though not because it made her madder, but because she could, and would, use that against me. "Again. We aren't getting married for a while."

"And what are you going to do when he leaves you for someone else?"

"Just because it happened to you doesn't mean it's gonna happen to me."

"It's not just me. I see it all the time. How do you even know you two will last through college?"

"Why do you always have to be so difficult? Why can't you be supportive?"

"I'm just trying to save you from a big mistake. You two have separate lives now. This won't last."

Mom was impossible. Dad didn't like the idea, but at least he was okay with us waiting. I left the room unable to talk to her anymore. She could never have a simple conversation without it turning into a yelling match.

"She's being ridiculous," I told David on the phone later that night. I paced my room, too amped up to calm down.

"She's just worried."

"Why? Why can't she be happy?"

"I don't see the big deal if you guys are waiting. Why didn't you just say it was a promise ring?"

"I don't know. I mean, if you told her you proposed to Abby, she would welcome it."

"I doubt that."

"I don't. I swear it's like she doesn't want me to be happy."

"No. She just doesn't want you making the same mistakes she did."

"But I'm not. Why can't she see how much he means to me? How completely in love with him I am. Or how much he loves me."

"Just let it go. Keep doing what you're doing. She'll get over it eventually. And then you can prove her wrong."

And that was exactly what I did.

Senior year started and having James text me every morning or randomly throughout the day helped. It was ridiculous how much we communicated, but we didn't care. It was strange being at school without him, since I had seen him practically every day last year.

I walked into English class, waiting for the bell to ring, and texting James. I was surprised he was up so early since he didn't have class until ten. I was jealous. When I looked up, I saw Lisa come inside and then take the seat next to me. Her thick blonde hair was now short, just coming past her ears. She looked a little thinner in her green short-sleeved shirt and black jacket.

"Hey," she said. She seemed different. Calmer. "How are you?"

"I'm fine. You?"

"I'm good." It was a little awkward, since we hadn't spoken in months. She had quit work and I hadn't seen her in a while.

We sat like that until the bell rang and Mike Malone entered. I could never escape him.

"Oh look," he said. "It's the two sluts."

"Shut up." Lisa glared at him. I guessed they broke up.

She sighed and sunk into her desk further.

"Don't listen to him," I said.

When class ended, Lisa followed me out into the hall and stopped me.

"I'm really sorry, Corinne. I acted like a complete bitch to you."

"Thanks. But don't worry about it. It's over. In the past."

"I wish I could be like you. You're so strong and know exactly what you want in life. And you don't let stupid little things bother you."

"I'm not perfect by any means."

"But you're smart. You don't make dumb mistakes."

"Everyone makes mistakes. We're human. And you're smart, too. Don't sell yourself short."

She gave a small laugh. "I wish you were my shrink."

"That'll be five cents, please," I joked.

Lisa rolled her eyes. "Ugh. I've missed you. And you were right about Mike. He was such a jerk."

"I'm sorry."

She shrugged. "I wasn't right in the head then. I started taking some new medication. So far, it seems pretty good."

"That's good."

"How are you and James?"

I could feel a silly grin form on my face and I held up my hand. "We're engaged."

She gasped and her brown eyes widened. "Wow." She checked out the ring. "So soon?"

"Well, it'll be a while before we get married."

"That's really cool. I'm really happy for you."

"Thanks."

"Do you wanna hang out sometime?"

After everything we had been through and all the drama, I was hesitant. But she seemed so different now. So I agreed.

Lisa and I hung out quite a bit and she did seem better. She still didn't like that I spent time with Amos, but it wasn't like before. Every so often James and I saw each other on the weekends. They lasted such a short time. But we made sure we took advantage of the time we had. And as always, we both hated saying goodbye.

CHAPTER SEVENTEEN

Emma and I found a spot underneath a willow tree and were laying in the thick grass. The sun was out and it was hot, but there was a nice breeze. As I looked up through the maze of branches and leaves, it didn't feel like I was a crazy girl in a hospital.

"So, Lisa changed," Emma said. "That's good."

"It didn't last long. She hates me now."

"She didn't seem like a very good friend. I really like James. He sounds amazing. It would be nice to find someone like that."

"And not ruin it," I said. "I ruined everything."

"Mmm, I don't think so. At least from what you've told me. And everyone was right about you. You are compassionate and have a heart of gold. You'd be great at helping people."

"Thanks." I smiled a little.

"Have you thought about having visitors?" She sat up and leaned against the tree. She played with a piece of pine straw, curling it around her finger and uncurling it.

I sat up cautiously. She seemed nervous, which was unusual behavior for her. "What's wrong?"

Emma sighed and tossed the pine straw. "I have

something to tell you."

"What?"

She bit her lip. "Well, Dr. Meisner told me yesterday, that, um, this is my last two weeks."

I stared at her, frozen. I wanted to tell her that I was happy for her and how proud I was of her. That I would miss her, but the words wouldn't come out. I looked away to hide my tears.

"Oh no, please don't cry." I felt her arms around me. "I'm not leaving you. You know I will keep in touch with you and visit."

I nodded. The words were still caught in my throat. I hated that I cried when I should have been celebrating with her. I only thought of myself and that made me feel guilty. I took a breath and pulled back from her slightly. "I'm sorry. I'm really happy for you, Emma."

She gave a sweet smile and a tear rolled down her cheek. "I promise if you just tell Dr. Meisner *everything*, you will recover. Don't make the mistake I did and just wait for it to happen. You are strong and I know you will survive this."

My chin quivered. "Thank you."

"I will give you every single piece of contact information I have so you can call or write anytime."

I nodded. "So are you done in two weeks for good?"

"I still have to come back for therapy. You know, to see how I'm doing in the real world. I'm really gonna miss you."

"Me, too."

We walked back to our room and I realized I only had two more weeks before I'd be alone in this room. Scott was gone, and soon Emma would be. Ginger was still there but we didn't talk much.

Someone knocked on the door, and then it opened. Nurse Smith came inside with her usual chipper smile. "Corinne, you have a visitor."

My heart dropped and my stomach clenched. It couldn't have been Dad, because she would've just said that it was him. And then she entered the room.

CHAPTER EIGHTEEN

Lisa smiled as if nothing happened the last time we saw each other. She actually seemed happy to see me. She introduced herself to Emma.

"Hi." Emma narrowed her eyes, and then looked to me for some sign. I nodded. "I'll leave you two alone." She walked out and closed the door behind her.

Lisa leaned against the dresser. "This room is so drab."

"Why are you here?" I asked.

"I came to apologize. How are you?"

"I'm in a hospital. How do you think I'm doing?"

She raised an eyebrow. "Chill out."

"Did my parents tell you I was here?"

"Yeah. I can't believe they put you here. Well, after the stunt you pulled, I guess I can understand. What do you do?"

"Mostly therapy." I wanted to forgive her for running out of the room that day, but I couldn't bring myself to do it.

"Why have you been here so long? Shouldn't you be out by now?" She paced the room.

"They won't release me until they think I'm okay to leave."

"But you're fine, right? I mean, you still don't think about those things you told me about. That was months ago."

How could I answer her? "Lisa, it's just really difficult."

She rolled her eyes. "Whatever. I started college and Jack broke up with me. Said I was too codependent and needy. Men suck. I swear all they ever do is lie to you and then leave you. So you wanna get out of here? It's kinda boring." She spoke really fast and couldn't be still. Was she on something?

"I can't leave."

"Why?"

"I mean, we can go for a walk outside, but that's about it. I don't have day pass privileges."

She stopped pacing and then she turned to me, eyes wide. "I could sneak you out. We could have an adventure." She giggled. "Oh it'll be so much fun."

I shook my head. "No."

She let out an exasperated sigh. "You are so boring. When are you ever gonna change?"

"My doctor says I'll get better once I start letting it all out. It's hard though. I don't want to relive it. I mean, the nightmares and panic attacks have calmed down, but I still can't get rid of this overwhelming guilt."

"Ugh, stop being so melodramatic. You're such a loser." She shook her head. "I dealt with enough of that with my father and it tore my family apart."

I clenched my teeth. "What did you want to apologize for exactly?"

"For running out on you. I figure since you're here you must be trying."

"You're sorry now. Until something else happens."

"What is wrong with you?"

"You always get upset about something and then apologize. But you never stop. I mean, I'm always waiting until your next outburst."

"And you don't do the same?"

"I haven't always been like this and you know it. I can't do this anymore, Lisa. So just leave me alone."

Her cold eyes glared at me. "Are you not grateful for

everything I've done for you? You are so selfish. I came here today, hoping we could resolve our friendship. I was hoping you would be back to normal. I'm so sick of you always playing the victim—like everyone is out to get you."

"It's not like that."

"I will never forgive you for what you did," she spat. She reached inside her purse and pulled out a bottle of ibuprofen. "Here." She tossed the bottle at me.

"Lisa, stop."

The door opened and I quickly hid it under my pillow. I didn't want to get caught with it.

Nurse Smith smiled. "Corinne, keep your door open when you have visitors." Then, she walked away.

Lisa turned back to me with such coldness in her eyes. "If you want to kill yourself and be selfish then go ahead. I don't care. No one would care or miss you. They'd welcome your death."

I felt sick. Why was she saying this? Words lodged in my throat. My breathing picked up and I was dizzy. My heart raced and I sweated. I remembered Dr. Meisner's tips. Count, and just breathe.

She sighed in exasperation. "Amos knows about you, too. I told him everything you did, and he agreed with me about your selfishness. He probably told James. Sorry." She shrugged. "I gotta go. This place gives me the creeps. Have a nice life, however short that'll probably be." With that, Lisa walked outside of the room.

I didn't hear Emma come back into the room or feel the tears that fell down my face.

"What did she say?" Emma shook me softly.

"I—." I couldn't talk. I breathed in and out until finally my heartbeat slowed.

"Don't listen to a word she said. I'm going to get Nurse Smith."

She stood, but I grabbed her hand. "No, please."

"Are you okay?"

"I'm fine." My head throbbed.

"What did she say?"

"It's nothing." I faked a smile and wiped my tears. "I'm fine."

I was fine when we ate dinner and came back to our room. I was just tired, at least that's what I told Emma. But the cramping in my stomach wouldn't go away and I couldn't get rid of the lump in my throat. All my friends knew about me. They hated me. I thought about all the angry letters from James waiting to be read on my desk at home. I shuddered. I was fine until it was time to receive my medications.

Instead of taking the pills, I stared at them. Rage grew inside of me. Why should I take them? I hated being here. Nothing changed. Emma was leaving. My friends hated me. Mom didn't even care enough to come visit. She just cared to know how long it would take for me to be normal again. She was embarrassed by the fact that her daughter was crazy. And it was clear she'd never forgive me.

I'd been here three months and was no different. Dr. Meisner's obvious impatience for me to open up pressured me, as if I could magically make myself better. Wasn't that *her* job?

And then I thought of Lisa's words again. *They'd welcome your death.*

"I hate it here," I screamed, throwing my cup on the ground. The pills scattered across the white glossy floor. "I've resolved nothing." Tears streamed down my face as I fell to my knees. I wanted out of there. Not just the hospital. I just wanted to leave everything.

"Corinne," Nurse Smith cried. "Please calm down." She came out of the nurses' office.

"I've been here too long. Can't you talk to Dr. Meisner about getting me out?"

"These things take time. You must be patient." She picked me up on my feet, and walked me back to my room. Everyone was quiet as they stared at the crazy girl. They whispered to each other.

Once inside the room, I sank onto the bed, and rested my

head in my hands. I tried calming my breathing. What had I become? I was a monster. I didn't know myself.

A few seconds later, Nurse Smith came back in the room with pills and water.

"I don't know what to say to help you." Her voice was calm. She knelt down, handing me the pills and water. "Just try. Try telling Dr. Meisner how you feel."

She made me so mad. "I've told her how I feel. She knows exactly what happened to me." I held my stomach as it twisted tighter and tighter. I took the pills and the small cup of water.

"Have you actually told someone what happened?" Her voice was barely above a whisper. I could hear a faint quiver in her voice. Was she afraid of me?

I popped the pills in my mouth, and then drank the water. I tossed both cups into the trash can.

"Open," she firmly said, referring to my mouth. My accusation of her fearing me had vanished once her stern voice returned.

I opened my mouth for her and lifted my tongue. "I swallowed the damn things, okay?"

Nurse Smith didn't say anything else as she left the room. I fell back on my bed, and waited. Waited for the right time to come. Waited to finally leave. While I lay there, Lisa's words blinked in my mind like a yellow caution light. *They'd welcome your death.*

CHAPTER NINETEEN

That night, after I made sure Emma was asleep, I pulled out the bottle of pills and poured them into my clammy palm. Their orange coating stained my hands. I sat on the edge of my bed and stared at them in the orange glow from the light outside. Would I really do this? *Could* I do this again? What would happen if I did?

I grabbed the glass of water I asked for earlier and popped the pills, a little at a time, in my mouth. My face twitched from the horrible taste. I drank all of the water and the pills rushed down my throat and into my stomach. For a second I felt them trying to come back up, but I forced them to stay down. And waited.

They'd welcome your death.

After what seemed like forever, my heart began pounding. I squeezed the sheets on my bed. Sweat beads trickled down my face, and I was cold. My hands shook violently and I kept swallowing. My eyes couldn't focus any longer and my breaths were short. I leaned over and winced in pain. The glass fell from my hand and clattered on the floor. My eyes watered and I fell forward onto the floor. I heard Emma's voice and saw her figure moving toward me. Her voice seemed so far away. I closed my eyes.

"Corinne, wake up," she yelled but it was muffled. "Nurse Smith!"

They'd welcome your death.

I felt their hands on me and heard their endless pleas to keep me awake. I kept my eyes closed and forced myself not to throw up. Again, I saw the blackness as Emma and Nurse Smith's voices became more distant. I felt relaxed. I saw him. Standing in front of me.

"Cor, don't do this." His blue eyes didn't smile.

"I can't live anymore. I want to be with you."

"Wake up, Corinne. Be strong. Please. Live your life."

"David, don't go."

"I'm here. I'm always here."

I blinked my eyes several times until they focused. I heard many voices and the light was so bright. And then I saw Dad leaning over me, holding my hand.

"You are strong," he said. "We love you very much. David would not want this. Neither do we."

I opened my eyes, tears dropping into my hands, and stared at the bottle of pills. I couldn't do it. I couldn't put my family or myself through that again. I got to my feet and walked into the bathroom. I opened the bottle, dropped the pills into the toilet, and flushed them.

CHAPTER TWENTY

When I woke up, I told Emma everything that Lisa said to me, and she told me not to believe it. I kept the pills a secret from her.

We had breakfast and then went to group. I listened to the others talk about their issues. Their alcoholic fathers. The need to cut themselves. Or whatever they wanted to talk about. Since Tracy had been absent again, the atmosphere was definitely less intense. I apologized for my outburst, but they all understood. They'd all done it once or twice.

I went to Dr. Meisner's office for my session. I had to tell her what happened last night. I knew I had to. It was the right thing to do, wasn't it?

"Lisa came yesterday," I said.

She nodded. "I know."

I told her everything Lisa said.

"Had I known she would be here, I don't think I would have allowed her to visit you, at least, unsupervised. She just cannot be trusted."

I nodded slowly, but didn't look at her. I wringed my fingers together. My palms were sweaty. I needed to tell her.

"Are you okay?"

"I-I need to tell you something."

"What is it?"

I could feel the panic coming, but I calmed myself. *Just tell her what happened.*

Dr. Meisner waited patiently.

I swallowed the lump in my throat. Just *tell* her. I fidgeted with my ring. I took a deep breath. The pulsating in my chest rang through my head. *Tell her.*

"Lisa threw a bottle of pills at me yesterday."

"What?" I could hear the shock in her voice.

"She told me if I wanted to kill myself, to go ahead. Last night, I thought about swallowing them all."

We were quiet for a few seconds.

"What happened?"

"I just stared at the bottle for the longest time and thought about what would happen if I took them. And then I decided, I couldn't do it. I flushed them." I cried.

"I'm proud of you."

"Why? I broke the rules."

"Because you told me. And because you decided to do the right thing."

"I want to get better. I know I've probably revoked my own privileges and have to start over and will have to be on suicide watch again."

"Do you think you need to be?"

I took a moment before responding to make sure it sounded true. And to be sure I believed it myself. "No. I want to get better. I want out of this."

"Then I won't put you on suicide watch, but I will have to tell the nurses about this, and they will have to check the visitors more closely."

I nodded. "Please don't tell my parents."

"Whatever you tell me does not leave this room."

"I don't want to see Lisa again."

"I understand. But something inside you was stronger than anything she could have said. It reached you. What was it?"

"I just imagined what my dad would say."

"Do you think your subconscious was really telling you those things?"

I hadn't thought about it. But I guess she could have been right.

After therapy, Emma and I talked in our room. I was going to miss her.

There was a knock at the door, and Nurse Smith opened it with a smile. "You've got a visitor," she told me.

The thoughts in my mind were like a thousand fireworks exploding. Who was it? Was it Lisa? I couldn't handle another episode like yesterday. Nurse Smith moved out of the way and ushered in a tall, round man with a red ball of hair. I froze and watched Amos hesitantly enter the room. I saw the anxiety in his brown eyes.

"Hey." He gave a timid grin. I had missed his accent. And him.

How did he know I was there? Had Lisa really told him? I cleared my throat. "Hey." I hated how feeble my voice sounded.

"How are you?"

"I'm okay."

"Good." He looked to Emma. "Hi, I'm Amos." He held out his hand for her, which was shaking. Amos was afraid of me.

She smiled. "I'm Emma."

I wanted to talk to him, but I was scared he would yell at me like Lisa. Several questions boiled on the tip of my tongue that begged to come out, but I said nothing. The silence was awkward.

"Can you go for a walk?" he asked.

"Sure." My mouth was so dry. He followed me outside to the sweltering August day. We both took a seat on mine and Emma's favorite bench.

"It's pretty here," he said, his fingers tapping his knee.

"Yeah."

It hurt me to see him so nervous around me. Walking on eggshells, Scott once said.

"Doctors are nice?"

"Yeah." I hated the awkwardness.

He nodded. "That's cool."

"Yeah."

Amos exhaled. "I know you're wondering why I'm here. Please don't be upset that I came."

"I'm not."

"I saw Lisa at school and she told me you were gone." He shook his head. I saw the muscles in his jaw twitch. "She said some unpleasant things and told me you tried to take your life and that you were in a hospital. I went to your house and practically made your father tell me which one. He said you didn't want anyone to know."

"He's right."

"When Lisa told me that, I freaked out. I had no idea things were so serious. I knew you were struggling, but then when you quit work, I never heard from you." He bowed his head. I didn't know what to say. "I feel awful, Corinne. I had no idea the pain you were in. I should've called or come by."

How could he feel awful? I was the one who hurt him. "It was probably best that you didn't. I haven't been a good person lately."

"You know I care about you. I don't know what happened. I only heard Lisa's story. But I want you to know that I'm here for you."

It was the complete opposite of what I had expected him to say. "Amos, it's so hard for me to be happy because it doesn't feel right. I'm constantly haunted by it. Like I'm meant to suffer. It's like I'm always walking through a foggy, black night. I can't see or feel anything. It's just...quiet. I only knew one way to end it all."

Amos took my hand in his. It was warm and comforting against my cold skin. We stayed like that for a while.

"So, you don't agree with Lisa?"

"Bloody hell no!"

I exhaled, unaware that I'd been holding my breath. Lisa lied. Why would she do that? "Did you tell James?"

"I haven't talked to him in months. I don't have his number." Awareness came over his face. "He doesn't know any of this?"

I shook my head. "No."

"Oh, wow. Hasn't he tried to contact you?"

I took a deep breath. "Dad says he's been sending letters. But the last time I saw him, we fought. Mom wouldn't let him come back or call. He still called a few times after that, but I told him not to."

"Well, what do his letters say?"

"I don't know. I haven't read them."

"Why?" he asked softly.

"I'm scared of what they'll say."

"Do you want me to call him?"

"No."

Amos stayed with me until the end of visiting hours. We talked about my being here, his school and work, and sadly I actually missed work. I started to get jealous because I wanted to be out there living my life.

"Corinne." Nurse Smith's voice came from behind us. I knew what she was going to say before she said it. "Visiting hours are over."

I sighed, not wanting to let go of the moment. It had been such a long time since I had felt this comfort. I felt for a moment, all my shattered pieces together again, not completely healed, but close enough.

I didn't want Amos to leave, and I guessed he could see that in my eyes. We both stood from the bench and followed Nurse Smith inside.

"It's okay." He squeezed my hand. "I'll come back if you want."

I nodded vigorously. "Yes."

"Are you sure you don't want me to call James?" he asked again.

I wanted to see him, but I didn't want him to see me like this. I didn't want anyone for that matter to see me like this. But I didn't want him wasting his time on me. "He needs to move on."

Amos pulled me to him, pressing me into his chest. His arms held me like that for a moment. "I'll come back tomorrow."

"I'm glad Amos came to see you," Dr. Meisner said. "He sounds like a very caring friend."

"Yeah," I said.

"How do you feel about him visiting?"

"I don't know. I don't want anyone seeing me here."

"Why is that?"

"Because I'm ashamed."

"Of what?"

I twirled my ring around my finger. "Of being here. Trying to kill myself. Any number of things."

"Why don't you tell me more of your memories? I've enjoyed listening to them."

"There are no more."

"You are making such great progress. You've come so close, and I don't want you to stop."

I chewed on the inside of my mouth. "It's not that easy."

"I understand."

"Do you? Do you really understand that it should have been me to die and not David?"

"Is that why you tried to kill yourself?"

"I thought we've already established this."

"I want *you* to tell me, Corinne."

I sighed in exasperation, and then stood from the couch and walked to the window. The mid-afternoon sun made the green leaves on the trees so vibrant. There was a steady breeze that moved the puffy clouds across the sky.

I closed my eyes and felt a tear drop down my cheek. I wiped it away and turned back to her. "Isn't our session over?"

She stood from her desk, and moved beside me. "I just want you to know that you can trust me. Once you face the issue and deal with it, you will eventually *learn* to accept and forgive yourself."

"I don't think I can relive it."

"The nightmares will end."

I glanced at her and then moved back to the couch and rested my head in my hands. My stomach constricted itself as if a snake was wrapped around me. My palms sweated.

"I know you're afraid. We are all afraid to speak our deepest fears or secrets. We fear the reactions of others."

I nodded. I didn't know when or if I would be ready to talk. What would Dr. Meisner think? Would she just think of me as a selfish person who is just taking up her time? Would she be ashamed of me like everyone else? Angry? But she knew what happened. Why did she want to hear it from me?

I left therapy with my stomach in knots and made it back to my room. Seeing Emma's belongings packed only made my stomach twist tighter. I tried not to panic at the thought of being in the room alone or someone new moving in. I felt comfort with Emma there.

Since she told me she was leaving, Emma and I talked incessantly about everything, well sort of. I wanted to tell her and Dr. Meisner what happened to me, but it was like I'd hit a brick wall or an electric gate. Amos visited every other day and I didn't overlook the cute smile on his face when he saw Emma, or the way her eyes lit when he came. I could tell they were attracted.

"Has Amos said anything about me?" she asked.

"He's asked about you."

She bit her lip. "I wanna get to know him more."

"He's a great guy. I think he likes you."

"Really?"

"You remind me of me."

She smiled a little, but then frowned.

"What?" I asked.

"Corinne, you—." She pressed her lips together, contorting her face as if in deep thought. "You should call him."

"I'm sure he'll be here tomorrow. He knows it's your last day."

She shook her head. "I mean James."

I shifted uncomfortably. "I can't."

Emma moved to sit beside me on the bed. "He will forgive you."

"You don't know that."

"He wouldn't still be writing letters if he was angry with you."

I hadn't thought of that. But I remembered Dr. Meisner mentioning the negative thought and how automatic it was for me to think so negatively. But I was ashamed to have people see me there.

"Tell Dr. Meisner *everything*, Corinne. Don't let this condition control you. You can trust her and you will recover. I know you can do this."

"But what if I can't? I don't want anyone leaving me again."

Emma leaned toward me, an arm around my shoulder. "Then don't leave them."

I took an uneven breath. "I-I just don't want to be angry anymore or have anyone angry with me. How can I stop feeling guilty?"

"These are questions and thoughts you need to share with Dr. Meisner. She won't judge you at all. No one will run from you. If you're thinking of Lisa, don't." Her soft voice was firm. "She wasn't a good friend. And Amos wouldn't be here every day if he was angry."

"What about my mom?"

She frowned. "I don't know. She might be having a hard time coping with everything. I can't tell you what to do or how things will turn out. But I can suggest that you focus on *you*. Focus on getting better and finding yourself again. She's still in there."

I didn't sleep much that night because Emma's words circled in my mind. Though, sleep hadn't really been great since I'd been talking about my past life. I would lie down, close my eyes, and see James. I wanted to hear his voice. Feel his arms around me. And gaze into his incredible blue eyes. It was like torture because I didn't deserve him. And then it would all start over. The guilt. The pain. Everything. I wanted to talk to my brother to hear his advice. Or just to see him. I hated what I did. But Emma's encouragement, and the support from Amos and Dad, and even Dr. Meisner pushed me to make the decision. I knew what I had to do.

CHAPTER TWENTY-ONE

Emma's party was bittersweet. Now that she'd gained weight, her face was full and not sallow and she smiled the whole time. She gave me a hug before she left. Later that day, I went to therapy with the courage to finally finish. It was time to take down the wall that prevented me from feeling happy, brick by brick. I could see bits of light coming through, but I needed to continue. As much as I was scared to relive it, I couldn't live with the nightmares.

I wiped the sweat from my hands on my jeans. I felt like I was going to lose my lunch right there on Dr. Meisner's couch.

"Corinne, are you okay?" she asked.

I nodded and then took a deep breath. "I tried to kill myself because it was the only answer I found to end my pain. It was all I could think of to make things right. After what I did to my brother, I don't deserve to live." I sighed. "It's something I've wanted to forget. Something I never wanted to think of again. But no matter how hard I try it always comes back to me in my dreams. I can't keep it inside any longer. I've lost so much because of the tragedy." Biting my lip and forcing the tears back, I met Dr. Meisner's curious look. "I killed my brother."

Dr. Meisner furrowed her eyebrows. "What do you mean?"

"I killed him.

"Everyone had come home for the holidays and I loved having them home. We had a good Christmas and New Year's, drama free. I had gone to see James on his last night before he went back to school. I wasn't feeling all that great, like I was coming down with something, so James and I just cuddled in bed and watched a movie.

David was hanging out at Charles's house. His car had died a couple of days prior, so I offered to take him back to school. I planned on staying with Abby and coming back the next morning.

"Corinne." I heard James say.

I opened my eyes and realized I had fallen asleep. I was a little upset because I didn't want to miss any time with James. "What time is it?"

"It's about nine. Your phone just rang."

It was David calling to let me know he was ready for me to pick him up. I reluctantly pushed the covers aside and slid out of the bed. I shivered, knowing the tell-tale signs of a fever.

"Are you sure you're gonna be okay?" James asked. "You're not looking so great. Maybe you should stay so I can take very good care of you." He gave a wicked grin.

I playfully smacked him in the shoulder and he laughed. "I'm fine." I slid my feet into my boots.

He sighed, wrapping his arms around me. "This is the part I hate."

"Me, too."

He leaned down to kiss me, but I stopped him.

"I don't want to get you sick."

James rolled his eyes and then kissed me, never holding anything back. The way his arms held me tight and the way his lips softly, yet eagerly moved with mine always made my knees weak.

He walked me to my car, and even though it was unusually

warm outside, I shivered. Stupid weather. Probably the culprit for my oncoming sickness.

James buried his face in my neck, giving me little kisses. "I'll see you soon, Mrs. Arion."

I never got tired of hearing that. "I'm not Mrs. Arion, yet."

He kissed my cheek. "You are to me."

I smiled. "I love you so much."

"I love you." I could hear the desire in his gravelly voice as his eyes gazed into mine.

I didn't want to leave, but if I didn't soon, we probably would have ended up in my backseat, delaying me further. I shook my head as if trying to get the image out of my mind.

I cleared my throat. "I'll call when I get there."

He chuckled and I assumed he knew what I was thinking. "I'll be waiting."

I kissed him once more and then left. I tried not to be too sad about him leaving again. I reminded myself that we only had a few more months of the long distance thing and then he'd be home for the summer.

I turned on the radio to distract me, and to keep me from yawning. I picked up David and we left.

"Did you have fun?" I asked, and then yawned. It wasn't that long of a drive, and my body started aching. As soon as I got there, I would take some medicine and sleep it off.

"Yeah. Played some games."

"Cool."

"What'd you and your fiancé do?" he asked.

I smiled. "Just hung out. I hate it when he has to leave."

"I know. You've been doing well with it though. Can't believe you got engaged before me."

"I can't believe it either."

"So, what are you doing tomorrow?"

"Driving back home, why?"

He cleared his throat. "I was wondering if you wanted to go ring shopping with me."

"Are you freaking serious? Omigod! That's awesome."

"Yeah. I think maybe Abby and I should get engaged. I

love her. I just came to the realization that I really want to spend the rest of my life with her. She's an amazing woman and she means a lot to me."

"It's going to be awesome that Abby will be my sister-in-law. I'm so happy for you."

"Well, I don't know if she'll say yes."

"Pff, you know she will."

"You really think so?"

I rolled my eyes. "Of course. She's head over heels for you."

I saw his smile in the blue glow of the interior lights.

David eventually fell asleep, and I turned up the radio to help me stay awake. It started to thunder and, off in the distance, it lightened. I hoped I made it before the rains came. I hated driving in the rain especially at night.

I couldn't believe David's confession. My own crazy engagement. And how I loved my life. I was very lucky. And then in an instant it was gone.

I heard a loud crack and opened my eyes. The car had veered into the other lane and I realized I had closed my eyes but I didn't know for how long. I jerked the wheel and then the car slid. I gasped and my heart skipped a beat.

And immediately, without thinking, I slammed on the brakes.

But it was too late. The car lost control and then the headlights flashed on an oncoming tree. I closed my eyes. And then, there was an ocean of noise. Glass exploded. Metal grinded. Piercing sounds hurt my ears. I felt debris cutting my face as my body lunged forward, but my seatbelt held me back.

And then silence.

Everything stopped.

Then, I heard the soft pattering of rain. Something trickled down my face, but I could barely see anything. A flash illuminated in the night and I saw metal crumpled up in front of me and blood. I tried moving my legs and arms, but it was like they didn't listen to my brain. I couldn't move. I felt paralyzed.

"David?" I could barely hear myself from the ringing in my ears. I cleared my throat and repeated his name. Queasiness settled in my stomach and I could barely breathe.

Another flash of lightning and I saw David bent over the dash, climbing through the windshield. I guessed his door wouldn't open.

"Are you okay?" I struggled with each word. Why wasn't he talking to me? I couldn't stand the silence.

The lightning flashed again, and I saw David in the same position as before. Was he stuck? Had he passed out from too much exertion?

I wanted to sleep, so I closed my eyes.

I woke to voices and random noises.

"David." My voice was so weak.

"Ma'am, please stay calm," someone said. "We'll get you out as soon as we can."

Get me out of what? I was cold and wet. And I couldn't move. My head ached and my mouth was dry. I licked my lips and tasted blood. What was going on?

Maybe I was having a weird dream.

I groaned and then closed my eyes as the voices and sounds slipped further and further away.

CHAPTER TWENTY-TWO

Enormous pain circulated throughout my entire body, which couldn't move. My head throbbed and it felt like something was crushing me. I felt a stabbing pain in my ribs every time I breathed. I tried lifting my left arm, but it wouldn't budge. I found a tube and traced it with my fingers it to my nose. I felt a bandage around my head. There was a needle in the crook of my elbow and a tube that went somewhere I couldn't see. I had a clip of some type on the tip of my finger. I brought my hand to my face and felt several long and short scratches along my cheeks, jawbone, neck. And my right eye was tender.

What had happened to me?

I searched the room slowly and stopped once I saw my parents holding each other as they peered out the window.

"Mom." My voice was barely audible.

"Corinne!" Mom cried as she and Dad rushed to my bedside. "Oh god, you're awake." Her face was puffy and her eyes were red. She grabbed my hand and squeezed it gently. "You're okay." She gave a pained smile.

"How do you feel?" Dad asked.

"I-I'm…okay. Just sore and a headache." It took more than I expected just to speak. "It hurts to breathe."

"I'll tell Dr. Andrews." Dad leaned down and kissed me on my forehead, but I couldn't feel it for the bandage. Then, he walked out.

"What happened?" I asked.

"Shhh, don't talk now," Mom said.

"Talk to me." I could barely keep my eyes open. I didn't want to go back to sleep, but I couldn't deny the lethargy that enveloped me.

"You were in an accident." Tears streamed down her face and her chin quivered. Her voice was on the verge of hysterics. "You've been unconscious for two days."

I was stunned. Two days? "Did I break anything?"

"We'll let the doctor explain it. You were very lucky."

"I saw David climbing out. Where is he? He never answered me. I wanna see him."

"Honey—."

The door opened and a tall man with a head full of gray hair walked to my bedside with my father.

"Good evening, Corinne," he said with a smile. "I'm Dr. Andrews. I'm glad to see you're awake." He had a loud voice that hurt my ears.

My parents backed away a little as the doctor began checking my IVs, heartbeat, breathing.

"How are you feeling?"

"I'm sore and my head hurts." I took a deep breath, and winced. "It hurts to breathe." "Anything else?"

"It hurts here, too." I traced the pain with my hand across my chest.

"That's where the seatbelt was." He pointed to my chest. "You have a large bruise from it, which should heal within a week or so."

"What else?" I made a sudden move to try and sit up in the bed, but Dr. Andrews placed a hand on my shoulder.

"Don't move too much. Just rest. You have a broken arm, two fractured ribs, fractured knee, a cut on your forehead, a bruised eye, and a few cuts on your face and arms. For now, I've put you on morphine for the pain"

"Okay."

"Your arm is in a cast and we'll give you a sling for it. Your left leg is in a brace and will be until your knee begins to heal from the surgeries. The soreness you feel will go away in a few days. Your ribs will heal on their own." I assumed he was also speaking to my parents because I kept closing my eyes. "Also, try to take a deep breath every hour so you won't develop pneumonia or a partial collapsed lung. I've given your parents all the instructions. You're very lucky to have survived that accident."

I inhaled and then exhaled, as I let the information soak in. There were so many injuries. I tried remembering them all, but gave up because of my sleepiness. Mom wept into my father's chest. He placed his arm around her.

"Tomorrow we'll run some more tests." Dr. Andrews nodded. "You get some rest, okay?"

"Okay." I said. "Where's David? Is he okay?"

Dr. Andrews looked up at my parents and I followed his sullen eyes. I knew something was up when they didn't answer me.

"What? What is it? Is he okay?" I tried sitting up again, but Dr. Andrews stopped me.

"Corinne, you must not move. You have to rest." He motioned for my parents to follow him. "I'm sorry, but she really needs to get some rest."

My mother immediately broke down and wailed. Hearing her pained cries made me sick to my stomach. She covered her face with her hands and rushed out of the room.

"Will someone tell me?" I yelled with everything I had, and ignored the immense throbbing pain, and it left me breathless.

"I'll leave you two alone." Dr. Andrews told my dad and then left the room.

I locked eyes with Dad's. Small tears filled in his brown eyes.

"Corinne, David—." He sighed and pulled a chair next to my bed and took my hand in his. They were warm and comforting.

My body tensed. What was he about to say?

He cleared his throat and took a breath. "I don't know how to say this."

Was David in a coma? We could wake him. I'd heard stories of people waking up because they heard their loved ones pleading with them. Everything would be okay.

"David," he said, but then a rush of emotion overwhelmed him. He squeezed my hand and couldn't seem to finish his sentence.

My mouth went dry. I didn't like this. I didn't like the way he clutched onto my hand as if it was the only thing he had to hold onto. I didn't like his sobbing. The only other time I'd seen my dad cry was at his mom's funeral. I didn't want to hear what he was about to say.

Dad took another breath, but kept his eyes closed. "David died." His voice cracked.

I froze. I couldn't breathe. A wave of nausea passed over me and my vision blurred. It had to be a dream. This wasn't real. I shook my head. "No. I saw him climbing out of the car."

"H-he wasn't wearing his seatbelt."

"No no no no."

"I didn't want to tell you as soon as you woke up." I could barely understand him through his thick tears.

I lost my voice, my mind a jumbled mess of incoherent thoughts. My heart sank deeper and deeper forming a hole beneath my chest. Goosebumps covered me as a chill passed through the room. I couldn't stop shaking. His face circled in my mind. I closed my eyes and saw him. The saliva in my mouth produced faster and faster and no matter how many times I swallowed, it appeared instantaneously. I leaned over the side of my bed opposite Dad and hurled. The pain in my ribs was unbearable. But nothing compared to this.

I barely felt Dad's hands and barely heard his murmurs.

A couple of nurses came in and cleaned up the floor and checked my monitors. One of them stuck a needle in the IV and whispered something to Dad.

I tried remembering exactly what happened, but my mind was clouded from medicine. Bits and pieces flashed in my mind. David was asleep. It was quiet and I had opened my eyes. The car veered in the other lane. I swerved and then slid. And crashed.

I stiffened. Had I closed my eyes? Had I fallen asleep at the wheel? Was that really what happened? I wished I could remember.

Oh God, what had I done?

CHAPTER TWENTY-THREE

I didn't know how long I'd been asleep, and I was so sore. It was hard to open my eyes because they were so dry. As my mind became clearer, I remembered the nightmare. My brother was dead. How could this be? I didn't even get to say goodbye. I'll never see his smile again or hear his laughter. My heart just...collapsed. I could feel the paralysis creeping throughout me.

This had to be a dream.

And then my memory of the accident came back to me. How could I have done that? How could I have been so reckless?

I didn't cry or move or talk. I just lay there like some corpse.

I was in and out of sleep through most of the day and the nurses constantly checked on me. I let them poke and prod me. I didn't care. Nothing took my mind off what I had done.

The rain hitting the metal sounded like popcorn popping. Redness blurred my vision of the crumpled metal. Thunder cracked, forcing me to jump through my skin. I stood outside of the car by the tree. I tilted my head and froze. His blue eyes stared intently into mine. Blood covered his face. I gasped for air as the rain suddenly flooded my lungs.

I opened my eyes, and gasped for air. I cried out as the deep breath vibrated my ribs. I peered out into the dim room. The only light was from underneath the door from the hall. The makeshift cot that Dad had been sleeping in was empty. He must have taken a break.

The door opened, and I closed my eyes. I knew it was the nurse coming in to check on me.

I heard the person shuffle near the bed, and then I felt him take my hand. It must have been Dad because I heard him softly cry. He kissed my hand and sat in the chair next to the bed. I knew I would have to confess to him what had happened in the accident, but I was scared. I couldn't break his heart any more than I had.

"Oh God, Corinne."

Warm tears rolled down my cheeks. "James." I attempted to sit up, but I winced and sucked in air. "I want to see you." I wanted to feel him and to know he was really there. I needed something.

I heard him blindly searching for the light switch, and then a soft light came on. I was glad it wasn't the fluorescent one.

The whites around his blue eyes were red and his hair was disheveled. He looked as if he hadn't slept or shaved in days. I knew I probably looked like hell with a swollen black eye and several cuts that serrated my face.

"Corinne." James quickly wrapped his arms around me, but I flinched from the pain. "Shit. Sorry." He slightly pulled back, grabbed my hand, and then tenderly kissed me. His lips kissed my cuts, as if he were healing them one by one. I was so touched by the gesture and his affection that I started crying again.

He squeezed my hand and pressed his forehead to mine. I wanted to be wrapped up in his arms, as if he could protect me from the pain that I felt. All of it.

"I never want to let you go," he said. His voice sounded as if he'd be screaming for hours. And I could hear his longing, relief, and sorrow. "I couldn't stand not seeing you."

"Have you been here long?" My breath made a grating sound.

"Ever since your dad called me. I don't know what I would have done if I lost you. I love you so much."

I started crying again. I couldn't control my emotions and I knew I would have to tell someone what I did. I just didn't know how.

His lips grazed my cheek, and though he was close, I wanted him closer.

"It hurts so much," I said. How could I heal if I kept hurting myself?

"I'm so sorry. Do you want me to call the nurses?"

I nodded, and he pressed the button on my bed remote.

A few seconds later, a woman in magenta scrubs with straight black hair walked in, and her warm black hand touched mine. "Hey hon. What can I get you?"

"I'm in pain."

"Okay, hon. Let me check when the last time you had morphine and if it's time, I'll get you a dose." She walked out and then returned a few minutes later with Dad behind her.

James got to his feet as the nurse came to the bedside with a needle. She stuck the needle and pushed its fluid into the IV tube. "She'll be out soon."

"It's okay," Dad said. "Get some rest."

"C-can I please stay?" James asked. "I could stay the night if that's okay."

Dad nodded and then turned to me. "Would you mind if I went home?"

I shook my head.

He leaned down and kissed my forehead but still lingered by the bed.

"I'll be okay."

Dad nodded again and then left, albeit reluctant, with the nurse.

James returned by my side and took my hands, kissing them.

"It should have been me," I said.

He shook his head. "Don't say that. Neither of you deserve this."

"I'm here. He's not. I did this."

My eyes were getting heavier and I could feel the morphine moving quickly through my veins.

When I woke the next morning, I felt as if I was suffocating. My brother was gone because of me. I didn't want to face another day, another second without him. I felt so empty. And I kept thinking, wishing, hoping that he would just walk right through the door with a big smile on his face.

But he never did.

I turned my head and saw James asleep on the chair-turned-cot. His feet hung over at the end and his arms were crossed. He looked peaceful, finally. All through the night, some machine would stop or break and an alarm would go off waking us both. How could anyone get rest in a hospital with so much going on?

I wanted James to be holding me, but I knew that wasn't possible. I felt like I was breaking into pieces. My mind taunted me. I had visions of me falling asleep and losing the grip on the wheel. But that hadn't happened. I just closed my eyes for a second. But that second cost the life of my brother. What would happen now?

I kept replaying it over and over in my head. The car sliding and slamming into the tree. The grinding and popping. And the silence. Seeing my brother leaning out of the windshield.

I stiffened. David wasn't trying to get out of the car. He went through the windshield.

Ohgodohgodohgod.

The room spun and my breathing labored. I couldn't take it anymore. I didn't want to remember these awful images.

"Hey, Corinne, what's wrong?" James asked, kneeling beside the bed, and taking my hand. "Are you in pain? I mean, physical."

I babbled and I tried curling into a ball to keep the pain

from hurting so much. But nothing I did helped. I held onto James's hand so tight, he reached for the nurse's button, but I stopped him.

I felt him sweep aside my hair and kiss my forehead and cheek. He never said a word, but he was comforting. I finally calmed down after a while and he stayed with me.

Mom and Dad came back, looking worse, and then I realized they were probably working on funeral arrangements. I felt sick at the word. This wasn't right. It wasn't happening.

Dr. Andrews ran test after test after test and then I finally got to lay down. They reminded me to take a deep breath every hour. I wanted to get out of this place.

When the door opened, I thought it was the doctor or a nurse, but then I saw her short blond hair and my stomach dropped.

"Oh, Abby," Mom cried and gave her a tight hug, and then Dad hugged her. James acknowledged her with a nod.

"We'll leave you two alone," Dad said and he and Mom walked out.

James squeezed my hand and then left.

Abby slowly lowered herself into the chair, as if she was afraid to sit. Her green eyes looked faded by the redness that surrounded them. Her once vivacious face held a grim look. What could I possibly say? How could I tell Abby that he was going to propose? Would she ever speak to me again?

"I just wanted to come see how you were doing." She painfully smiled.

"Thanks."

An awkward silence filled the room. We had never experienced that before. We always talked over each other or knew what the other would say before we said it.

She sighed. "I know this is hard. But, I-what hap-how could you lose control of the car?" Her chin quivered and an endless stream of tears fell down her face.

No words came to my mouth. I looked away from her.

"I-I can't do this, I'm sorry." She jumped out of the chair and ran out of the room.

I closed my eyes and tried swallowing the lump in my throat. Would it ever go away? *How could you lose control of the car?* was all that paced in my mind, backwards and forwards. Forwards and backwards. Each word being dissected as if it were something to study for a test. Except, my mind changed the words. *How could you fall asleep at the wheel? How could you kill your brother?*

"Corinne," James said, as he was by my side again, comforting me. I didn't deserve it. I took away something precious from everyone around me. I was ashamed. Disgusted. Angry.

Over the next few hours, my grandparents, Lisa, and Amos came to see me. There was more crying and whispering, but I was numb to it all. Then, the doctor came back with my test results. I tried listening to every word he said, but it seemed all so insignificant. I picked up the gist. Suffered mild concussion. Very minimum damage. May cause daily headaches. Pills to help with anxiety and sleeping problems. Heal within six to eight weeks. Get plenty of rest. Take deep breaths. Should see a grief counselor. Rehab. Lucky to have survived.

But I wasn't lucky.

Mom kissed me before she left. I felt worse for her having to split her time between seeing after a child in my condition and having to make arrangements for the other. It wasn't fair. And I only felt guiltier.

Dad stayed behind and made James go home to rest for a little bit. They planned on releasing me the next day, but the thought of going home made me ill. How would it ever feel like home without my brother?

"Dad," I said.

"What is it?"

"It was my fault."

"What are you talking about?" His eyebrows furrowed. "They said you might have swerved to miss something."

I bit my lip, hard and squeezed my eyes shut. "I fell asleep.

But my eyes were only closed for a second."

"Oh, Corinne," he said, after a moment of stunned silence. I could hear the disappointment in his voice. "We'll get through this. We'll get through this." He kept repeating. He told me he loved me and that he wasn't upset with me.

But I'd made a mistake. A very costly mistake.

The door opened, and for a second I thought it was James, but then I saw an officer. Dad stood and shook hands with him. My heart pounded. It was like having the principal come into a classroom and single me out, but worse.

"Hi, Corinne," the short, black man said. "I'm Officer Chancellor and I'm here to ask some questions about Saturday's accident." He had a calming voice and a friendly disposition.

I nodded, squeezing my father's hand.

Officer Chancellor opened his notepad and clicked his pen. "I got your general information from your driver's license that I found at the scene. Corinne Elliot, seventeen."

"Yes," I said.

"Do you remember what happened?"

The room blurred, and I wiped my tears. Dad wrapped an arm around me.

I drew in a shaky breath. "I-I was taking my brother back to school. He fell asleep. I-I—." The words lodged in my throat.

"It's okay," Officer Chancellor said. "Take your time."

"I closed my eyes, and then when I opened them, my car- it went into the other lane. I swerved and lost control," I sobbed.

"How fast were you going?"

I shook my head. "I don't know. Sixty five. Seventy."

"She never speeds," Dad added.

"How long had you been awake before driving?"

"I don't know. Since mid-morning."

He nodded. "Did you fall asleep at the wheel?"

I nodded, feeling completely ashamed.

"Okay. And then you woke up and your car had veered in

the other lane. You overcorrected and lost control and then the car hit the tree. Is that right?"

"Yes." My voice was barely above a whisper.

"Did you know your brother wasn't wearing his seatbelt?"

I shook my head.

He closed his notepad.

"Is she going to be charged with anything?" Dad asked.

I hadn't thought of that. Would they send me to jail for killing my brother? I closed my eyes and gripped Dad's hand.

"No. Her actions weren't reckless, but she was clearly negligent. Your son died because he wasn't wearing his seatbelt. I'm really sorry," he said, and then I heard the click of the door behind him.

Dad pulled me close and kissed my temple. David always wore his seatbelt. How could they know for sure he wasn't wearing it? If he had worn it, would he still be here?

I shook my head. He'd still be here had it not been for my complete negligence. Why weren't they hauling me off in the police car? Why was I the one laying in the hospital bed alive and not David?

When we got home, Dad helped me inside, his arm around me. Booger calmly wagged his curled, fluffy black tail and let out a soft whine. He cautiously watched me as Dad helped me hobble up the six stairs to my room. Pain stabbed me with each step. When I reached the top, I glanced down the hall to the closed door to David's room. Tears clouded my vision as Dad gently pulled me toward my room. Once I reached my bed, I froze. David's Auburn hat rested on my pillow.

Dad cleared his throat. "We thought it would be best if you kept this. If you're not ready for it…"

I shook my head and picked up the hat, holding it close to me. Dad eased me down onto the bed and propped me up against several pillows. I was already dressed in pajamas, thankful I didn't have to go through that process again.

After he left, I sat up, ignored the pain, and slowly

staggered toward my door. I listened for him to walk downstairs and when he did, I opened my door and made my way to David's room, dragging my useless leg behind me. My balance was off, but I didn't care. Booger quietly followed me as I slowly turned the doorknob and entered the room. He whined and placed his tail between his legs before he followed me inside.

David didn't look up from his computer game to say hello. He wasn't relaxed on his bed watching a movie or football. He wasn't even air guitaring to any music or tossing his football in the air. He wasn't there. I told myself that he was just away at college. This wasn't real.

I slowly slid to the floor next to the bed. Booger nudged me softly and sat next to me. I rested my head against David's bed while Booger laid his head in my lap.

The bulge in my throat grew and never went away. The tears never stopped falling down my face. There was nothing but the silence and the piercing pain.

CHAPTER TWENTY-FOUR

The sun shone beautifully through the thin, white clouds in the deep blue sky. Its rays shimmered through the bare trees, showing the only life on the morose winter day. The harsh wind cut through my clothing like knives. I wore a knitted beanie to cover my ears, but the wind felt like thousands of tiny needles pricking my face.

It was an unusual day for a funeral. David's funeral. My brother. It didn't seem right. Family was supposed to live forever.

I don't remember the drive to the church or to the cemetery. I don't remember anything anyone said to me. When they spoke, it was as if their voices were garbled murmurs.

At the gravesite, I vaguely remember James helping me to my seat and holding my hand the whole time. Everyone wore black, as if displaying my feelings all around. Dad sat next to me holding my weeping mom. My grandparents were near along with Charles and Abby. The numbness hadn't left me; the physical pain resonated all over, but I welcomed it. It was the only thing I felt.

I stared at the dark wooden casket in which my brother slept. The preacher spoke, but it was miles away. I didn't cry.

Breathing still hurt, but the doctors gave me medication for just about everything. Except *this* pain. The tears that my parents and Abby cried provoked a guilty pang. Charles hung his head low. Why wasn't it me inside that casket? Wasn't there enough room for both of us?

Memories of David swept through my mind like a filmstrip. Riding bikes. Playing baseball and football. Listening and talking about music. Going to concerts. Hearing his laughter. Having his protection. His humor. He would never get married. Never graduate college. Never have kids.

I'll always protect you…

I knew then, I could never think about David again because it hurt too much. If I saw his face, or played his voice in my head, or even imagined him hugging me, it would break me.

Once the preacher finished his sermon, everyone gave their condolences and left. A few of us stayed behind and waited until they buried the casket. We walked back out to the gravesite. The empty marker was at the head of the freshly buried plot. The cemetery director told us they'd have it engraved within a week—as if to make it permanent that he was gone. A mixed array of carnations, roses, and violets lay upon the plot. Their colors were lost on me as I stared at them.

Abby bent down and took a red rose, and Dad handed Mom a yellow one. My grandmother took a carnation, then grabbed a white rose and gave it to me.

She hugged me tight. "I see it in your eyes," she said. "Don't blame yourself, baby girl."

At home, I barely listened to the quiet whispers of random people while I sat on the couch in the living room. The same green couch David leaned against a week ago. The same couch he fell asleep on most times when we had movie night. Or when we would stay up late chatting on Christmas Eve. My parents didn't have too many people over after the funeral, but I didn't pay attention to a lot of them. I was numb. Frozen. Completely lost.

At one point, Amos bent down and hugged me and I wasn't sure if I even moved.

"Please call me," he said, with a slight quiver to his voice. He squeezed my shoulder and then left.

"Do you need any medicine?" James asked.

I nodded.

"I'll get it," Lisa offered.

She returned shortly with Dad and handed me a couple of pills and a glass of water. She kneeled down beside me. Her face was tear-stained like the rest of ours. "Look, Corinne. It'll be okay. I'm here for you."

I couldn't hold back the emotion. The crying hurt so much. The cuts on my face stung from the salty tears. "I'm so sorry," I said.

James squeezed my hand.

I looked up and met Abby's eyes. "I'm so sorry Abby. Dad."

Abby bit her lip, arms holding herself. Her chin quivered. "I'm sorry. I-I have to go." She walked out of the room, and that was the last time I saw my best friend.

Her reaction only brought more tears and I didn't want to be there anymore. I was spent.

"Come on, let's go upstairs, sweetie," Dad said. He helped me up the stairs and into my room with James and Lisa behind us.

"I'll help her change, Mr. Elliot," Lisa said.

"Thank you." Dad and James stepped outside.

I stood next to my bed while she undressed me, which took a while with the cast and leg brace. She put me in a gray short-sleeved shirt and white pajama shorts. She helped me lay down along the length of the several pillows that crowded my bed. I heard Booger's soft whimper, but couldn't see him.

Lisa bent down to face me. "Don't worry about a thing. I'll be back tomorrow to take care of you," she said, and then left.

James and Dad came back inside.

"I can't begin to know what to say," James said. "But please know that I'm here for you. I love you. I'll be back tomorrow."

I met his eyes and didn't let go of his hand. "Don't leave me."

"I'll stay until you fall asleep."

"No," I yelled. "Please stay."

He looked back at my father.

"Sweetie, James has to go home."

"Please, Dad. Not tonight."

"Do you mind staying?" Dad asked him after a few minutes.

"Of course not."

Dad kissed my forehead. "Get some rest, sweetie. Please let me know if she needs anything."

"Of course."

Dad closed the door slightly, leaving Booger inside. I heard his paws softly brush across the carpet and then he rested his body down on it.

James untied his black tie and tossed it onto my desk. He kicked off his shoes and then carefully lay down beside me and took my hand. His thumb gently caressed against my fingers. I wanted him closer, but with all the pillows and braces and casts I took up a lot of space.

I wanted to sleep, but I couldn't get over the way Abby feared being around me. Or was just so angry that she couldn't stand to be in the same room with me.

"She hates me," I said.

"Who?" James raised his head to look into my eyes.

"Abby." I inhaled a deep breath and exhaled, remembering what Dr. Andrews instructed.

"She doesn't hate you. She's just…lost."

I grabbed David's hat and clutched it to my chest. No tears came the rest of the night. I figured it was just that my body couldn't produce enough to shed for David.

The pain that I caused everyone, I couldn't handle. David

wasn't there for me to call and talk to about it. The guilt overpowered me and nothing could make it better. I shouldn't have left that night. I should have waited until I had rested. Why had his car stopped working? *How could you lose control?* I didn't deserve to live after what I'd done.

Abby stood next to me inside the morgue. An autopsy table was to my left and a wall of silver drawers was on my right. I shivered and as I exhaled, my breath came out in a small cloud. Her glaring eyes made me tremble. Her lips pressed tightly together as her fingers curled into fists. I opened my mouth to speak, but nothing came out. I tried moving, but I was paralyzed.

"How could you?" She hissed. "How could you do such a thing? You should be here instead of him. You should be the cold dead body in the drawer. Not him," she screamed. She lifted a knife and clasped it tightly in her hand.

Again, I tried moving but something pinned me down. A flashing light forced my eyes to close. A loud snap, like the sound of metal breaking, rumbled inside the room, making it shudder.

I opened my eyes to a dark room. I tried taking a deep breath, but my lungs wouldn't cooperate. I clutched my chest and panted. A tingling sensation ran the length of the veins in my arm. I closed my eyes as the onslaught of nausea appeared. I grabbed my queasy stomach and groaned. I couldn't catch my breath. Thunder rumbled outside and I jumped.

"Corinne, are you okay?" James asked with alertness in his voice, and then he turned on the lamp. "It's okay. Try to focus on slowing your breathing." He helped me sit up slightly, and then pressed me to his body. "It's okay. Just a storm. It's out there. It won't hurt you." His soothing voice helped me relax.

My breathing finally became normal again. Then, as quickly as the symptoms came, they vanished.

Booger whined as he walked closer.

"Did you have a bad dream?"

I nodded. The thunder sounded once more and I flinched, trying to pull him closer. He held me against his chest, and he kissed the top of my head.

James lowered me back down on the pillows, and placed his arm on my stomach. He kissed my cheek and then our foreheads touched. I calmed down, but I didn't want to close my eyes. I couldn't see Abby's fierce glare again.

The next day, I woke up after a restless night. The nightmare of Abby still haunted me. From the weary look in James's eyes, he hadn't slept either, but he never left my side.

"Good morning." He kissed me and then sat up. "Are you feeling better? I know that's probably a dumb question, but I just meant after last night..."

I nodded, but I wasn't persuasive.

"I think you might have had a panic attack. Scared me half to d—," he stopped himself. "Sorry. I suck at this." He sighed and rubbed his eyes.

I squeezed his hand. I wanted to tell him that I couldn't do this without him or that I appreciated his being there. But I didn't say a word. I didn't want to talk.

"Are you hungry?"

I shook my head.

"You have to eat. I'll go make us some breakfast." He got up from the bed. His long-sleeved shirt and suit pants were wrinkled. I seized his hand and he turned and met my eyes. "It's okay, I won't be gone long. Besides, I think Booger needs to go outside for a bit." He half-smiled at the patient dog lying by the door.

I nodded and released his hand. He opened the door and followed Booger out of the room. I was left with only my inescapable thoughts. I peered outside at the dreary day. A thick fog blanketed the motionless bare trees. The unmoving sky was gray and white. I closed my eyes tight as a pulsating rhythm moved from behind my eyes to each side of my head to the back of my head. I took a deep breath, and pushed him to the back of my mind. I wouldn't think of him. I couldn't.

A light knock on the door startled me, making my heartbeat speed up, and I flinched

"Hey." Dad greeted with a pained smile. Nothing could hide his pure agony. "How did you sleep?" He sat on the edge of the bed.

I shrugged, but then winced. A sharp pain centered inside my arm. I wished I could rub it to make it better, but the cast prevented me.

"James is bringing your medicine along with some food. Lisa will be by today since your grandparents aren't able to come. Well, actually your mother insisted they go on their vacation and *try* to have a good time," he rambled. "I'm glad James and Lisa are here for us. I'm not sure what we'd do without their help." His eyes watered and he rubbed his hands together. "I'm trying to help your mother and myself. I'm just glad you have someone in case your mom or I can't be there." Dad squeezed my hand. "We'll get through this."

James returned with a plate of food, water, and my medicine. He left again and came back with his food and Booger in tow. Booger wagged his tail and sniffed at me until he was finished and then licked my hand.

"I made some toast, eggs, and bacon," James said. "I made some for you and Mrs. Elliot."

Dad helped me sit up and James carefully set the plate in my lap.

"Thank you, James." Dad patted his back. "I'll go see if Carolyn wants to eat." He closed the door behind him.

I looked down at the steaming food, but the idea of eating was repugnant. I moved the plate aside.

"You have to eat a little. Just enough so you can take your medicine."

I picked up the toast and chewed it slowly. I ate it so slow that my eggs and bacon were cold. James had finished his and urged me to take a couple of bites of the eggs. I did and then I took my meds.

"You did well. It'll be enough so the medicine won't make

you sick."

He collected the dishes, took them to the kitchen, and was back almost as fast as he'd left. He still wore his black slacks and blue button-down shirt from yesterday and I felt guilty that he hadn't had a chance to change. He took his place next to me as close as he could, and took my hand, kissing it.

"Do you need to check your email?"

I shook my head.

"School work?"

I shook my head.

He scanned the room. "Want me to read some sonnets or a story?"

I mused over it for a moment and then nodded.

James went to browse my bookshelf and then pulled a book from it. He resumed the previous position as before, and I lay my head against his chest.

He opened the book. "'Who am I? And how, I wonder, will this story end?'" He began, and I immediately knew it was the first line of *The Notebook*, my favorite. He went on to read the first chapter, while I listened intently to his smooth voice. Anything to keep my mind from racing. He stopped once we heard Lisa enter the house. Anyone could hear her loud voice anywhere. She was louder than Booger's barking.

She slowly opened the door and entered my room. "Hey." She had a wide smile, showing her perfectly white teeth. Her blonde hair was pulled away from her face with small barrettes.

What could she possibly be smiling about?

"Hey. How are you?" James asked.

She shrugged. "I'm okay. I came to help out around here. Tidy up the place and do some laundry. Did you need a break? Just to go home for a bit. I could sit with her."

He looked longingly at me. "Would you mind?"

I reluctantly shook my head, and then he turned back to Lisa. "Yeah, that would be nice. I just need to run home and freshen up. I promise I won't be long." He kissed me. "I'll be right back."

I didn't want him to leave, but I knew he needed to. I was relaxed with him, talking to me, as if he were my protector. He was my wall, blocking the pain from entering my mind. I wondered if he could help stop the nightmares.

"How are you holding up?" Lisa asked after James left the room.

I shrugged my one available shoulder.

She picked up the book that James was reading, closed it, losing his place, and tossed it aside. "I know it's hard. But you'll get through this. Because I'm here to help." She paused. "And James."

She kept talking, but my mind didn't focus on her words. Her voice was so loud I grimaced as it rang through my ears. The more she spoke, the more I longed to hear James's soft, gentle voice. She talked with her hands and moved in front of my mirror on my closet door to unclasp and clasp her barrettes. "You know my boyfriend Jack is coming into town soon for Valentine's Day. We planned a weekend getaway. I wonder if James will plan something nice for you."

Booger stood and left the room as Lisa continued primping herself in front of the mirror. I wanted to tell her she looked fine and to stop. At least she didn't look like the freak I was now with the scars and bruises on my face.

But I deserved this. I wasn't *dead*. I might as well be.

"Do you need to take a bath or something? How long's it been?" She twisted her face as she looked at me.

Another shrug.

She sighed with a hint of annoyance. "Are you ever going to speak again? You'll have to eventually."

Why should I? It seemed pointless. I had nothing to say. Except that, I was utterly sorry for what I had done. Nothing I could say could take away the pain. My jaw clenched and I closed my eyes. I really wished James was back. He didn't make me think of it. He never asked questions about it.

"So have you heard from Abby?"

Her name felt like a knife cutting inside me. Twisting it. Tears welled up in my eyes and I tried to force them back.

"Guess not. Look, please don't cry." She plopped down next to me a little too harshly and a stab of pain shot through me. "It doesn't help much. I learned that. You just have to be stronger than that. Besides, all that crying is depressing and it can't be good for you now." Her eyes roved over me. "Aren't you tired of sitting? Wanna try and walk around?"

If it would get her to be quiet, sure, I'd walk around. But I actually did need to use the restroom. Something that annoyed me because it took so much out of me just to walk that short distance.

I carefully moved my leg closer to the edge of the bed, waited, and then stood awkwardly. I slightly lost my balance, but Lisa was there holding me. I limped out of my room and down the dark hallway. The bathroom was across from his room, but I didn't look once. I closed the door behind me while Lisa waited. I welcomed the silence in the room. I hoped she wouldn't start talking again.

I took my time, not that I could've done it any other way. And once I finished, she helped me back to bed. It did feel nice to stretch some of my muscles. But my ribs ached.

Lisa started talking again and I had grown tired, so I feigned sleep hoping maybe she would leave. It wasn't that I didn't appreciate her. She just talked too much. She finally left after a few minutes.

I waited impatiently for James. I began to feel scared that he wouldn't come back. I couldn't handle the idea. I took a deep breath and tried thinking of something positive. But nothing came to mind.

Booger's bark from downstairs startled me and I hoped it was James. Relief washed over me as I faintly heard his voice. And then Lisa's telling him I was asleep. Would he ignore her and check on me anyway?

As my door opened, I turned to see him enter, and closed my eyes once I saw a glimpse of Lisa.

"I told you she was asleep," Lisa scolded him in a whisper.

"It's okay. I'm just dropping off my bag."

"Don't wake her. She needs her sleep."

I realized I wouldn't be able to fake my sleep if I wanted James to stay since Lisa was determined not to leave.

I slowly opened my eyes as I felt James near me.

"Hey sweetie." He smiled and then kissed my forehead.

"You came back." My voice was barely above a whisper, and groggy. It sounded tired and unused. It didn't sound like me at all.

"She talks to *you*?" Lisa frowned and crossed her arms in front of her chest.

I saw a muscle in his jaw twitch and then he looked at her. "This is the first time."

"Hmph," she huffed. "Well, maybe her voice is coming back. I tried to see if she needed a bath, but she never said anything."

"It's okay. We'll worry about it later." He gave me a sweet smile as his blue eyes stared into mine.

"Fine. I'm gonna do laundry and then I'll start dinner," she said and then walked out.

"You're tense," James said.

I realized I was stiff, but then relaxed. Had Lisa made me so uptight?

"I tried to hurry, but I was visiting a little with my parents and Tony."

I nodded. After hearing the horrible sound that came out of my mouth, I didn't want to make it again, especially since there was a much better sound I could hear like James's voice.

"Your dad and I talked before I left and decided I could stay this week. I called my professors at school and explained the situation, so I get this week off, but I still have homework to do over the computer."

I frowned—a guilty frown. He had his own life and I didn't want to prevent him from living it. I couldn't do that. But I did want him to stay.

"Hey, it's okay." He lifted my chin with his fingers. "I'm a great multi-tasker. I can take care of you and do homework. I have a laptop so I can still sit here with you."

I looked at him, a little doubtful.

"It's really okay. Don't worry about me." He picked up *The Notebook*. "Shall I continue?"

I nodded and he continued reading.

I opened my eyes to a dimly lit room. I looked around and saw James sitting next to me with his laptop. I watched him type and his forehead creased a little, the way it did when he was in deep thought. He looked exhausted, but as soon as he saw me, he immediately smiled.

"Hey." Always a warm, beautiful smile on his face. "You fell asleep while I was reading." He closed his laptop and set it on the nightstand.

I frowned at the news. His reading didn't bore me and it seemed like we always had interruptions. Like when Lisa came in earlier for dinner. I didn't feel like eating, but both James and Lisa encouraged me.

"You were really tired," he said. It was like he could read my mind. "You needed the sleep. Didn't even twitch."

Didn't dream either. He *was* my protector from the nightmares.

"Are you in pain? Hungry? Need to stretch?"

I shook my head at each one, except the last one.

He nodded and helped me up. I got to my feet and he steadied me with his hands on either side of my waist. The cast and brace were so bulky and in the way.

"He was my *son*!" I heard Mom yell from their room. Her voice was so angry. My good hand clutched onto James and he pulled me close.

"Carolyn, please." Dad tried calming her.

"She fell asleep." I hated the panic-stricken sound she made.

My knee lost its strength and I sank onto the bed. James held me tight.

"What was she thinking? Why was she driving if she was so tired? How could she do such a thing?" The fierce words punched me and my breath hitched.

Dad said something, but it was muffled through the walls.

James tilted my chin up to look into my eyes. "Please don't listen to that. She's just upset. She doesn't mean it."

"David is dead!" Mom screamed. "How could she be so reckless?"

My pulse quickened and I couldn't catch my breath. Knots twisted in my stomach and I started sweating.

"Please, she doesn't mean it." James said, and I could hear the panic in his voice. "You weren't reckless."

Something shattered against the wall on the other side and I jumped. I covered my face, blocking the glass from shooting its way toward me. The grinding noise of the metal bending made my teeth clench.

"I'm here for you." I heard James. "You're okay. Take a deep breath."

I did, and eventually my breathing slowed. It was quiet, except for the soft sobbing coming from the other room.

"She didn't mean those words," he whispered.

How could my presence make things better? I should've died in that crash. It was my fault he died.

I had ruined my family.

CHAPTER TWENTY-FIVE

The days that followed, James never left my side, and Lisa was there every day after school. She was a good caretaker. She comforted all of us, cooked dinner, fed Booger, and checked our mail. James helped during the day since she was at school. I knew he would eventually have to return to his life, but having him there made me feel whole and I knew the second he left, I would fall apart.

Amos dropped by a few times, but I didn't talk to him.

I rarely saw Mom, but Dad would check in every so often. No one explained the shouting match from the other night. At least not to me. And it wasn't the only one that week. They argued about James staying every night. Mom didn't like the idea of him being in my room, but Dad reasoned with her that James was a big part of my recovery. She didn't say another word about it, but I knew she wasn't done.

James and I stayed in my room for the most part, and when I needed a bath, he would help because I didn't want anyone else but him.

A week had passed since the funeral, and Mom and Dad were able to pick up some of their everyday tasks, but Lisa still came over. Mom seemed to be getting better, but still didn't speak to me. At least until today.

"Your dad and I are going back to work on Monday," she said. Her eyes held such a cold look. Like she was disgusted with me. They were starting work so soon after? It had only been two weeks since the accident. "I suggest you go back to school on Monday as well. We've worked it out with your teachers, and all you need to do is make up a few items." Her voice held no emotion whatsoever.

School? How was I going to do that?

"James, I think you need to go home. You have school to get back to. Lisa's here if she needs anything."

He squeezed my hand. "Could I possibly stay until Sunday, please?"

"I think you've coddled her enough."

"But I—."

"James." She warned.

"I just don't think I could be away from her right now. Just one more day."

Mom sighed. "Sunday then." She turned on her heel and marched out of the room.

I bowed my head, feeling the tears coming. James held me while I cried.

"I'm sorry."

Why was he sorry? What did he do? It was me who should be sorry. I thought of him leaving Sunday and more tears poured out of my eyes. How could I do this without him?

"Why is she crying?" Lisa's shrill voice came from the doorway. "What did you do?"

I looked up at her.

"It wasn't me," James said. "Her mom just told her she needed to go back to school, but she isn't exactly consoling right now."

"Well, she needs to go back. It'll help strengthen her. Give your mom time. She'll come around eventually."

"I know school will help her keep her mind off things, but right now I don't think it's a good idea." He pointed to my cast and brace.

She crossed her arms. "Now's a good a time as any, James.

You can't always protect her."

"Yes, I know. But that doesn't mean I don't want to."

"Well, come Sunday, she won't need you anymore. I'll help her the rest of the way." She jutted her chin out. "You have your own life."

"She's a part of my life, Lisa."

"I know, but you can't do everything for her."

They conversed as if I wasn't even in the room and it annoyed me.

I sighed which made them turn their attention to me in an instant. I felt the heat rise to my cheeks.

Booger sneaked past Lisa and then jogged closer to me and placed his head at the edge of the bed. I rubbed Booger's smooth, velvety fur.

"I'm going to help your mom prepare dinner," Lisa said and then walked out.

Booger jumped up onto the bed next to James and lay down.

James took my hand. "You're tense again." I relaxed. He gazed into my eyes and placed his hand on my cheek. "I wish there was something I could do."

"You are." I grimaced at the sound of my voice.

"It's nice to hear you speak." He gave a half smile.

"My voice sounds awful."

"I think it's the most beautiful sound."

I looked away. "How can you still look at me?"

"Because you are still stunning. Scars or no scars."

"Even after what I did?" My voice cracked.

"What you did?"

I hoped my silence would answer him. I didn't want to say it aloud.

"You haven't done anything wrong."

"But Mom and Abby…"

He lifted my chin and our eyes met. "They're hurting, Corinne. Just like you. Everyone grieves differently. Don't blame yourself."

"I just miss him so much."

"I know." He cleared his throat and I saw his eyes water. "What if I stayed?"

"What do you mean?"

"I could quit school this semester and stay with you."

I appreciated the gesture more than he could ever imagine, but there was no way I was allowing that. "No, James. You can't quit."

He sighed. "But school can wait. You're my fiancée. I mean, if we were married, it would be my job to care for you. Why can't I do that now?"

"Because you need to go back. We'll get through it."

"What if I don't want to leave?"

"I don't want to be the reason you quit school. I'll be fine." But even as I said it, I had doubts.

He kissed me. "Then, I'll visit every weekend."

And I believed he would. It took everything I had not to break down in front of him the day he left. I saved the shower of tears until after he left and then Lisa came inside my room. She held my shaking body close to her broad shoulders.

"I can't believe he actually left you. *I'll* never leave you."

"He had to," I sobbed. "I couldn't keep him here."

"Ugh. He didn't *have* to, Corinne. He *wanted* to."

"That's not true. He offered to quit school for me."

She gave me a doubtful look. "He was just saying that. You should've seen the way he was when he wasn't around you. I swear, he constantly complained about you. He couldn't wait to leave. He only stayed because your dad asked him to."

I stopped sniveling. "What?"

"Seriously. I don't even know why he was here to begin with. Maybe he thinks he'll get some from you again. Who knows?"

"I don't believe it."

"I wouldn't lie to you. You're just blinded by love. But give it time. You'll see."

"I don't believe you."

"Just wait. He can't be perfect all the time. He'll falter. They all do. Except Jack. He's really good. Very supportive. You should find someone like Jack."

I shook my head. "James is perfect for me," I insisted through my broken voice.

"Just wait until Friday. I bet he won't even come. Can't believe he left you," she said under her breath.

She was wrong. James wasn't like that. Did he really complain? I couldn't blame him. I deserved worse.

I hugged my knees and rocked my body. I tried wiping the blood from my fingers, but it wouldn't go away. There was so much of it. His intense eyes stared at me through the curtain of blood that draped over his face.

"Look what you did," James shouted and I jumped. He hovered over me with an icy glare that bore right through me. "You murdered your own brother."

"You killed my son!" Mom yelled from behind him.

"What kind of monster are you? I never want to see you again."

"You are no daughter of mine." Mom glared at me.

I woke up to a dark room, my heart pounding. I gasped for air and winced in pain simultaneously. I remembered James's voice calming me. And slowly my breathing returned. It was the first nightmare in over a week. Now that my protector was gone, I didn't sleep well. But did James really care? Was Lisa right? Was he just going to abandon me?

CHAPTER TWENTY-SIX

There was no way I could go to school. I couldn't even dress myself. I'd ripped a couple of shirts trying to put them on. I cried and then picked up the nearest thing and threw it. I wanted to talk to James, but my cell phone had stopped working during the accident and the only phone we had was in the kitchen.

Whether I was allowed to be up and walking around, Mom didn't care. She needed me out of the house. I was the reminder of David's absence. And I felt it every time she looked at me, even though I never heard her say it.

Dad always left really early for work, and Mom didn't want to take me. Lisa had a doctor's appointment, so Amos offered to take me to school. I felt like such a burden to everyone.

Amos showed up that freezing cold morning and helped me down the concrete stairs to his car. I stopped, staring at the large death machine.

I shook my head. "No. I can't do this."

"I'm so sorry."

The garage door opened and Mom backed her car out a little, and then she got out.

"What are you doing?" she asked me.

"I can't get inside that car."

"Would you rather take the bus?"

There was no way I was getting on a bus like this. I hated how small she made me feel by just the tone of her voice.

"Either get in the car, or I will force you."

A tear slid down my cheek. "Please don't do this. I'm not ready."

I thought I saw a sliver of pity in her eyes, but then they turned cold again. "I'm not ready for this either, but you know what? We have no choice. So get in the car and I'll see you when I get home."

She turned, got back in her car, and peeled out of the driveway.

I took a deep breath and it came out in a large cloud. Amos guided my crutch into the backseat and held my arm while I slowly sat into his passenger seat. My ribs didn't hurt as much, but my head throbbed.

Amos slid behind the wheel and closed the door. The engine was already running so he put it in gear and backed out of my driveway.

"How the hell am I gonna do this?" I yelled. "Look at me? I can't do anything on my own. I have to have to someone there helping me every inch of the way. I can't bend my leg. I can't straighten my arm. My face looks like someone butchered it. What are people going to say? Or think?"

"Ya can't worry about them, love. It really doesn't bother me to help you. And you still look beautiful."

I gripped the door handle and willed my nausea away. "I don't like riding in cars, Amos."

"I'm sorry. I'll drive slowly."

We arrived at school and it took an embarrassing fifteen minutes to get me out of his car. My face flushed as onlookers walked by whispering to each other. I felt like yelling at them, but I remained quiet.

Luckily, Amos and I had the same first class, but then for my second class I was left alone. In either class, I couldn't concentrate on anything but my physical pain. People constantly stared at me. Stared at the scattered cuts on my face or the large bandage stuck to my forehead or the annoying leg brace. Some gave me pitiful looks and apologized. But I knew others laughed.

I sat in the back of the room since my leg had to stretch out, but the lack of blood flow made it pulsate. Amos pulled an empty chair and lifted my heavy leg onto it. Moving around as much as I had was really taking its toll.

I tried listening to the teacher drone on about *Hamlet,* but my mind wandered. Wandered to the time I'd spent with James listening to his voice as he read to me. Lisa's warning cut into my thoughts. *Blinded by love. You'll see.* He doesn't care.

Mom's face came into view as she yelled. Her lips never moved. *He was my son!* And then Abby stood next to my mom. Both with a rigid stance and icy glares in their eyes. *How could you lose control?* Behind them was David on the cold ground. Still. *Too* still. A sound climbed from my throat and through my lips.

"Corinne?" I heard a whisper.

I blinked and saw thirty faces staring at me with a surprised look. I blushed.

"Corinne, are you okay?" Mrs. Lee asked.

I nodded and the stares ceased. I looked at Amos. His clammy hand touched mine.

Mrs. Lee continued with her lecture. Had I just hallucinated in class? How could I stop thinking of them?

The rest of the day, I focused hard on the lectures, even taking notes. But none of it made sense. I heard the words, but they came out like gibberish. I had a hard time keeping up with what the teachers said and I felt like my brain couldn't process the information. News of my screaming in class reached the whole school. By the end of the day, I felt like my eyes were going to pop out of my head or my head was going to explode. School was too much to handle.

Lisa took me home and I wanted to check to see if James emailed me. Communication was going to be difficult.

Lisa checked it for me and gave a wicked smile. "He

emailed you." She read it aloud only because I was lying in the bed and she sat at the computer. James missed me and couldn't wait to see me and wrote that no matter what, he would always be there for me and that we'd get through this.

But I didn't hear from him the rest of the week. And every time I called, it went to voicemail. Thinking about him only made it worse. What made me think I deserved James after ripping my family apart?

In school, I focused on the lectures, and since the first day, I hadn't hallucinated or had visions. The nightmares only happened at night. And weird things started happening. Like I would jump any time I heard loud noises. Lisa asked why I had such an exaggerated response, but I didn't know why. I couldn't be calm. It was like I was paranoid. A couple of times, for no apparent reason, I would freak out in class like I was having a heart attack or something.

The end of the week finally arrived, and Lisa offered to take me to the doctor, since my parents were at work. My CT scan came back normal. The bandage on my forehead was taken off, revealing a crusted, hard scab over the deep gash. The bruises had healed, but the cuts were still on my face. My arm remained in a cast and they changed my leg brace to one that just covered my knee.

They refilled my prescription for my headaches, and Lisa and I left. The violet sky bled over the orange horizon. The air was harsh and cold. I was nervous, only because James was supposed to come over. But I wasn't sure that he was anymore since I didn't hear from him.

We got home, ate, and then I fell asleep, waiting.

Lisa woke me up and told me James had called, but that he wasn't coming at all. She told me he said he had other important things to take care of and left it at that. I couldn't believe her. But when I called him, I always got his voicemail.

Was Lisa right? Did he really hate being around me? I didn't know why I even asked myself those things. Of course he did.

Lisa was the only one who stood by me every day. She

said we were connected. But even with that, I still felt *nothing*. I was drowning in a pool of sorrow and I couldn't breathe.

I broke down that night after Lisa left. All their disappointment and anger forced guilt to wallow in my stomach and move through my veins. Guilt for taking him away. I would give anything to talk to him. I needed him. I needed to be near him. And I wanted to make it happen.

CHAPTER TWENTY-SEVEN

"Look, I know it's painful," Lisa said and hung a sweater in my closet. "But trust me, school will get your mind off things. You have to do *something* so you don't keep moping around all the time."

"Are you sure James hasn't called? Dad said he hasn't heard from him either. Why hasn't he called or emailed?" It had been two weeks since he left my house, and while I didn't hear from him, I still held onto some shred of hope that maybe something had happened that prevented him from talking to me. But I knew what he was doing. He was cutting the ties.

"I can't believe you still think about him. You need to get over it. I mean, the way he acted when he wasn't around you, he got agitated. He hated being here."

"Really?" I tossed a pen in the air.

"Yes. He told me he couldn't be with you because of how much you changed. Ugh. Can you believe that?"

My stomach dropped and I let the pen drop to the floor. "You talked to him?"

"I wish you wouldn't toss things up in the air." She bent down and picked up the pen. "It's kinda annoying."

"Have you talked to him? Did he call you?"

"No, he hasn't called." She sighed and then sank onto the edge of my bed. "Look, I didn't want to tell you, but I called him, trying to persuade him to come see you, but he refused. I mean, if he really cared to see you, don't you think he would've come?"

"He refused to see me?" My voice cracked.

"Yes. He completely deserted you and probably moved on to someone else."

I believed every word she said. Even as I stared at my ring. Why would he want to be with someone who killed her brother? James. Mom. Abby. Their hate was justified. I caused all of this, so I deserved what happened to me.

"What's going on inside your head? You know I don't like it when you start thinking for a long time."

"Sorry. Just thinking about Abby and—."

"Ugh. Don't even say her name." She shot up and snatched a sweater, roughly putting it on a hanger. "Not after what she did to you. You had an accident. It wasn't like you murdered him."

I clenched my teeth. "You *know* it was my fault."

"I'm not arguing this with you again," she insisted. "I've already told you that you could've had better control, but you didn't. You freaked out. Unfortunately, it caused your brother's death."

"It should've been me," I mumbled.

"Would you stop saying that?" she snapped. "How many times do I have to remind you I hate it when you talk like that?" She dropped her hands by her side, and kneeled down beside me as I sat in the desk chair. "Look, your parents and I are the only ones who care about you. I know what you're going through. To the others you're just a problem. A nuisance. They think you're a burden. Only I know what that's like. I've been there. I know what it's like to feel dejected. And to be abandoned. And that's exactly what Abby and James have done. It's obvious they don't care about you. If they did they would've tried to contact you. Remember, you and I are connected." She smiled.

She hugged me and then went home. I tried focusing on my homework for a couple of hours, but as usual, got frustrated. I could not care less what x equaled or the history of U.S. government. Besides, it was merely impossible to think about anything when James refused to see me. I decided to check my email for the hundredth time that day.

I sifted through the spam mail and stopped when I saw an email from James. My heart stopped, and I hesitated but then clicked on it. An error message popped up explaining that the message had already been deleted. I frantically searched the trash folder, but it was empty and by the time I reached my spam folder again, it was gone.

What was going on? Why was it deleted? I was scared to call him and ask what the email said. Afraid of the words he might say to me. If he really cared, wouldn't he come back?

I felt like Marianne from *Sense and Sensibility* when she'd always ask the butler if she had gotten a letter from Willoughby. I always asked if James called. But, like Marianne, every day the answer was no.

Lisa was right. I wouldn't think about him. It was too painful. He deserved better. I took off my ring and put it back in the little black box. I hid it in my dresser and then closed the drawer, shutting him from my life.

CHAPTER TWENTY-EIGHT

A couple of weeks later, I got the cast and brace off my arm and leg. A little physical therapy and I could walk on my own. My ribs healed, but the one thing that never left me was the sadness. Guilt. Anger. It all still weighed heavily on me.

Lisa and I became inseparable, except when Jack was in town, and she was at his side the whole time. She helped me focus more on school and Mom forced me to go back to work. She and I still didn't talk and if we did, it was mostly yelling.

Lisa or Dad took me to school and to work because I had no car, but even if I did, I wasn't going to drive. Work was just as bad as school. People constantly pitied me and working the register frustrated me. I got so upset over little things, like if the computer locked up, or if I scanned something twice. Brandon, my supervisor, felt it would be better to put me on the floor stocking. Anything to keep me away from the front.

But even that had its nuisances. I wasn't as strong as I had been and dropped things, which broke and spilled everywhere. Amos always helped and I wondered if they had assigned him as my babysitter. People constantly asked me where things were and I was completely rude to them. I didn't care. Sometimes I hid in the backroom because I couldn't deal with the noises or the people. And I always ran and hid like a scared little girl whenever I felt the panic attacks coming.

I only worked two nights a week, but with school and work, it left me exhausted every day. Homework piled up and I couldn't keep up. That was the only reading I ever did. And I stopped listening to music. Lisa occupied a lot of my time after school, unless I worked. But when she left, thoughts of David, James, Abby, everything consumed my mind. The nights were the worst because of the nightmares and those stupid panic attacks.

Friday night rolled around and I asked Lisa what she and Jack were up to. I did not want to spend another night at home listening to Mom nag about my moping or the constant reminders of him. I didn't care if I was going to be the third wheel. I just had to go.

"I'm going to his house for a party. He lives on campus."

"Can I come?"

She looked at me dubiously. "Really? You really want to come?"

"Yeah, why not?" I shrugged.

"Finally. It's about time you had some fun. There'll be lots of guys there, too."

"Lisa, I'm not looking for—."

"Just to talk to. I'm not suggesting you hook up or anything. Although, I find it helps to get over a breakup."

I cringed at the word. "I'll keep that in mind."

"Anyways, the party is about forty-five minutes away. Is that okay?"

My body tensed. Forty-five minutes in the car. I could feel the panic coming.

"I know you don't like cars, but I'm driving so…"

I took a breath. "It's fine."

"Awesome. But you are so not going like that." Her eyes roved up and down and she grimaced.

I looked down at my jeans and black sweater. "What's wrong with this?"

"Ugh. Don't you have any cute party clothes?"

Sure. I shop for those all the time.

Lisa let out an exasperated sigh and moved to my closet. She sifted through top after top and finally pulled out a turquoise sweater and skinny jeans.

"I'm not wearing that sweater."

"Why? You look good in it."

"I don't like blue."

"Since when?"

"I just don't, okay?"

She sighed and then pulled a dark purple sweater from the hanger and tossed it to me. "I'm also gonna put makeup on you. It'll cover that hideous scar on your forehead."

I changed and slid my boots on over the jeans. Lisa acted like she was a Mary Kay lady and put all kinds of shit on my face. Heavy black eye shadow surrounded by black eyeliner and mascara that made my lashes grow. It didn't look like me. But she did manage to cover the hideous scar.

When she finished, we left, and drove to Tuscaloosa. My parents were both glad I was getting out of the house. I was nervous, partially because it was the first time I'd actually been anywhere, and because the last time I went to a party with Lisa was New Years and she went off on me.

Lisa pulled her car next to one of several cluttered around the green house. People gathered in groups all around the yard and I could see a lot of people inside. Music thumped so loud that it rattled her car windows.

Why was I here? My hands started to shake, but I got out of the car and followed Lisa toward the front door. We slogged through plastic cups and dead leaves.

"What do you want to drink?" Lisa shouted over the music as we entered. It looked to be an old house, maybe from the 30's or 40's with hardwood floors and a paned door.

"Nothing," I said. But as I looked around at all the people, they each held a cup or bottle in hand, laughing and smiling.

They were all *happy*. I wanted that feeling. "A beer?"

"Cool. Everything will be okay." She winked and then grabbed my hand, dragging me into the kitchen.

I didn't know anyone there and felt incredibly out of place.

Lisa dug in the fridge and pulled out two beers. She twisted the top off of one and handed it to me. "Here you go." She opened hers and then clinked our bottles. "Cheers."

I took a sip and almost gagged at the awful taste.

She smiled. "You'll get used to it, I promise. Let's go find Jack."

I trailed behind her to a few rooms until we finally found Jack in the back room playing a football video game with another guy. The TV was huge in the small room and a few guys and girls gathered around hollering as if it were a real football game. I tried to not let the noises bother me.

"Hey, babe." Jack paused the game, and then stood. His bushy blond beard made him look so much older than a college student. He wrapped his huge arms around Lisa and planted a kiss on her lips. I looked away and someone threw an empty cup at them.

"Get a room," someone yelled.

"We will after I finish beatin' your ass," Jack said, and then looked at me. "Hey. Corinne, right?"

I nodded.

"Cool. Glad you're here." He picked up Lisa and pulled her into his lap. "Everyone this is Corinne. Corinne, this is everyone."

I heard some drunken 'heys' and then they all returned their attention to the game as Jack and his friend continued playing.

I watched them play and drank the beer. But I was getting antsy. I wanted to feel what all the others were feeling. I was even jealous of Lisa's happiness.

Once the game finished, there was even more yelling and cheering, which made me jump.

The thin guy next to Jack stood up, raising his arms, and let out a celebratory howl. "I beat your ass," he shouted at

Jack.

"I had a distraction," Jack said, and then kissed Lisa. "I gotta relieve some tension. But I'll be back."

The guy laughed. "And I'll still beat you."

"Want another beer?" Lisa asked me.

"Sure."

Jack slapped her on the butt as she got up and she squealed. "Where you goin'?"

"To get more beer. I'll be back."

"Well hurry up and meet me in my room." He sounded so demanding. Was he like that all the time?

"So, do you go to Alabama?" The guy on the couch asked. He had a Southern accent that I found to be kinda cute. A red Alabama hat covered his dark hair and he wore glasses.

I shook my head. "No."

"You go to school with Lisa?"

"Yeah."

"Here's your beer," Lisa said as she handed it to me. "I'll be right back, okay? Just mingle around." She smiled.

"Okay."

When I turned back to the guy on the couch, there were two different guys sitting there, beginning a new game. I drank more of the beer. How does one mingle? Do I just walk up to someone and start talking? A twinge of sadness hit me when I realized I didn't have any friends. And the one I did have was off with her boyfriend.

I felt a hand on my shoulder and I jumped and my heart raced. I whirled around and was face-to-face with the couch guy.

"Hey, sorry. I didn't mean to scare you. Too many beers makes you go to the bathroom."

I nodded, trying to calm myself. I took a large gulp of the beer. It was kinda growing on me.

"I'm Will." He held out his hand and I shook it.

"Corinne."

"Nice to meet you."

I could feel the alcohol running through my bloodstream.

I could also feel the incredible heat rising in my entire body.

"Would you wanna dance? I see a few people starting the dance trend." He pointed to the other room.

"Sure." I chugged the last of my drink and tossed it into a nearby trash can. Then, Will led me to a dark room with flashing lights like it was some club. I couldn't believe people actually went this far for a party. But whatever.

The loud thumping music drowned out any other sound. People grinded against each other. Some made out. Others jumped with the music. Will's hands were on my arms, hips, and back as we danced. I didn't care though. I was having a good time. Will didn't know who I was or what I had done. He wasn't judging me and I liked that.

After a few dances, we went to the kitchen for more drinks. I didn't know what was so funny, but I couldn't stop laughing. I felt so high. So free. Why couldn't I feel this good sober?

"Give me a minute, I've gotta make a bathroom run," he said.

I giggled and watched him hurry out of the room. I waited for him in the kitchen and drank some more. I watched a beer pong tournament which no one was good at playing. And then the conversations around me blurred. It was really hot. The room swirled.

"Hey, you okay?" Will asked.

"Of course. Why?"

"Your face is red. Need some air?"

"That would be great."

We walked outside into the bitter cold night, but it felt great. I didn't realize just how hot it was in the house. He found a chair for me and motioned for me to sit.

I did, and then sighed. "I haven't had this much fun in a long time."

He smiled. It was a sweet, shy kind of smile. "I'm glad. Pretty girl like you deserves to have a good time."

The porch light made it a little easier to see his face, but it was still rather dark. He was attractive and quite tall. His skin was tanned and he had baby blue eyes.

"How come I haven't seen you around here before?"

"I don't know. I guess I just never felt like it."

"Well, whatever the reason, I'm glad you came out."

"I take it you go to Alabama."

"Yeah. I plan on eventually going to law school."

"Wow. Cool." I took a sip of beer.

"What about you?"

"What about me?"

"Where do you plan on going after high school?"

"I haven't thought that far ahead."

"Isn't graduation comin' up?"

I shifted uncomfortably. I didn't want to talk about the future. "Can we talk about something else? School is just stressing me out lately."

"Okay. Are you an Alabama fan?"

"I don't really like football."

"Oh. Guess that's better than bein' an Auburn fan," he teased. "What kind of music you listen to?"

"I don't."

"Oh."

I took another sip. "You wanna go dance some more?"

He chuckled. "Sure."

We danced and I drank more than I should have, especially since it was the first time. Somehow, we wound up on the couch and Will had his arms around me and I fell asleep. If I didn't move, I wouldn't be sick.

"Hey, wake up, Corinne," I heard James whisper.

I slowly opened my eyes with a smile, but it faded once I saw someone else. I blinked several times, waking myself up. At first I didn't remember anything, but then it all came back to me. Will, the dancing, the drinking.

I sat up and groaned. "Oh, god, my head."

"How much did you drink?" Lisa asked.

I shrugged. "What time is it?"

"It's like three."

"Great. I'm in trouble."

"Can you help me carry her out to the car?" she asked Will.

"Yeah," he said.

"I can walk," I mumbled, but I let him help me to Lisa's car.

"Are you doin' anything tomorrow?" Will asked.

"Not that I'm aware of."

"I'd really like to see you, if that's okay."

"Sure." I didn't care. He hugged me and kissed my forehead. I wasn't sure why. I just wanted to go to sleep.

Will closed the door after I settled in the seat.

Lisa plopped down in the driver's seat, shaking the car a little, and then started the engine. "Well, someone sure did enjoy herself tonight. Who knew you were such a good dancer? And Will was practically falling all over himself for you. He and Jack are best friends. I think you two will be good for each other."

"Lisa, stop." I playfully hit her arm.

"What? I'm just saying."

It was almost four when we got to my house. I had to sneak inside somehow without Booger hearing me so he wouldn't wake up my parents. He was notorious for hearing the slightest sound. I shouldn't have stayed out so late, but who cared? They wanted me to go out and so I did.

Lisa helped me up the stairs outside. I tripped and fell, laughing.

She let out a laugh. "Shh, you're gonna wake the neighborhood."

We couldn't stop giggling.

"Are you going to make it?" she asked.

"Yes. Help me up."

She grabbed my arms and pulled me to my feet.

"By the way, thanks for letting me come out tonight. I enjoyed it."

"No problem. I'll call you tomorrow and let you know when I'm on my way."

"Okay." I walked as quietly as I could inside the house.

Making my way up to my room without making a sound was quite difficult, but I made it.

I closed my eyes for the night, but I found myself not being able to stop the car that was heading for the tree. No matter how hard I pressed the brakes. Glass covered me and I bled. David flew through the window. I shuddered once I heard the crack of his skull against the glass. The seatbelt held me back and I couldn't catch him. He was too far out of my reach.

I woke, unable to catch my breath. My chest tightened and I doubled over in my bed.

Oh god! Not again.

The prickling sensation shot through my arms. My stomach turned over and over. *Focus on your breathing*, I heard him say. I closed my eyes tightly and concentrated.

Once the attack was finally over, I lay back against my bed. I curled up and sobbed into my pillow. Screaming as if it would somehow get rid of the pain.

CHAPTER TWENTY-NINE

When I woke up, it took forever for my dry swollen eyes to open. They stung from the tears and lack of sleep from the nightmares. My mind was in a daze and an uneasy feeling churned in my stomach. It never went away. I exhaled noisily as I rolled over and watched the sunrays dance through the window. My head felt as if it were splitting in half and my throat was dry.

I stumbled down the stairs to the kitchen for some water.

"Good morning." Dad said, setting his coffee down on the table.

"Morning."

He gave me an apprehensive look. "How late were you out last night?"

I shrugged. "I don't know."

"Did you and Lisa have fun?"

"Yeah. We're hanging out again today. And I might stay with her tonight." I reached inside the cabinet and grabbed a glass.

"Wow. Good for you, honey. Are you hungry?"

"No."

"Have you talked to James lately?" he asked after a moment.

My teeth clenched and I almost dropped the glass when he

said his name. "No. And I don't want to."

His eyebrows furrowed. "Why? What happened?"

"I don't want to talk about him. He's a jerk." I filled the glass with water.

"Did you two break up?" I still hated that term.

"Dad, stop," I snapped. I didn't mean to sound so cruel. He went back to his coffee and I went back to my room.

Lisa picked me up later that afternoon and Jack and Will were already in the car, so I took the backseat next to Will. Lisa turned down the radio and gave Jack a reproving look when he asked why she did that.

"Hey girl," Will said. "How you feelin'?"

"I'm fine."

Jack spun the tires out of the driveway and I gripped the door handle.

"Stop doing that," Lisa told him.

"I'm just havin' fun."

"Don't be like that when she's in the car." She tried to keep her voice low, but I still heard her.

"Sorry, Cor."

David flashed in my mind. He was the only one who called me that. And then I saw his bloodied face.

Take a breath. Focus.

I closed my eyes and tried not to let the panic come. But that was the thing about the attacks. I never knew when they'd come. I could be working on homework and suddenly I felt like I was having a heart attack. I constantly feared them because I didn't want people seeing me freak out over nothing.

"My name is Corinne," I told him once my breathing steadied.

"Sorry," Jack said, but he didn't sound like he meant it. "You ready for some football?"

"I guess." I didn't care what we did. I just wanted out of the car.

"Cool. My folks have a house on the lake and there's a huge yard so we can play football."

Jack drove like a crazed lunatic, which I guess was normal since no one said anything except Lisa, but I knew she only did that for my benefit.

"Corinne, are you okay?" Will asked.

I nodded swiftly.

"You're looking very pale."

"She just gets car sick," Lisa said.

"That sucks." I felt his hand on mine, but it didn't comfort me. "Jack, maybe you should slow down."

"Fine." He acted like a jerk, but I was grateful that he finally decided to drive somewhat normal.

We arrived at a house with dark wood siding right on the water. The sun peaked through the thick pine tree forest. It was quite secluded. Once we got inside the large lake house, Jack offered us a drink, and I immediately took a beer. I needed something to calm my nerves.

We watched some TV and waited until others showed up and once they did, Jack encouraged everyone outside to play football. Lisa and I huddled together, since it was freezing. She said we'd be warmer as soon as we had more alcohol in our systems. I already had a few beers, waiting for that feeling again.

Will went over the rules with Jack like it was some science, and as he did, he tossed the football constantly in the air.

Up.

Down.

Up.

Down.

My eyes fixated on him and I saw David tossing the football. My breathing sped up and I clenched my teeth.

"Ooh, does someone have a crush?" Lisa asked as she placed her arm around me.

"Can we just play?" I asked them.

Will chuckled and stopped tossing the ball. "Of course."

I learned that I wasn't the best football player, even though I thought at one time I was okay. But the other girls were good. I thought I would enjoy it, but I really didn't. It was cold and boring and reminded me too much of playing with David and Charles. And the alcohol didn't help make me happy.

"You'd better be careful." Will grinned as he crouched down before me.

"Oh yeah? Why is that?" I asked, crouching, too.

"Cos you're gonna get tackled."

Jack finished his count and drew back to throw the ball. Everyone scrambled around like they knew what they were doing.

I ran a short distance and then felt arms around my waist. Will softly tackled me to the ground and removed his hat. He leaned closer and I saw James. His lips touched mine and I reached around his neck and pulled him closer, wanting to feel something.

But the kiss was wrong. It wasn't slow and focused, like he wanted to savor every second of it like James did. Will's kiss was rushed and I felt nothing. Would I ever be able to feel anything anymore? Would I ever stop being reminded of everyone who left?

"You're a good kisser." Will smiled.

I cleared my throat and pushed against his chest. He moved and helped me to my feet. I brushed my backside. And then I felt the tingling sensation in my arms. Something bad was going to happen. I had to get out of there. My pulse quickened and I curled my hands into fists.

"Hey, you okay?" Will took my hand.

"I'll be right back." I darted toward the house. Once inside, I found the nearest bathroom and closed it. I bent over, my hands resting on my knees, and my breathing accelerating. My throat closed and I was sweating. The room spun. I slid to the floor and put my head between my knees. I couldn't stop shaking. I was going to die and I couldn't stop it.

Focus your breathing. It's okay. James's voice was the only thing that helped stop the attacks. His voice soothed me and after a little while, I finally calmed down.

I brought my knees up and rested my head on my arms. I felt like I had just ran a marathon or something. I was exhausted. And seeing James in my mind before Will kissed me, I knew I missed James more than I led on. I wanted to be with him. I needed him. How could he refuse to see me? Had he really found someone else?

But I knew the answers. I deserved this hell.

I had no one to talk to anymore. I needed my brother more than anything. Lisa hated it when I talked about him or James or Abby. It was like a forbidden topic with her.

The tears came and I let them. I decided I never wanted to leave my house. But maybe I just needed more alcohol to get rid of the pain. Maybe I hadn't drunk enough.

Someone knocked on the door and I jumped.

"Are you okay?" Will asked.

I cleared my throat. "I'm fine. I'll be out in a minute."

"Did I do something wrong?"

I just needed a moment to myself. I didn't want to answer questions. "I'm fine," I said and then another crying spell started.

"Okay. Let me know if you need anything."

I knew I had to hurry because Lisa would be up to check on me soon. The sobbing was more than my breathing could handle.

But I had to stop. I couldn't do this all the time. I inhaled and closed my eyes and forced the tears to disappear.

A few minutes later, I joined everyone on the dock of Jack's house to watch the sunset with Will. He wrapped his arms around me. I could tell he really liked me, and for the time being, I played along. I drank even more than the night before until I felt as happy and alive. And that was what my life had become for several weeks. Just a blur of partying, drinking, making out with Will.

I lost my focus on school and every time I sat down to do my homework, I just stared blankly at the books. They were filled with scrambled words and letters that meant nothing. I did everything I was told. School. Work. Went out. But I was like a mindless drone. I couldn't sit still for very long and I hated being in my room all the time.

Will called often, but I always kept the conversations short. He acted like we were dating or something, and asked if he could take me out, but I always declined. He complained that all we ever did was drink and he got a little suspicious about why that was the only thing I wanted to do.

The weeks were slow and dreadful and I couldn't wait until the weekends. I longed for them, not to see Will, but to forget everything, even if only for a few hours. I hardly ate. My muscles were always tense. My nerves were frazzled and my mind was crazy from the nightmares and panic attacks. The only time I ever felt *good* was when I was drunk.

One night, I sat at my desk staring at my blank computer screen, frustrated that I couldn't come up with something to type for a stupid paper I had to write. Someone tapped on the door startling me.

"Corinne," Dad said, and walked in.

"What?" I asked with a hint of agitation in my voice.

He sat on the edge of my bed. "Are you okay?"

"I'm fine." I stared at my notebook, pretending to read.

"I don't think you are."

I looked at him. His eyes were sad and I couldn't get over how much he seemed to have aged in the last three months.

"What do you mean?"

"It's just that for the past few months you seem…*empty*. I'm glad to see you going out and doing things, but it's like you're just here physically. You don't talk very much, at least to your mom and me. You don't eat very much and you look so tired all the time."

Because I am.

"You seem jumpy and tense all the time. I just want to know if there's anything I can do."

I forced myself to smile. "Oh Dad. I'm fine. Really. I'm just stressed out from school. It's a tough semester."

"Do you hang out with anyone besides Lisa? Or talk to them?" I knew he was sugarcoating it. *Them* being Abby,

James, and Amos.

"I see Amos at work. And I'm seeing someone now." The words burned at the back of my throat and my stomach coiled. "His name is Will and he makes me happy." My chin slightly quivered and I turned back to my book hoping Dad didn't catch that. I knew I didn't sound convincing at all. I couldn't convince a two-year old to eat candy with my tone.

"Corinne—."

"Dad, it's okay. I promise. I really need to get this paper done."

After a few minutes, he surrendered and left the room, and I exhaled. I hadn't fooled him for a second. How on earth could I keep this up? I was miserable and I just wanted all of it to stop.

Lisa and I went to Tuscaloosa as usual on a Friday after school. We partied hard, but it was the last party I went to. I was so drunk and Will and I started making out, and I didn't stop him when he wanted to go further. Afterwards, I cried like an idiot because I felt as if I had cheated on James, which only made me sick. I was mortified, but it wasn't the first time I threw up with Will around. He didn't ask questions, but I knew what he was thinking. Some crazy drunk girl who couldn't keep it together.

We'd fallen asleep, his sweaty body against mine and his arms around me. I didn't want him touching me, but I did nothing to change that. I felt like a slut. That wasn't me. None of it was me. What had I become?

The leafless trees swayed in the breeze as the darkening clouds moved across the sky. I pushed open an iron gate, cutting my wrist on a jagged edge. I ignored the trickling blood as it steered toward my fingertips and dripped onto the dead ground. I followed a narrow dirt path up a hill to a large oak tree. My hands touched the cold bark and I rounded the tree to the other side, stopping short when I saw hands on the ground. Narrowing my eyes as if it would help me see better in the dark, I moved closer.

The hands moved and suddenly *he* stood before me. A glare in his blue eyes. A scowl on his mangled face. His hair was caked with dried blood. His hands curled into fists. My breath caught in my throat.

"D-David."

"Look what you did to me." Anger and hatred in his voice.

"I-I'm s-sorry."

"This should be you. You should be here. Not me."

He looked larger than I remembered him. His stance was like a lion about to attack a gazelle. I stood frozen, afraid to look at him. I closed my eyes, waiting for what I deserved to come to me.

My eyes darted open. I clenched and unclenched my hands, trying to force the tingling sensation to disappear, but it didn't. I panted and clutched my chest. Knots tied in the pit of my stomach as I tried to force the nausea away. The images from the dream swarmed around my head.

"Corinne," Will said. "Calm down. Hey, calm down." I knew he meant well, but it was like telling someone with allergies to stop sneezing. I got out of bed and paced. I didn't want anyone seeing this, let alone some guy I barely knew.

Will got up and wrapped his arms around me. "Hey, calm down," he said in a soft voice. He kissed my forehead, but he was smothering me. I pushed him away. "What's the matter?"

I walked back to the bed and knelt beside it, listening to James telling me nothing was going to hurt me and to focus on my breathing.

When I calmed down, I got dressed.

"Are you leaving?" Will asked, sliding on his jeans.

"I have to get out of here."

"Why?"

I pulled my shirt over my head and grabbed my jacket.

He took my arm and pulled me back. "Will you talk to me?"

"What do you want me to say?" I snapped. "This shouldn't have happened."

He furrowed his eyebrows. "What, last night?"

"All of it. This isn't me."

"You mean the drinkin'?"

"I mean everything." My eyes blurred.

"Including us?"

I blinked and the tears fell. "There never was an 'us.' Don't you get it? I feel nothing when I'm with you."

His face twisted as if he was hurt. "So what am I to you? Just some guy you can play with and toss in the end?"

"I just want the pain to go away," I shouted. "But it won't. I hate the way I feel all the time. I hate how I keep hurting people."

He let out a long breath. "I'm not gonna pretend that you're obviously hidin' something." Will stepped closer. "You kept saying 'David' last night in your sleep. But it wasn't the first time I'd heard you say his name."

"What?" Now I was *talking* in my sleep.

"Who is he? An old boyfriend or something?" I didn't miss the hint of jealousy in his voice.

"He was my brother," I yelled.

"I didn't know you have a brother."

"I don't. You don't know anything."

"You're right. Because you stay locked up inside your head. And it's like the only time you're ever really happy is when you're drunk."

"If it bothers you so much then why do you hang around me?"

"Because I like you and I care about you."

"That's what they all say."

"I don't go sleepin' around with just any girl, Corinne." Will moved closer and pulled me to him. "You're such a mystery to me." He took my face in his hands and I looked into his baby blue eyes. "This isn't all that you are. I know there's more to you, and I just wish you'd let me in."

"It's not good."

"I doubt that. I want to know you. Everything. The good, the bad, whatever."

I didn't understand why he liked me so much. I hadn't

been nice to him at all.

"Let me in," he whispered. He leaned down and kissed me, but as usual my heart didn't go crazy and there wasn't a nervous feeling in my stomach. There was nothing.

"I-I need to go home."

"Don't put up a wall. Please."

"I have to go."

His shoulders slumped and then he nodded. "Okay."

Will pulled up into my driveway and I glanced at the clock on the dash. Six in the morning.

"Will I see you tomorrow?" he asked, hopeful.

I bit my lip and shook my head with my hand on the door handle.

"The next day?"

"This isn't going to work."

"We don't have to party anymore or have sex."

"I can't do this."

Will sighed. "Why? Why are you being like this?"

"We should've never met." I opened the door and got out, closing it before he could say another word.

"But we did meet." I heard him behind me. "And you're just gonna walk away like it never happened?"

I turned around. "You should do the same. Don't call. Just forget about me." I went inside and exhaled once I heard him drive away.

"Where have you been?" Mom's severe voice came from the kitchen.

I lingered in the doorway. "With Lisa."

"Unless Lisa has been taking steroids and testosterone, then you're lying."

I rolled my eyes. I did not need this right now. "That was Will. He gave me a ride home."

She raised her eyebrows. "Do you have any idea what time it is?"

"Yes. And I'm tired so I'm going to bed." I took a step toward the stairs.

"Oh no you're not. You get back here right now." She

crossed her arms in front of her and glared.

"What do you want?"

Mom moved closer and looked at me in disgust. "Are you drunk?"

"No. That wore off hours ago."

"Don't get smart with me. Do you realize I have been sitting here all night wondering where you were?"

"You knew I was with Lisa. I'm tired. I had a bad night and I just want to get some sleep."

"You've had a bad *night*? Well, I am so sorry. I've had a bad few months and your nonsense hasn't helped at all."

"I'm sorry that you're left with the problem child," I yelled. "I'm sorry I can't be perfect like David was or that I'll never amount to anything."

"I never said that."

"No, but you haven't exactly been the best mom lately. I know you blame me for everything that happened."

Her eyes widened with rage. She seized the large framed picture from the wall, ripped it off, and smashed it over my head. Glass broke into a several tiny pieces. I fell backward on the stairs and then Dad charged downstairs toward her. It all happened so fast I wasn't sure she had really done it.

I could see the hatred in her cold eyes. Her chin quivered and she couldn't control her tears.

"Carolyn, stop," Dad demanded. "What were you thinking?"

I crawled up the stairs and saw Booger cower in the corner. I went to the bathroom and locked the door. My hands shook and I held my stomach from the ache. Miraculously, I wasn't bleeding.

I had to end this. The pain. The constant yelling and hate. It seemed like the only who understood my misery was Lisa. She'd been there. She'd dealt with death. But I wondered if she would understand my solution to the problem. I thought of several ways out. Pills. A knife. Hanging. They wouldn't miss me. Everyone would be so much better off with me gone.

CHAPTER THIRTY

Spring break came and I couldn't have welcomed it more. Except my mind wouldn't stop remembering last year's beach trip. It was as if my own mind haunted me. Tortured me with the memories. Showing me what I had lost. Any time I remembered things, I got angry. I threw things, cursed. I hated myself for what I did and I didn't need my mind reminding me.

Lisa and Jack were going to the beach and constantly asked that I go, but I didn't want to. I hated the beach. Besides, I had my own plans.

"Jesus, Corinne, I'm beginning to not like being around you." Lisa groaned. "You're like a robot or something. What happened to you? We were having a lot of fun and then you just stopped going out."

Two weeks had passed since that night with Will and the confrontation with Mom. I stayed out of Mom's way and she stayed out of mine. Dad tried to keep the peace, but I knew it wasn't easy for him.

"Are you afraid of your mom going off on you?"

I nodded, but that wasn't the real reason.

"She won't. She was just upset that you came home with a guy. I can't believe you broke up with Will." Lisa shook her head and plopped onto my desk chair.

"We never dated."

"You know, he's torn up about the whole thing. I mean, you're right back where you were a few months ago. It's annoying."

"Sorry my mood is dampening yours."

She let out an exasperated sigh. "Why are you like this all of a sudden? Did Will do anything to you?"

"No. Nothing has changed. Abby and James and Mom—they all hate me."

"I can't believe you *still* think about Abby and James. They are so worthless. Why do you still pine after them like they are the greatest beings ever? Just stop moping around. It's driving me insane."

"If you don't like being around me, then don't. Why don't you just leave me like everyone else has?"

"I can't believe you're being like this to me. I saved you from the heartache of all those people who inevitably broke your heart. I—."

"It won't stop," I cried. "He's always in my head. His face constantly surrounds me. I can't think about anything else."

"I hate to be mean, but just because your brother is dead doesn't mean you can't live your life. He's not coming back, so stop holding on."

"*I* can't live without him," I yelled.

"You need to learn how to live without him. And stop feeling so sorry for yourself. This is seriously straining our friendship."

"You don't get it, do you? How can I possibly have a *life* when I deprived David of his?"

"Ugh. I can't talk to you right now. You're making me too mad. I hate it when you talk like this. Reminds me so much of my dad. Look, what are you going to do when I'm out of town? Who's gonna watch over you?"

I clenched my teeth. "I'll be fine, Lisa. You don't have to babysit me anymore."

She raised her eyebrows. "Oh no? Then why won't you

eat? You look like hell all the time, now. When was the last time you actually showered? You won't even attempt to cover up that awful scar on your forehead. You won't try to make yourself pretty anymore. I think you need some sun and the beach."

"I don't like the beach."

"You sure as hell liked it last time you went."

I sighed and shook my head. How could she not understand me? She told me she felt it all before. She knew what it was like to lose something so close. So why was she suddenly *not* understanding me?

"Wait, are you not going to the beach because David was with you the last time?"

I winced at the mention of his name.

"You've seriously got to get over this. I had to get over my father's death. He's not here, he'll never be here."

Her words did nothing but pierce my hollow heart. They rang so loudly through my head and I swallowed the lump in my throat, but as always, it came back. *He'll never be here.*

"I have to go home and finish packing. But think about what I said. And call Will. He'll cheer you up. He misses you so much. I'll come by tomorrow before I leave."

"You don't need to come. Just go enjoy your trip. I'll be fine. And I'm sorry for my attitude. I promise I'll be different when you come back." I gave a smile.

"Okay. I'll see you when I get back then." She hugged me rather aggressively and then left.

She didn't know that was to be the last time we saw each other. Or so I thought.

With Lisa gone, no school, and my parents at work, David consumed my mind even more. The house was insanely quiet. I missed his goofiness. His laughter. I even missed him playing video games and ignoring me. Or the stupid B movies he insisted we watch. Why did I have to fall asleep that night? I wished I could call David and talk to him. Tell him how miserable I was. Tell him how miserable I was making everyone else. I needed David here to help me through it.

Though, if David were here, I wouldn't be in this much pain. None of us would be.

I fell asleep that night, but not without a nightmare scaring me out of my sleep. It was four in the morning, and I just stayed in bed waiting until the sun rose. I pretended to be asleep when Dad came to say goodbye before going to work. Mom never did anymore. I remembered some mornings when it was cold and rainy she would curl up in the bed with me and we'd lay quietly together. I missed that.

I finally got out of bed at some point, and let Booger out before the rain came. The godforsaken rain. I sat at the kitchen table, waiting for Booger to be done, and was left with my thoughts. Same thoughts every single day. They annoyed me, but there wasn't anything I could do to end them. Today was the day.

But how?

I could jump off a bridge. But that might hurt. I could use a gun. But that would leave a mess. Maybe I could drown myself in the bathtub. Or hang myself. Or swallow a bunch of pills.

I shuffled to the back door and let Booger back into the house. His claws scraped against the linoleum kitchen floor as we started to walk back upstairs.

The phone rang and startled me. It was Lisa calling to check on me and I kept the conversation short. I tried to convince her that I was fine, but I wasn't sure I did. She urged me to call Will and I told her I would just to get her to shut up about him. I finally got off the phone, and just as I started walking up the stairs, someone knocked at the door, and Booger barked. It startled me and I just stood there not knowing what to do, for some reason.

Another knock. Another bark.

I scuffled my bare feet across the cold hardwood floor of the foyer and turned the deadbolt lock. I opened the door and couldn't move. My breath hitched as I stared into his blue eyes.

CHAPTER THIRTY-ONE

Booger immediately brushed past me to greet James, happily. James's slightly wet hair was disheveled and his eyes were bloodshot. He had a little bit of stubble on his face. I dropped my gaze. I didn't know what to think or say.

"Hey, Corinne." It had been so long since I'd heard his voice. Or say my name. "H-how are you?" The rain poured behind him, and hit the bottom steps with an irritating pat.

"Fine."

There was a long awkward pause. Why was he even here? What did he want? I hated what he did to me.

"How are your parents?"

"I don't really feel like small talk right now. So just get to the point."

"I just came because I-I." He struggled with his words. Something I'd never seen him do. And then it dawned on me. He was there for the ring.

I sighed and turned back toward the stairs. "Come on."

I heard him close the door behind him and then he followed me to my room. Of course, he'd only come back to get it. Had he found someone else to give it to? My stomach clenched and unclenched as I dug around in my drawer for the stupid thing. I couldn't stop shaking. I finally found it and tossed it at him.

"There," I said. "You can go now." I couldn't keep the bitterness out of my voice. He'd left me. Couldn't stand to be around me.

But why did his eyes water?

I crossed my arms in front of my chest. "Why are you so sad? This was inevitable."

He met my eyes and cleared his throat. "Why are you doing this?"

Was he serious? What kind of question was that? Did he not think what he did was a valid reason? "Because you left me," I yelled. "You never came back. Or called." I batted at the tears that fell down my face. "You couldn't even tell me. I had to hear it from Lisa." I was so angry with him and I didn't know why. He had every reason to leave me.

"Your parents told me not to." His voice cracked.

That brought me up short. "They said that?"

"Well, Lisa did."

"What?"

"I called that Friday I was supposed to come to let you know I had the flu and couldn't make it. Lisa answered and started crying and I finally got it out of her. She said your parents asked her to tell me not to come back or call you again."

That didn't make sense. If my parents really told her that, then why did Dad seem sad that James and I broke up? And Lisa was the one who begged James to come back.

"Don't lie to me."

He took a step closer but I moved back. "I'm not. I couldn't believe it, but Lisa said it was because they didn't want me to make it worse. I emailed you a thousand times because I couldn't stand being away from you. It drove me crazy, but I didn't want to go against your parents' wishes. And then you finally emailed me back. You were angry and said you hated me and never wanted to see me again. You said to stop emailing. So I did. But I came today because I just, I need to hear you tell me that this is really over."

"Why are you lying to me?"

"I'm not. Why do you keep asking that?"

"Because I never got a single email from you. I haven't talked to you since you left that day. I called you every day that week, but you never answered or called back."

"I did call, but Lisa always answered and said you were asleep. And I kept missing your calls because I had the flu so I was out of it for a couple of weeks."

"Why don't you just admit that you hated being around me and that you refused to see me? Lisa told me she begged you come but you refused. How could you?"

He shook his head and then ran his hands down the length of his face. "You've got to be fucking kidding me," he mumbled. "I never said that, Corinne. Or felt that way. She never begged me to come. She told me to stop calling because your parents requested it. She lied to you. I have not stopped loving you."

My heart stopped and my knees wobbled. The churning in my stomach made me dizzy. I couldn't seem to breathe properly. I felt like all the blood drained from me. I had to sit down. What was going on? This was too much for me to grasp. Had my parents really asked that? Or was it just Mom? Why would Lisa lie to me?

"No. Lisa wouldn't lie to me. She's the only one who's been by me this whole time."

"Please believe me, Corinne. I swear to you I never said those things."

We were quiet again, my mind racing with the knowledge.

He moved closer. "You said you didn't get any of my emails. You never got a single one?"

"No. I didn't get any from you." Except once when I clicked on it, it had already deleted. Lisa knew my password and would often check it for me. Oh god. Had she deleted all of his messages? Could she have sent an email to him from me?

"What is it?"

"I think she deleted them and wrote you that message

from my address." My voice was barely above a whisper. But why would she do that?

The muscle in his jaw twitched and I could see the anger in his eyes. He turned away and gripped the back of my desk chair so tight his knuckles were white. "Lisa always sounded so sincere and apologetic and told me that you just weren't yourself. I can't believe this. I don't even know why I ever believed her." He took a deep breath, and then turned to me.

I couldn't hold the tears back. "She told me you didn't love me anymore. That you couldn't stand to be around me. That's what I've thought for three months. My dad seemed so surprised when I told him we'd broken up."

He sighed and shook his head. "All this time I thought I was doing the right thing. I didn't want to be the reason you couldn't heal, so I stayed away."

"How could she do this to us? Why would she keep us apart?"

"I don't know. She never liked me and hated that I took up so much of your time."

I looked up at him, his eyes were lost and sad. "I feel awful." I covered my face with my hands and then felt the bed dip beside me. He slid his arms around me and pulled me to him. It was comfortable. Familiar.

"Don't feel bad. And this is yours." He slid the ring on my finger. "*You* are the only one for me. You know that. No matter what. There is no one better than you."

His words only made me feel guiltier for believing Lisa. For sleeping with some guy that I didn't love. "I don't deserve it. Or you."

James pulled away, and tilted my chin until our eyes met. "Why? Because of what Lisa made us both believe? Trust me, I'm ashamed of it. It's you who deserves better."

"Because I cheated on you," I said through thick tears. My whole body shook and I couldn't look at him. He eased his grip on me. "I slept with someone else because for months I thought you hated me. I went out with Lisa and we drank and partied for weeks. That's all I did, because it kept my mind off things. Off of you and how much I hurt. How much I hurt everyone. But it only made it worse. I hate myself for what I did. I'm trying so hard to feel something else other than this sadness. I can't. No matter what I've tried, it won't go away, James." I buried my face into his chest and felt his arms tight around me.

James kissed the top of my head. "I'm so sorry." His voice shook. "I wish I could take away your pain."

"I can't do this anymore. I can't keep pretending that everything is fine. Lisa hates it when I talk like this, but I'm the reason David is dead. The reason why everything is so messed up. I'm so sorry, James. Please don't hate me." I was apologizing for everything. For believing Lisa. For sleeping with Will. And for what I had to do.

"I don't hate you. And you have nothing to apologize for."

We stayed like that for what seemed like ages.

The rain started and it sounded as if rocks were being thrown against the house. Thunder quietly rumbled.

I didn't want to say goodbye to James, but I had to. I wanted to kiss him one last time and be with him. Just one more time.

I lifted my head and gazed into his eyes. I placed my cold hand upon his cheek and leaned forward. I kissed him, and moved my mouth with his, but there was no electricity. I pulled him closer until he lay on top of me.

"Corinne," he said between kisses.

I wrapped my legs around his waist and kissed him harder. I slid my hands under his shirt feeling his soft skin. I missed him and I wanted to remember what he felt like. One more time.

"Corinne, wait." James stopped my eager hands and held himself up, his breathing labored. His eyes held an intense gaze.

"What?"

"We-we can't do this."

"We don't need protection." I reached up and tried to pull

his mouth to mine, but he grabbed my hands.

He took a deep breath. "Stop. This isn't right."

I tried to swallow the building lump in my throat. "You're rejecting me?" My voice cracked.

"No. I want to be with you so much, but I don't think it's the right time."

He didn't know just how right the time was. "No, please. I'm sorry I cheated. I made a mistake and I—."

"It's not that. You didn't cheat on me. You haven't done anything wrong. It just doesn't seem right, right now."

I pulled myself into a sitting position and leaned against the iron bars of my bed. He still held my hands in his. The tears couldn't be held back now. The stabbing pain returned and I bit my lip. "What are you saying?"

"I just think with everything that's been going on, we don't need to focus on *that*. I'm not blind, Corinne. I know you're going through a lot. And I know you're still in a lot of pain. I love you so much." Both of his hands held my face in place and his thumbs wiped away my tears. "But you're not yourself and I understand that the circumstances would change anyone, but I don't think you're healing at all. At least from being around Lisa. I just want to do whatever it takes to help you."

The rain assailed my window just like the tears on my face. We heard Booger bark downstairs while the garage door opened, announcing Mom's arrival, followed shortly by Dad. We waited a little while to see if they would come and greet us, but they didn't.

"I don't know what's wrong with me. I can't eat. I always fear sleep because of the nightmares. I hallucinate things and I can't concentrate on school. I tried being happy for everyone else's sake. But all I feel is anger and guilt. My mom doesn't understand why it's so hard to just get out of bed sometimes. Why I can't stand to be in a car. I'm afraid all the time because I might have another panic attack. I just think it would be better if I wasn't here."

He furrowed his eyebrows. "What do you mean exactly?"

he asked slowly.

"I just want to be happy. But I can't." I sighed. "This is going to be hard."

"What is?"

"Losing you again."

"I'm not going anywhere." He cleared his throat. "Have you," he paused for a moment. "Have you tried talking to someone?"

"Like who? I thought Lisa would understand, but she never wanted to talk about it. She says I'm too melodramatic and thinks I should have gotten over this a while ago."

He sighed. "I can't believe her. Why would she say that?"

I stood from the bed and walked to my desk. "I can't talk to Mom because she hates me. And Dad's been busy taking care of her and himself. You're the only one I've talked to."

I felt his arms around me from behind and I leaned my head back against his chest, and relaxed.

"I just meant that maybe you should." He paused and I felt him stiffen. "see a professional."

"Professional what?" I asked, twisting in his arms to face him.

He hesitated. "Like a counselor or something."

"What? Is that what all this is about?" I struggled out of his grip and he released me. "You think I'm crazy and need to be locked away?"

"No, Corinne. You're not crazy, but you need to talk to someone about this."

"I just tried talking to you."

"But they can give you the help you need. You can get beyond this. You can learn to move on."

"Move on?" I raised my voice. "I can't leave my brother, James."

"You're not leaving him behind. You're just learning to live without him." He garbled the last part. James placed his hand on my arm, but I batted it away.

"Live *without* him? How can I *live* when I'm the one who killed him? How can I move on from this? Answer me."

He frowned and grabbed the nape of his neck, the way he always did when he was nervous. "I-I don't have the answers."

"It should have been me. It's all my fault."

"But it wasn't."

"Don't say that." I hit his chest with my fists. "I fell asleep. I couldn't stop. I couldn't stop him from going through…" The tears plagued me and he tried to draw me into an embrace, but I held him back.

"I can't pretend that I know what you're going through. And I know nothing I say will make it better but I care about you and you're not alone in this. I'm here."

I let out a groan. "I don't need help and I don't need you," I shouted. "You're nothing to me."

"You don't mean that." His eyes watered.

"Get out of here."

"Please, Corinne. I don't mean to upset you." I could hear the panic in his voice, but I wanted him gone. To be left alone. Because no one was going to stop me tonight.

"I said go!"

Lightning flashed and a loud pop echoed. The room went black and then I saw it all over again. The car slammed into the tree. The shattered glass. And David. His bloodied body crashed through the windshield.

I steadied myself against my desk and clenched my jaw from the constant moistening in my mouth. I wiped the perspiration from my forehead and closed my eyes. I couldn't breathe. The tingling was coursing through my veins. With every flash of light, his mangled body appeared, covered with blood.

I blinked several times and saw Dad and James hover over me in the dim light from the stormy dusk. The power had gone out and I was on the floor trying to catch my breath.

"Slow your breathing," James said, gripping my hand.

"What's wrong with her?" Dad panicked, which only made me breathe harder.

"She's having a panic attack. Focus, Corinne. Breathe in."

I did.

"Breathe out."

He helped me through it, and then I sat up and leaned against my desk. How long had I blacked out? And how long had Dad been there?

Mom came in the room with a lit candle. "What the hell is going on in here? Why were you two yelling?"

"I-I was just trying to talk to her," James said.

"Why were you yelling, Corinne?"

"It was my fault. I'm sorry."

But it wasn't James's fault at all. It was me. I was the problem. I felt sorry for the harsh things I said to him.

"I think you need to leave," she told him.

"No, please."

"James, now," she insisted. "I think it's best not to come around here anymore until she gets better."

"No, please. I just want to help her."

"James, don't make this any worse."

"How could you think that?"

"Because you just did."

"I can't leave her," he yelled. He had never raised his voice to her. "She needs as many people who love her. I don't think you realize she needs help."

"I know what she needs," she shouted back. "I have everything taken care of. You need to go."

"Please. I'm so sorry. Just don't make me leave her again."

"I'm not going to ask again."

"Carolyn," Dad said as he held me.

James turned to me and the look in his eyes was heartbreaking. It haunted me. He mouthed, I love you, and then walked out of the room and Mom followed.

Their voices faded as they walked down the stairs. I wanted to call his name, but I couldn't speak. I couldn't move. It was best that he left. At least I got to see him one last time.

I glanced into the hallway. Booger peered into the room, but his tail hid between his legs. Even my dog was afraid of me.

"I shouldn't be here, Dad."

"What do you mean?"

I heard Mom trudging up the stairs. "What the hell is wrong with you? Why are you so angry all the time? What did James do to you?"

I didn't want to fight with them on my last night. But I wished she would understand. "I'm sorry, Mom. I'm sorry for everything."

"We need to talk," Dad said.

It was dark so I couldn't see their faces. But I imagined Mom's face red from anger, and the sadness in Dad's eyes.

"Corinne, we think you should see a doctor," Mom said.

So they all thought I was crazy. I wanted to scream, but I held it all inside. "Okay."

"I've already set up an appointment with a very good psychiatrist. Thursday, your dad will drive you to Dr. Venable's office."

"If you think that's best," I said. But I wouldn't be here Thursday. Or tomorrow.

"We do."

The lights flickered back on and I saw both their faces were wet with tears.

"It'll be okay," I told them. "I'll make it right."

I ate dinner with them and even sat with them and watched TV. We didn't talk. After a few hours, I hugged and kissed them both goodnight.

"I love you," I told them with a smile.

"We love you, too," Dad said.

I walked up the stairs to the kitchen, fixed myself a glass of water, and grabbed a paring knife out of the drawer. I hid it under my shirt and then climbed the stairs to my room. I closed the door and exhaled. Pulling the knife out from under my clothes, I placed it on my desk and sat down.

I buried my face into my hands and let the tears consume me. I would make things right. I had to do what was right in order for everyone to live again. I opened my notebook to a blank page, and pressed the tip of the pen to the paper.

I can't explain how much the pain hurts, how much it kills me inside to know that my brother is gone. I can't tell you how sorry I am for the hurt I have caused. I don't deserve to have anything after what I've done. It was my fault. I fell asleep and lost control. I killed him and I can't survive this pain. I need to do this so I will not be a problem to anyone. I just want to end all this pain. My head aches constantly from the tears I cry. I'm too afraid to close my eyes to sleep because I will see him. My mind makes me see him over and over. Forcing me to relive the memory. Making sure I know what I did. Please God make this go away. I stare at this knife and I'm afraid, but I know it's the right thing to do. It's the only thing to do. I've caused too much pain for everyone around me. I cannot be this burden any longer. I see your agony and it hurts to know it was me who caused this. You have always given me what I needed and all I did was hurt you. I love you, always and will never forget you. I have to let you move on. Please forgive me. I love you.

Corinne

I tore the page from the notebook, folded it, and scribbled 'Mom and Dad' on the front. I reached for the Shakespeare book from my small bookshelf and searched inside for the sonnet. The only words I could leave for James. I was never good with words, and hoped he would understand my feelings. Once I found it, I ripped it out of the book, and read the sonnet, once more.

"No longer mourn for me when I am dead
Than you shall hear the surly sullen bell
Give warning to the world that I am fled
From this vile world with vilest worms to dwell.
Nay, if you read this line, remember not
The hand that writ it, for I love you so
That I, in your sweet thoughts would be forgot,
If thinking on me then should make you woe.
O, if, I say, you look upon this verse,
When I, perhaps, compounded am with clay,
Do not so much as my poor name rehearse,

But let your love even with my life decay,
Lest the wise world should look into your moan,
And mock you with me after I am gone."
"Sonnet 71", Shakespeare

    I folded the sonnet, and wrote his name at the top. I picked up the knife and stared at it for what seemed like forever. Something deep inside of me didn't want to do it and was scared. But I *had* to. It was the only thing I could do to end everyone's misery, including my own. I was tired.

    I closed my eyes and pushed everything away, all the pain, the anger, the thoughts. I only focused on one thing. Ending it all.

    I opened my eyes, placed the cold blade upon my flesh, and held the knife tightly in my hand.

    I took a breath, then cut deeply and vertically against my left wrist. Blood quickly squirted out, staining my white shirt. I grabbed the knife with my left hand and weakly cut my right wrist. There was so much blood. The carpet underneath me turned red. I didn't want to make a mess. I had to clean it up.

    A wave of dizziness rushed over me as I tried to stand. I collapsed to the floor and looked around. I felt a hollow beating in my chest. My wrists throbbed, as they lay flat on the carpet, still bleeding.

    So much blood.

    I closed my eyes and saw David. Abby. Mom. Dad. My breathing slowed. And I saw James. I didn't feel the carpet pressing against my face.

    And then everything went black.

CHAPTER THIRTY-TWO

It took eighty-seven stitches to close both gashes in my wrists. They wrapped each of them with white bandages, but my wrists throbbed and stung as if someone was jabbing them constantly with needles.

Thank God your father heard you fall, Mom had said. And then asked how I could have done such a thing to them. I felt ashamed, but I was disappointed that I was still there.

They kept me in the hospital two days for observation. Observation for what exactly, I wasn't sure. And some guy had come in to ask all kinds of dumb questions and his indifferent demeanor told me I was just some other patient to him. He never looked at me, which made me feel even more ashamed. When he was done, he told my parents I needed to seek psychiatric help immediately.

That was his suggestion. After all the questions, that's all he had to say. Like doctors were some miracle cure.

Wasn't it obvious that I no longer wanted to live? Why should they go through all this trouble for me? I was a killer, a monster. I was my own worst enemy and they couldn't see what they were trying to do for me.

I was exhausted, in pain, and miserable. We were silent the whole way home. And when we came inside, Booger warily greeted us. My grandparents were there. I couldn't look them in the eye, but they each gave me a tight hug.

I turned to go upstairs, but Mom stopped me.

"What?" I asked, my foot lingering on the first step.

"We need to talk." She pointed downstairs to the den.

"I'm tired."

"Yeah, well, so am I. Downstairs."

I reluctantly consented and they all followed me. Mom pulled me into a hug and held me there while she cried.

"I never realized you were this ill," she said and then let me go.

I plopped down on the couch. The dark clouds outside made the room darker, so Mom clicked on a couple of lamps. I watched her pace in front of me. She stopped and placed her hands over her face and sobbed loudly. Dad pulled her close to him and I looked away.

When she finally quit, Dad kissed her forehead and then he and my granddad went upstairs to the kitchen. I heard a few things being tossed into a box, like silverware.

Maw sank down onto the couch next to me, holding my hand in what felt like a vice grip.

"I don't even know where to begin." Mom's voice trembled and she looked at me. "We can't trust you anymore. And we can't afford to just take off all the time, so Mom and Dad are going to watch you. I don't even know how we're going to afford this doctor, but we'll figure that out."

You could just not send me.

"Your dad and granddad are collecting every single thing in this house that you could possibly harm yourself with and hiding it or throwing it away. We've decided that you are no longer allowed in your room alone. You are not allowed to leave this house alone. You are not to have visitors until you are well."

"I can't go to my room? Where am I going to sleep?"

"You can sleep on the couch from now on. And one of us will be watching you."

"Like I'm a baby?"

"You leave me no choice," she shouted. "I'm real tempted to send you to a psychiatric hospital right now, but I think seeing a psychiatrist will help. She can give you medication."

"What, like that's supposed to solve all my problems and make everything go away?"

"I don't know! Don't argue with me. I'm so angry with you." Tears flowed once more, as she darted up the stairs. When she came back, she tossed a couple of blankets, sheets, and pillows on the couch and left again.

Booger whimpered.

"I never wanted to hurt anyone," I said.

Maw held me tight and rocked me. "I know, baby girl. We love you very much. Don't you forget that."

Later that night, I hugged a pillow as I lay on the couch under the blankets. I trembled, but I wasn't cold. Maw was asleep in the recliner next to me. She was a very light sleeper, so any sound I made I knew she'd hear me. So I didn't move.

The grandfather clock ticked loudly from the foyer upstairs. A radio from a passing car outside vibrated the windows. The ceiling fan hummed monotonously above. Leaves scraped against the small windowpane above the television. Each sound amplified inside my head. But the loudest sound of all was the grinding metal and shattering glass.

I was lying in a grave with everyone looking over me in revulsion. They screamed at me. Mom called me a killer. James called me a whore. David shook his head and walked away. They all followed him, leaving me alone in the cold dark grave.

I woke up in a panic. I hated the tightness in my chest and stomach. I hated the lack of breathing and I certainly hated the dreams. Didn't they understand why I wanted it all to end?

The next day, Dad drove me to Dr. Venable's office. It wasn't far from home. Having her so close made me nervous. Easy access.

Once we arrived to a small gray office building with dull red doors, a chill ran up my spine. Bushes surrounded the two-story elongated structure. Sinister clouds loomed over us, hiding the sun. I shivered with the trees from the April wind.

My father met with her first and then I was called into her office. It had a modern look to it, fancy lamps, chair, leather couch. Diplomas cluttered the middle of the wall above me. She probably didn't pay attention to her patients because she probably ogled her diplomas. There was an ugly painting of circles and squares with simple colors for each shape behind her.

"How are you?" Dr. Venable asked. She took tiny steps in her high, black stiletto heels since the gray pencil skirt wouldn't allow much movement from her legs. She sat down, rested her elbows on her desk, and leaned forward. Her skin was mildly tanned. Blush circled her high cheekbones and her nose was slender. Her dark hair was pulled back tightly and neatly into a bun. I wondered if it hurt.

I didn't feel like talking, especially to her. I never looked her in the eyes. There wasn't a window so I stared at the dark green wall. The room felt small.

"Would you like to talk to me?" Her voice was articulate but rather stern.

"Not really."

"I spoke to your mother on the phone today before I met with your father. Your mom tells me you weren't doing so well in school and have shunned away from your friends. Would you like to tell me about that?"

I guessed she didn't care that I didn't want to talk. I looked down at my ring and rotated it around my finger. I missed James, but I had ruined us. He wasn't allowed to see me and it was real this time. It wasn't just Lisa lying to us.

"What are you thinking about?"

"Nothing."

"Don't be afraid. You can open up to me." She clicked her pen constantly. I hated the noise. It annoyed me to no end.

Click. Click. Click. Click.

"Do you mind?" I asked.

"That's a pretty ring."

"How long is this going to last? I really don't think I want to sit here and listen to you badger me with questions."

"How long have you been feeling depressed?"

"I don't know. A while."

"Your mom says you've become angry and despondent."

"Did she tell you that she has become angry and despondent, too?"

"We're here to talk about you."

"Didn't think so."

For the rest of the session, she scribbled whatever bullshit she could conjure about me and asked questions. Why was I not eating? Why did I push away my friends? Did I have panic attacks? And in the end, she prescribed an antidepressant. As if all of my problems would dissolve from one little pill. It wasn't like I had a headache that went away from taking medicine. But she didn't seem to care. She or the other two psychiatrists that I saw. They all told me I was angry and depressed and that I just needed to control it. But no one ever told me how. My condition was always 'complicated' and they just sent me away with some new pill that I never took.

I only had a little over a month of high school, but I dropped out. And I'd quit work. My grandparents stayed with me and took me to whatever psychiatrist I was seeing. I liked being with them. They never asked questions, and didn't judge me.

The weekend after my attempt, Lisa called, but Dad told her I was sick and couldn't have visitors. And a month later was when she stopped by to talk. Because of her reaction, there was no way I was going to tell anyone else.

James called every day, but I wasn't allowed to talk to him. Not until I was 'well enough' as Mom put it. But I didn't want to talk to him. Not that he did anything, but he shouldn't have spent so much time on me. He needed to move on.

CHAPTER THIRTY-THREE

I waited for Dr. Meisner's response and twisted my ring around my finger. I'd been telling Dr. Meisner everything. Just like she wanted, but as I sat there, I was scared that she would yell and tell me what an awful person I was or how ridiculous I was being. That it was all in my mind.

But when I looked up and met her gray eyes, a hint of a smile played at her lips.

"I'm proud of you," she said. "That was a very brave thing you did in telling me your story. I know it was not easy."

"It wasn't, but you helped." I had learned to redirect any negative thoughts, and while I wasn't completely cured, I felt better.

"I'm glad. In the last few weeks, how many nightmares have you had?"

I had been making an honest effort the past few weeks, and with Dr. Meisner's help on my thought process and with the workshop she'd placed me in, I wasn't angry. And the nightmares had diminished. I hadn't been on edge and my head felt clearer. "Not many at all."

She nodded. "You are recovering from this. You are coming to terms with the accident. You've also become less angry with yourself and others. How are you feeling right now?"

"I-I don't know. I haven't felt much of anything lately," I said, but even as I spoke the words, they felt too automatic. I took a breath. "Maybe I feel lighter. Like I'm not under a dark cloud or something."

"Good." She smiled and then it grew wider.

"What?"

"You're smiling."

I hadn't felt that in months. "Why didn't you get mad or run away like my mom? Or Lisa."

"Because I'm here to help you. Your mother has been dealing with a lot. It is hard for any parent to lose their child, but she does not blame you at all. She put a wall between you because it was the only way she knew to cope."

"I guess I did, too. I know she loves and cares for me. It was just hard to see it because all we did was argue."

"She was consumed with anger and grief, as with you. As for Lisa, she had trauma in her life and hasn't exactly dealt with it like she should. That's why she acts the way she does. And I am sorry she lied to you and James. Because of her abandonment issues, I believe she wanted you think everyone had left you, so you would only need her. And I think her fear of being alone controlled her relationship with you. I'm sure she thinks she meant well, but it unfortunately hurt you worse."

It made sense. And I remembered James mentioning her possessiveness of me way before the accident. Maybe I just clung to the one thing I thought I had.

"I have good news."

I looked up. "What?"

"I am granting you day passes now."

"A day pass? Are you sure?" A pass to leave the hospital for a few hours. Was I ready for such a thing? If only I could use it to see David, if only for one more time.

"Yes. You seem saddened by this."

"It's just that, well, I still think about David. Part of me still feels missing."

"You will always think of him and he will always be a part of you. We never completely move on from a death of a loved one, but we learn to accept. As each day goes on, it gets less difficult. It's not that you are forgetting that person—they'll always be there in your memories—it's just learning to live without them."

I nodded. "But I still feel guilty."

"What do you think David would tell you right now, if he was sitting next to you?"

I tried to imagine him sitting next to me, smiling, not glaring, and without a mangled bloodied face like in my dreams. I closed my eyes and thought about what he would say to me. *If any of my friends or family were ever in that situation I would do anything and everything I could to save them.* He would save me. But since he couldn't, he would tell me it wasn't my fault. And that he would not blame me. He would put the blame on himself. And tell me to live.

So many thoughts went through my mind once I left therapy on my way to my room. Guilt was still there. But it was a different guilt. Not for David's death. But for putting my friends and family through so much because of my pain. Saying it aloud had a different effect on me. I never thought telling someone everything would help. Sharing with Emma made me realize I wasn't the only one. Telling Dr. Meisner forced me to face the issues and work on them with her incredible patience. And with Amos, it strengthened our friendship. Now I could tell him anything and I was learning to trust again.

But there were still others I needed to reconcile with. And I started that afternoon.

I came upon the two small wooden cubby holes with chairs along a wall. A phone rested on each table, pulling me like a magnet. I needed to call, and I couldn't postpone it. I bit my lip as I sat down. My hand shook as I lifted the phone from the receiver and then slowly dialed the number.

Two rings later, a weary voice answered. My heart lodged itself in my throat.

CHAPTER THIRTY-FOUR

"Dad," I said. My chin trembled and I rested my elbow on the table and held my head against my hand.

"Corinne?"

"It's me."

"Hey, sweetie. How are you? Is everything okay?"

"Yeah."

After a few seconds of silence, Dad spoke again. "Did you need me to come up there today? I was going to come tomorrow."

"It's okay. Tomorrow's fine. But I'd like to come home with you. For a couple of hours."

"You got a day pass?"

"Yes. I'd really like to see Mom."

"Of course. She wants to see you, too."

My eyes blurred and we were silent for a few seconds.

"Abby called," he said.

I didn't know what to think. "She did? What did she say?" My voice cracked.

"She apologized for not ever calling. She'd really like for you to call her."

"Okay. I will. Dad, is Mom around?"

"Yes, she's sitting right next to me."

"Can I talk to her?"

"Of course."

I heard him handing the phone to her. "Corinne," Mom said. I could hear her eagerness.

"Hi, Mom."

"Hi."

I wasn't sure what to say. Emotions flooded my mind. I clenched and unclenched my fist. "I'm sorry for what I did to you."

I waited, but it was still quiet on the other end.

"I told Dr. Meisner everything," I said. "I just couldn't see beyond my own pain. She said that she could help me with my thoughts. Mom, I miss you," I finally said.

"I miss you, too," she said through thick sobs.

I had dinner with Ginger, and a new girl named Mia, who'd lost her parents in a car accident. She was the only survivor like myself. But I couldn't imagine losing my parents at the same time. And to think I almost left them for good. I liked Mia, and not because I saw a little of myself in her, but because of the fight in her. Ginger was on the mend, and Scott kept his promise to visit often.

We hung out in the common room and watched a movie, and laughed. It felt so good and that was what we had done for the past few weeks. As usual before bed, I wrote in my notebook, and sifted through my pictures. Seeing the smiling girl, and almost coming to recognize her again and my brother. What I would give to just have one day to tell him how much I love him.

I stopped on the last picture of James and me. His sweet smile. Dark blue eyes. Feeling his forehead pressed against mine and his arms around me. I missed him so much, but I was afraid to call him because of what I said to him. It had been five months since I'd seen him. But he still wrote me. Every day. And I still feared what the letters said. I held the picture near my heart and closed my eyes.

A slow song came from the speakers in the large room. Soft blue and pink lights held the room in a calm atmosphere. Several couples enveloped in each other's arms, gently swaying to the slow music. A piano played with a wispy drumbeat. A soft voice began singing, almost in a whisper.

"Will you dance with me?" I heard his silky voice behind me in my ear.

I slowly turned around and looked up. James's dark blue eyes held mine captive. My heart beat in a sporadic rhythm. I nodded to the handsome man in front of me. He wore a black tuxedo and I was wearing a long, satin, silvery-blue, dress with one shoulder.

His arms pulled me closer to his body, my right hand placed itself into his left, and we began moving in sync.

I laid my head against his chest as we swayed.

"I've missed you," he said.

"Me, too."

We stopped moving and he released my hand to lift my chin. My favorite smile spread across his face just before he leaned down.

I felt the familiar tug of my dream ending and I tried to cling to it. I didn't want to let him go.

But then I opened my eyes and looked around the room. I was sitting on the couch in our living room thinking about the weird dream I just had. James and I were at our prom, but the words were different.

"Cor, what's wrong?" I stiffened. Only one person ever called me that.

"David?"

"Hey. What are you doing up? We're going to the beach in the morning. Gotta get some sleep."

"I've slept enough. But I can't wait. It's going to be fun."

"I know." And then he turned to me with a serious look. "I want you to know that I'm okay, Cor. I'm *okay*."

"What?"

"It wasn't your fault. And I need you to do something."

"What?"

"Stop blaming yourself and live your life. Promise me that."

"Okay. I promise."

Like before, I lost my grip on the dream. I didn't want to lose it, but when I opened my eyes, I searched frantically around the room for him. I was in my bed at the hospital with the blanket up to my chin.

Two bizarre dreams. But something filled inside me. Resolution? Culmination? Whatever it was, I knew that wherever my brother was, he was okay.

I hadn't been in a car in months, but it wasn't as bad as I thought it would be. I was nervous, not because of the car, but because I was going home. Granted, it was just for a few hours, but it didn't matter.

"Booger misses you," Dad said.

I smiled to myself. "I miss him."

Dad drove on the interstate and my eyes peeled to the window. We'd just hit the city and I looked all around at the familiar buildings and various landmarks. The statue of Vulcan stood tall and strong atop of the mountain. I remembered going there with David and going to the observation deck at the top to see the city. David refused to come out for the view because he was insanely afraid of heights.

"What's funny?" Dad asked.

"David's fear of heights."

He gave a half smile. "Like when we were in the Smokies and he absolutely refused to cross that swinging bridge that your Paw had to carry him kicking and screaming."

I laughed. "But when we hiked to the top of mountains it never fazed him."

"He was a little quirky."

"That he was."

We were quiet again and I thought of random memories of my brother. Or things I was told that he did when I was a child. Like sing to me to get me to sleep. Although, it wasn't a soft melody by any means. I wondered if he would have done that with his own child. He would have made a great father. I could see him playing on the computer, baby in lap, teaching it to play, while Abby reprimanded him for letting the baby see such graphic images.

"You know David was going to propose to Abby," I said, but then I almost regretting saying it because Dad's eyes watered.

"They made a great couple." He cleared his throat. "Just like you and James."

I bit my lip. "Thanks."

Dad pulled into the driveway and the house looked just as I remembered it. The maple trees were full and green and the little pink flowers on the bushes in the front were still in bloom even though it was September. Fall never really hit the South until about November and only lasted for a month.

We got out of the car and I trembled. Dad opened the door and Booger barked. He bounded up to me, his tail wagging, and a big smile on his face. He jumped on me and I knelt down and petted his soft fur. He licked and sniffed me and then ran to grab his hedgehog, squeaking it.

I rolled my eyes and went to the kitchen where Mom stood next to my grandparents. She was thinner and her once dyed blond hair was now brown and gray. The whites of her eyes were covered in red veins. Her face looked ten years older than the last time I'd seen her.

When she saw me, she broke down, which made me break down, and then Maw broke down. We were definitely an emotional trio.

Mom grabbed me and held me tight. Her shoulders quivered as she quietly wept.

"It's okay," I said.

Mom held me at arm's length. "You look good. You look really good." And then she hugged me again.

I gave Maw and Paw a tight hug.

"I'm so proud of you, baby girl," Maw said. "I know it wasn't easy for any of us, but you've come so far and it's good to see you smile."

I nodded and wiped my tears. "I'm so sorry. I—."

"It wasn't your fault," Mom said. "It was never your fault. I never blamed you. I was angry and I didn't know how to be around you. And then things just worsened and I was afraid of you. But I should've been there to protect you."

"You can't be held accountable for everything I do, Mom. I couldn't see that any of you cared for me. I just saw that you were angry with me and I felt so guilty."

"I wish you had told us, but I probably didn't make that easy."

"I tried talking to Lisa, but she just waved it off like it was all in my head. She made me think James and Amos and Abby hated me and made them think the same of me."

Mom frowned and her chin shook. "I did a horrible thing to you and James. But I never asked Lisa to tell him to stop coming around. But when I told James myself, I just thought I was doing the right thing. I was so consumed by my own grief and anger that I never saw just how much pain you were in. I'm so sorry."

We hugged again and Maw handed out tissues.

Mom shook her head. "You know David would be laughing at us by now with all of our crying."

"Getting too emotional, he'd say."

We laughed and then we spent the day talking and laughing. That was what I loved about my family, why I loved being with them because of how close we were and how hard we worked to get back together. I loved the stories, the laughter, and that day I really lived in the moment.

I clung onto that as Dad took me back to the hospital. Just before I got out of the car, Dad handed me a plastic bag filled with letters.

"You should read them, Corinne," he said.

When I got to my room, I stared at them. There were so many. I sifted through them and found a padded envelope. I opened it and inside was an mp3 player and earphones with a small note attached.

I made this playlist for you, and I hope the music helps you. It does me. I think of you when I hear each and every one of these songs. They say music can heal, and I hope they are right. Just listen to it. I love you.

My heart sank at his gesture. It was written a few weeks after he stopped calling. I twisted the ear buds in, pressed play, and then listened. The songs were a mix of beautiful love songs. They weren't sappy, but they were romantic and filled with a need to be with that person, or help them, and see them through their pain. I loved every song. And it was the first time I'd really listened to music since before the accident.

I listened to the songs and picked up James's first letter he'd written me. I took a deep breath and then opened it with a shaky hand. My heart pounded.

Corinne,
This is the only way I know to talk to you. I called but your mom told me to stop. I hate every day that passes without you. After that night I left your house, I fell apart. Because there isn't anything I could do. I never meant to hurt you, and I only hope you won't give up. And when you feel like giving up, just tell yourself to hold off just one more day. Please remember that you are not alone in this. I am and will always be here for you. I will wait for you if that's what it takes. I love you.
James

I wiped the tears from my cheeks and took an uneven breath. I had to read more. I read about his life in the past few months. While I was miserable in the hospital, he was miserable out in the world. He'd driven by my house, hoping to see me through the window or hoped to bump into me somewhere and see that I was okay and happy. He ached for me, longed to touch me, kiss me or just feel me in his arms. I was what he wanted and that we had a love that would always bind us and no matter what we'd be together. There wasn't a day that went by that he didn't think of me.

The more I read, the more James became lost. Lost in the confusion and not knowing what to do. He didn't want to believe that it was over, and he would continue writing until he heard from me. No one else, but me-my voice. He wrote poems, some were sweet and loving, others were dark and desperate. He needed me, he loved me and still waited.

In the last letter I had, he wrote another poem.

The clouds separate in the dark sky
It tries to separate us, but I refuse
You're all I'm wanting
Your heart is broken
And I wait

Someday, the clouds will no longer separate your soul
Those tears will eventually stop rolling down your cheeks
And I wait for you

Your broken heart will mend one day
And mine will ache for yours
You're all I'm wanting
And I wait

CHAPTER THIRTY-FIVE

I paced in my room, wringing my hands, and tried to breathe. Every time someone walked by my room, I stopped, but then went back to pacing.

"For the love, would you please sit?" Amos asked. He was on my bed, legs stretched out, and leaned against the headboard, playing with his phone.

"I can't."

He shook his head. "Did you know there's an app for bowel movements?"

I couldn't tell if he was serious or just trying to keep my mind settled. But I took the bait. "What?"

"Yeah, I can track my bowel movements now."

I couldn't help but laugh. "That's disgusting."

"What, it's healthy."

"You're so weird."

"But think of how cool that is."

"Maybe you can brag to Emma now about how often you poo."

He smiled, a silly grin on his freckled face. Just as he always did when I said her name. "I just might."

There was a knock on the door, and my breath caught in my throat. I wasn't nervous anymore. I felt a smile on my face as she tackled me into a hug.

"Omigod," Abby cried. Her arms were tight around me, and mine around hers. I had never seen Abby cry until that day in the hospital after the accident. I could feel her shoulders shaking.

"I think Guinness could record that for the world's longest hug," Amos joked from behind us.

Abby pulled away, removed her glasses, and wiped the tears from her green eyes. "Don't make me come over there and kick your ass."

"Fair enough," he said.

She stood back and looked at me. "You look well."

"Thanks. You do, too."

"So what have you been up to lately?" She closed her eyes and cursed. "I'm sorry. That was dumb."

I shrugged. "It's okay. It happened. It's a part of me now."

"Don't you have a roommate?"

"I did. Emma. She left in August though. She's doing so well." I gave Amos a private smile and his cheeks reddened a little.

"She's awesome."

Abby cocked her eyebrow. "So you're dating her?"

"How can you tell?"

"I never miss a thing." She looked at me. "Except you."

We ventured outside and walked around. It was still humid and hot outside, but my hands were cold. As always. I told her about living in the hospital and the people I'd met along the way. But I still didn't tell her how I got there. How would I even explain that?

After a lull in the conversation, Abby stopped and turned to me. "I've missed you so much, Corinne. I'm such an idiot. You didn't deserve what I did to you. I don't even deserve to be called your friend. I couldn't be around you or your family because I would be reminded of David and I couldn't handle it because I'm a dipshit and I suck at these things. I don't know if you can ever forgive me, but I hope that one day we can be friends again."

"Of course I forgive you. After David passed away, I couldn't get over it. He was everywhere. In my head. In my dreams. I had nightmares almost every night since the accident. I hallucinated about it. I was angry because of what I did. I fell asleep for a second and I always crawled his butt for not ever wearing his seatbelt, but I didn't know he wasn't that night. I blamed myself."

"What?"

"For so long I felt like it was my fault. I hid from everyone, but Lisa. I believed everyone ran off, but it was just her cutting me off from them. She told me James never wanted to see me again, and I believed her. She told me that Amos never wanted to have anything to do with me. I couldn't handle it anymore." I wiped the sweat from my palms on the back of my jeans. "I just wanted it all to end."

She looked confused, but then comprehension registered on her face. "Oh no."

I had told Amos all this before and he was still by my side. He gripped my hand because he knew what I was about to say. I felt my breakfast trying to make its way back up, but I forced it down. I took a deep breath and exhaled. "I tried to kill myself."

Silence hovered around us, and then she hugged me. "Please don't let it be what I said."

"It wasn't."

"I'm the worst friend. I feel terrible."

"Please don't blame yourself, Abby. You didn't do this. No one did."

"Omigod. I'm so glad you are here. More than you'll ever know."

I felt a smile creep on my face. "Me, too. I wanted to tell you that David was going to propose to you."

Tears welled in her eyes and she smiled. "I would've said yes."

We started walking again and I realized it was easier talking to Abby than I remembered. I had forgotten how true and strong our bond was.

"How long have you been visiting, Amos?" she asked.

"For a few months now. I saw Lisa at school one day and she told me, but she wasn't very nice about it. So I came to see her."

She shook her head. "I should've been here."

"Don't beat yourself up."

"So, what was up with Lisa? I mean, what was she doing?"

Amos and I exchanged a look and then filled in the gaps about Lisa.

"What a bitch," Abby shrieked. "I ought to find her and give her a taste of my mind."

"Just let it go. I'm done with her and I never want to see her."

"Of course I can't exactly say I was the best friend either. You haven't mentioned James. Are you two okay? I mean, you're still wearing your ring."

I looked down at it. "Um, I haven't talked to him since April."

Her eyes widened. "What?"

"But he's written her a bunch of letters," Amos said. "That she refuses to read."

I rolled my eyes. "I read them."

"Okay. So are they the angry letters you thought they'd be?" Amos asked.

"No. He misses me and said he was waiting for me. And he talked about how confused he was."

"So, are you going to call him?"

"What am I supposed to say?"

"The truth," Abby said as if it was the most obvious answer. "You need to call him."

"Abby's right."

"What if he runs away or gets mad?"

She gave me a look that said *'are you kidding me?'* "You know he won't."

"If you don't call, we will," Amos said with an impish grin. "You know she has day passes now. We could take her to his house."

My stomach dropped. "No."

"Hmm. That's not a bad idea." Abby smiled with him. "I seem to remember David and me convincing you to go out with him in the first place."

"That's not true. I said yes when he asked."

Abby raised an eyebrow. "You still had your doubts. Come on. You should go see him before school starts."

"I'm not ready."

"You are. And you know he wants to see you."

"So, it's settled then," Amos said. "You call him tonight and we'll take you to him tomorrow."

"O-okay. Yeah. I'll call him tonight," I told them, but then they looked at me, clearly not believing me.

"We should make sure she does it," Abby said. Leave it to her to be able to read my thoughts. "Here, you can use my phone." She whipped it out from her pocket and handed it to me.

There was a tightness in my stomach and I started to sweat. My jaw clenched and I felt as if my heart would explode right through my skin.

"Hey, look at me." Abby placed her hands on my shoulders and looked right at me. "You can do this. You have to talk to him. You owe it to yourself, and to him."

I nodded. I slowly dialed his number, trying not to let my shaky thumb mess up. I put the phone to my ear and breathed. Or tried. I thought I was going to puke.

It only took one ring and then he answered.

"Hello?" he asked again.

Abby nudged me to say something.

"Hey, it's me. Corinne."

There was a long pause and that felt like forever. Had I made a mistake in calling him? What would he say? I heard him exhale.

"Corinne."

"It's me."

"It's so good to hear your voice."

I bit my lower lip in an attempt to make it stop quivering.

It was good to hear his silky voice. Much better than hearing it in my dreams. "Yours, too. H-how are you?" It was sort of a dumb question, but I didn't know what to say.

"I'm okay. I guess. You?"

"Yeah. I'm okay, too."

"Tell him," Abby whispered. She had a determined look in her eye that I knew if I didn't say something to James, she would take the phone and ask him to meet up with me.

"What are you doing?" he asked.

"Um, I'm hanging out with Amos and Abby." I took a few steps away from them.

"Oh. That's good that you and Abby are talking again. I'm glad to hear it."

"Yeah. It's the first time I've seen her since everything."

"Oh."

I sighed. "James, I called because I—." I wished my stomach would calm down and that I would stop shaking. "I know it's been forever and I know I haven't treated you very well and it's okay if you're mad at me. But I'd like to see you. To explain everything. It's okay if you don't. I'll understand." I sped through my words and hoped he picked up on them.

"I thought you'd never ask."

CHAPTER THIRTY-SIX

I was a complete mess. I got dressed, but I didn't like what I was wearing. So when Abby, Amos, and Emma came to pick me up that day, they took me by my house so I could change. Of course, that took forever because I couldn't find anything. Finally, Abby and Emma made me settle on a baby blue wrap sleeveless top and jeans.

We went to the botanical gardens to meet him. I loved the exotic smells it brought and it was cool in the shade from the trees. James and I had been there once before and counted frogs in the lily pond and played hide-and-seek like we were little kids. And then it started to rain, but we didn't care. We were both soaked to the bone, laughing without a care in the world. I remembered going back to his house, peeling our drenched clothes off, and showering together. But what I remembered most is the way he looked at me, his eyes so full of love and desire. I wondered if we would ever be like that again.

I felt myself smile at the memory as I sat on a swing, my knee shaking. My palms were sweaty while the same familiar nauseous feeling swirled in my stomach. I couldn't sit still with a trembling body.

"If you don't stop shaking, you're going to break this

swing," Amos said.

Emma pinched his arm. "Be nice."

"Ow! That hurt you, know."

"Whatever. I didn't even leave a mark."

"You'd better kiss it then." She did.

Abby rolled her eyes. "Kids."

I laughed with her and then I saw him walking toward us. My breath hitched and I slowly got to my feet. As soon as my eyes locked into James's beautiful sapphire eyes, I felt several things at once. Embarrassed that I hadn't contacted him sooner. Guilty because he was standing in front of me—obvious that he hadn't moved on. Angry at myself for saying horrible things to him. An overwhelming emotion of having him there—and not in a dream. And finally, reconciliation with myself, that I did deserve happiness.

James closed the distance. He greeted Abby and Amos, Emma introduced herself. Abby said she remembered seeing something in the gift shop that she wanted and the three of them walked away. It was just James, me, and my crazy beating heart.

"Hey," he said.

"Hey."

Then we stood there like two awkward people who didn't know how to talk. I wanted to wrap my arms around him and hear him tell me that we were okay.

"I hate this," I said.

"What?" I could tell his body stiffened.

"Being nervous."

"Oh." He gave a relaxed smile. "I know. I am, too."

We started walking on the paved path and silently made our way to the rose garden. Pink, yellow, red, white, orange roses were all in full bloom. They smelled wonderful.

"These are so pretty," I said. "I'd like to have a rose garden someday."

"I know."

Meandering into the crape myrtle garden, I pointed out the pretty pink, purple, and white flowers. I was stalling, but I wasn't ready to talk about the heavy stuff. But I could tell he wondered why I had finally called and wanted to see him after five months.

"It's been a while since I've been here," I said.

"Same for me."

"At least it's not raining."

"I liked the rain."

"Me, too." I cleared my throat. "So, how's school?"

"It's fine." I could tell by the slight agitation in his voice, he didn't want to small talk, but I couldn't help it.

"What classes are you taking this semester?"

"Just some core courses. Mostly boring stuff. What about you? Are you about to start college?"

Heat rose to my cheeks. "No. I never graduated," I mumbled. "So when do you go back?" I asked before he could question me about school.

"In a week."

"Oh." I was saddened by this, but there wasn't much I could do. "How are your parents and Tony? You mentioned in your letters Tony starting a band. That's exciting."

"So you got the letters."

"Yes."

"Oh. I kinda thought for a while I was writing to a ghost."

That stung a little.

"Sorry." He tugged on the back of his neck and let out a sigh. "That was a dick thing to say."

"There's an orchid exhibit here. Wanna check it out?"

"Sure."

We walked through the conservatory which had a desert garden and camellias and gorgeous orchids. The vibrant purple color centered inside white petals. I loved how they snaked downward from the trellis above making a curtain.

"These are my grandmother's favorites," I said. "David and I used to give her orchids every year for her birthday. Guess it's up to me now."

I felt his hand slip into mine and my pulse accelerated. He squeezed my hand and we continued walking hand-in-hand through the wildflowers, lilies, irises, Alabama woodlands, which looked just like the woods in my backyard, but it was still quiet and peaceful. He talked about Tony and his band and how it was getting popular at school. I was glad he talked because I didn't know how much more small talk I could handle. I found myself laughing and falling back into a comfortable rhythm with him and it seemed as if he felt the same.

We walked under the curved top of the torii gate for the Japanese gardens. It was called the 'gate to heaven.' This type of gate was considered sacred according to the sign that I'd read several times before.

I was almost afraid to go inside the bonsai house, but I did. "David loved these," I told him. "There's a place off the interstate that has them for like twenty bucks. It's no wonder he never got one. Abby probably wouldn't let him have one because she'd probably would have been the one to take care of it."

James lightly chuckled and then we made our way on the arched bridge that crossed over the pond and then went inside the lush green bamboo grove. The sun trickled through in little rays of light and it was so secluded. It seemed like a good place to finally tell him everything since we'd been walking all over this place and I hadn't said one word about it.

"I read your letters the other night. For the first time."

He released my hand and moved in front of me. "Why the first time? Did your mom hide them from you this whole time?"

"No. I didn't want to read them."

"What is all this, Corinne?" I could tell he was having a hard time holding back his frustration. "Why are we here? I just wanna know what's going on. I mean, you're still wearing your ring."

"Of course I am."

"What does that mean? Are we here so you can tell me that it's really over? That the last few months spent pining and aching for you was worthless because you've already moved on?" A tear slid down his cheek. "That when you told me I meant nothing to you, you really meant it?"

My heart sank with regret and I felt my shoulders slump and my breath struggled. His words, his pain made me falter. "I was scared."

He furrowed his eyebrows. "Of what?" he asked, his tone calmer.

"I didn't read your letters until now because for so long I feared what you said in them. I was scared because of the way I treated you. For pushing you away. Emma made me realize that if you were so angry, you wouldn't still be writing me. But I still couldn't read them until now."

"Why? Why couldn't you just talk to me?" he asked, desperation in his voice.

I took a deep breath. It was time to stop stalling and finally tell him the truth. "Because I haven't been at home since May. I've been living at Fairview Psych this whole time." I tried holding back the tears, but it was useless. I looked away.

"Corinne?"

"Please don't hate me."

He grabbed my arms and I met his eyes. "I don't hate you."

"I-I couldn't handle it anymore. When you came over that day, I had already made the decision."

The muscles in his jaw twitched and his arms went rigid.

I dropped my gaze and my cheeks filled with heat. "It never gets easy saying this." The words refused to come out of my mouth. I feared his reaction and losing him again.

"You can tell me anything."

I closed my eyes. "That night I-I took a knife and slit my wrists." My voice was barely above a whisper.

James drew me hard against him and I buried my face into his chest.

"Oh god." He tightened his arms around me and I felt his body shake. We both cried, but it was my turn to comfort him, so I held him until his tears ended.

"I could've lost you," he said. "I should have been there. I should've—."

"But you were." I pulled back to look at him. "It was always you, James. You helped me through this. Whenever I have a panic attack, I think of your voice telling me to breathe. That it's okay. When I got to the hospital, I never wanted to talk about anything, which is why I've been there so long. But then Emma and others convinced me that if I told Dr. Meisner everything it would help. But I wasn't ready to talk about my feelings. I just wanted to remember what it felt like to be happy. So I talked about us. And then I started reliving memories of us and David and Abby. I got all the way up to the accident, but I stopped. I hit a snag. And that was when Lisa came."

"Lisa?"

I nodded and I started walking again, and he stayed at my side. "She came to visit me."

"Are you two still friends?"

"No. She came over shortly after my attempt and completely went off on me. And then she came to the hospital, but I'd had enough. I told her I didn't want to be friends anymore and then she got upset and told me that—." I struggled with my words and James once again took my hand in his. "She told me that everyone would welcome my death and that she told Amos, who agreed with her, and said that he probably told you." My chin quivered. "She threw a bottle of pills at me and told me if I wanted to so bad, to just go ahead." I swallowed the lump in my throat. I was not going to cry over what she said to me. Not again.

James pulled me close. As a sigh escaped his mouth, I felt the air travel over my hair.

"That night, I thought about swallowing the pills."

His hold on me tightened.

"But I couldn't bring myself to do it. I flushed them."

He held me at arm's length.

"I eventually told Dr. Meisner everything. And she was

incredibly patient with me. I cleared my mind of all the thoughts and everything. She's helping me redirect my thoughts and overcome the negativity and guilt."

"I should thank her personally." His eyes watered again. "Do you still live there?"

"Yes. I'm here because I get day passes now."

"How much longer will you have to stay there?"

"I don't know. There are still some things I need to work on, and I'll never be perfect. I still get jumpy and panic, but it's not as much."

"You were never perfect, Corinne, nor will you ever be. But you are perfect for me."

"So are you."

"Can I visit you?"

"Yes. But only for a couple of hours. I'm sure you're still busy wrapping things up for school."

"It can wait."

We were quiet for a moment.

"I'm so sorry for causing your pain. I never contacted you because I wasn't ready. I was so cruel to you that day and I didn't want to do that to you again."

"Corinne, it wouldn't have mattered. I am here no matter what. Through the bad and good. I love you and I know I was being selfish this whole time, but I couldn't give up on you. I refused. And I hoped that one day you'd come back to me."

"I never wanted you to leave. I needed you and still do. And I don't want anyone or anything to separate us again."

His dark blue eyes held a familiar gaze that I missed. He took my hand and brought it to his face. "Is this okay?"

I nodded and then our foreheads touched, filling me with warmth and desire.

James tenderly kissed the scar on my wrist. "I never want to lose you."

"You won't."

His hand stroked through my hair and rested at the nape of my neck. Our lips were so close and my heart hammered against my ribs. Then his mouth was hungrily on mine. All the bridled yearning and tension we released in our kiss as we tried to make up for all the lost months. It was like we couldn't get enough of each other. His arms wrapped around me pinning me against him as if he was never letting go. I lost myself in the electricity that surged through my veins and held him just as tight.

James pulled away, but our foreheads still touched, and both breathless. "This can't be real."

"Why?"

"Because all I've wanted for nine months was you."

I felt myself smile. "It's real. I'm here."

He took a deep breath, as if he was relaxed, or relieved. "I've missed your smile."

"Yours, too."

He kissed me again, softer that time, and I smiled.

CHAPTER THIRTY-SEVEN

James and I wound our way back to the entrance of the gardens and met up with Emma, Amos, and Abby. We held hands and both grinned like silly fools, but we didn't care. We'd found each other and through it all came out stronger and more in love.

"Are you ready?" Amos asked.

Of course I wasn't ready to leave James. But I had to, even if it was for a short while.

"Can I take you back?" James asked. "I just want a little more time."

Abby chuckled. "That's a really stupid question."

"You don't mind?" I asked.

"You two are morons. No, we don't mind. You can have her tonight, but just remember mister, curfew is at eight." Abby looked at James as if she were a suspicious parent.

"Yes ma'am," he said.

I hugged them and then I rode back with James to the hospital. We talked the entire way about everything Dr. Meisner had told me, about how James had withdrawn a little from his friends and family and how running and music had kept his sanity. Then we talked about Tony's band and how they had made their own video and people loved it. They also had made a CD and were trying to get more listeners.

"Do you have it?" I asked.

"Yeah."

"I wanna hear it."

"I wonder if you'll like it." He raised the console and dug around for it.

"Why wouldn't I?"

James slid the CD in the player and I leaned on the console, waiting. The first song started and it was a hard fast beat with a punk sound. Tony's voice came through and I was taken-aback. His usual soft voice was powerful, full of emotion, and raw. James skipped to the second song after about a minute or so, and this one was filled with screaming, like a pop punk emo band, and loud guitars. It was okay, but I could have dealt without the screaming.

James chuckled. "Yeah, that was my reaction when I first heard it, sadly enough." I must have grimaced.

"It's good."

He rolled his eyes and shrugged. "He likes it." And then he skipped to the next one and we listened to the rest and talked. We pulled into the parking lot of the hospital and dread washed over me.

We were quiet, and he turned off the engine but left Tony's music playing. The next song came on with a quiet acoustic guitar and Tony's smooth voice sang with such heartbreaking real emotion. Then the drums joined, sounding like a heartbeat. The music amplified into the chorus and Tony poured his heart into the hauntingly beautiful words. I could feel his longing and need for the girl he sang about. I focused on the lyrics. Something about them sounded familiar. And then it ended with the same sad guitar as the beginning.

James reached to take the keys out of the ignition, but I stopped him. "Wait, I wanna hear that again."

I pressed the back button and listened again.

I lie awake dreaming of your face

PIECES OF ME

Thinking of how I could have changed things
But I'm left with only memories of you
And I cling desperately

I've made my mistakes
I never meant you harm
But the distance and time
Only makes me yearn for you more

Come back to me
I'm drowning in this misery
And in this haze, I wait for you
I'm not letting go
Until you tell me so

I write a letter every day
Just like the guy in your favorite novel
Hoping you'll pick up the phone
And call
Just call

I've made my mistakes
I never meant you harm
But the distance and time
Only makes me yearn for you more

Come back to me
I'm drowning in this misery
And in this haze, I wait for you
I'm not letting go
Until you tell me so

I am nothing without you
I need you
I miss you
I just wanna hold you
Taste your lips

And hear your laugh

Come back
Come back to me
Come back
Back to me

The lyrics spoke to me. And then I realized it was about me. "Did you write this?" I asked, but I had read enough of his writings to know it was him.

He grabbed the back of his neck and nodded. "The lyrics. Tony and his band wrote the music."

"This is really good."

"I told him not to put it on there. But when he read it, he practically begged me for it."

"Why didn't you want him to have it?"

"Because it's so personal. I was hurting and I didn't want others knowing my pain."

"But maybe they can relate to your pain and find that they aren't alone. I mean, that's why you and I like music so much, right? Because songwriters write from the heart which helps us through anything."

"Yes. It's just, I didn't want anyone seeing that side of me. Especially you."

"I can understand. I mean, I shared my writings with Emma and Dr. Meisner, and it was hard, but they didn't judge me."

"You wrote?"

"Yes," I said, feeling my cheeks warm. "But my point is, you don't have to hide who you are, at least around me. That's one of the reasons I love you, James. Because you're never afraid to be you. Of course there are parts of us that we don't want others to see or know about, but if you find someone who is still there through it all, then there's nothing to be afraid of."

"I think you're braver than me." His lips curled into my favorite smile.

I rolled my eyes. "Something inside you made you want Tony to use that song."

"Maybe. Maybe it was the same something that made you want to talk."

"It took a while."

"But you got there. And I'm proud of you." He glanced at the clock and sighed. "I don't want to say goodnight."

"You can come inside for a bit. If you want."

He agreed and then we walked inside, hand-in-hand. He signed in and then I took him to my room.

"So, this is it." I said.

He looked around, and then frowned. "I will never forgive myself."

"What?" I squeezed his hands.

"I can't help but think I had some part in all this. Because I wasn't there for you and you were here. Alone."

I reached up and placed my hand on his cheek. Remorse filled in his blue eyes. "James, you didn't do this. This was my own self destruction. And I've already told you that you helped me. So, no more apologies. Deal?"

He nodded, but I could tell he still felt regretful. I pulled his mouth to mine and kissed him softly. When we pulled apart, he still held my hand.

"What's your day like tomorrow?" he asked.

"Therapy. And more therapy. Maybe some reading. Writing."

"Is that your journal?" He pointed to the yellow notebook on the nightstand.

"One of them. I have quite a collection." I moved past him to the dresser and pulled out a drawer, revealing a stack of them.

"Wow. What did you write about?"

I slightly chuckled. "Everything." I wondered if I should let him read them. I hesitated for a moment, but I would be a hypocrite if I said no since he let me read all of his journals once. And I didn't want to say no. I wanted to share everything with him. Even if it wasn't always good. Because I knew he would never judge me and would still love me the same, as he had this whole time. And I would never again doubt his love for me. "Do you want to read them?"

James gave me an uncertain look. "I—."

"It's okay." I handed him the stack. "You shared your most intimate thoughts with me."

"Corinne, visiting hours are over, hon," one of the night nurses said as she passed by the room.

James placed the notebooks on the dresser and then he looked at me with such a heavy gaze. My heartbeat edged higher as he softly put his hands on either side of my face and then pressed his lips to mine. He kissed me long and deep.

"I could kiss you forever," he whispered.

I gave a soft laugh. "I don't want you to leave."

"I could always stay. I mean, there is another bed."

"I wish you could. Come on. I'll walk you to the door." I clutched his hand, not wanting to let go, and we walked to the entrance. We kissed once more and then he looked back before leaving. I knew I would see him the next day, but it was still hard to say goodbye.

CHAPTER THIRTY-EIGHT

"Perhaps one of the reasons you survived this is because you are surrounded by people who love you very much," Dr. Meisner said.

I was in her office for our usual session, but I couldn't stop fidgeting. I was so nervous about seeing James again. We could only see each other for four hours a day, but I didn't care. Any time with him was more than I could have asked. "I was just scared," I told her. "After the reactions of some, I just didn't think they still cared, or maybe I wouldn't allow myself to know the truth."

"We are sometimes our own worst enemies."

"I just can't believe I allowed myself into such a dark place."

"Unfortunately, that is the worst side effect of trauma. People react differently to circumstances, but because of the adverse things that happened after your trauma, it made you fall deeper. But I believe you are at a point in which you are fully capable of learning how to move on. You have made quite a bit of progress in the past couple of months."

"Why did I believe Lisa so much? Why couldn't I just heal properly?"

"Our minds are already very fragile. And when faced with such trauma, it shuts down and can't cope with everything.

Sometimes we reject the reality and refuse to accept it."

"That makes sense. I just wish it hadn't happened."

"Of course. How do you feel now?"

I thought for a moment. "Bittersweet, I guess. I haven't been very nice to myself, but I'm finding that girl I used to know and getting to know her again. I've learned to accept my mistakes and understand unfortunate things happen. But a small part of me will always feel responsible for what I did. Even though I know it wasn't all my fault. But, how can I possibly move on? I mean, do I just live my life normally and ignore the fact that David has died?"

"It's not ignoring him. It's living with the knowledge that he has moved on to a better place, and from what you've told me about your brother, he would want you to move on. He would not want you dwelling on this tragedy. I'd like to think that our loved ones who have passed are still with us, watching us."

Thinking of David sitting next to me, holding my hand, and hearing every single one of my confessions, I wondered what he would say. And then I remembered my dream of him. And even though it didn't make any sense, I never forgot what he told me. That he was okay.

"I still miss him. I miss talking to him and just being around him."

"Of course you do. We will always miss them. You are allowed and it's okay to feel sad. It's healthy."

I nodded. "It's taken me so long to get here."

"It doesn't matter how long it takes, just as long as you get there. I have some very good news for you, Corinne."

"What is it?"

"I see no reason for you to stay here anymore. You are going home."

"You're sending me home?"

"Yes. But keep in mind this is a probation period for two months. I know that sounds bad, but it's just a precaution. We have paperwork, and we have to present your case to the board. You will need to figure out what you're going to do though. Either go back to school or work."

"When?"

"Thursday."

I couldn't believe it. I was going home to be with my friends and family and James. Relief swelled inside me. I wasn't sure what the protocol or if there was any rules to hugging your psychologist, but I leapt up and hugged her. "Thank you."

She gave me a tight squeeze. "It was all you, Corinne. You were strong enough to overcome it."

On the way back to my room, I looked around at the shaded campus, remembering the walks I had with Emma, Scott, and Ginger. I thought of how they were a part of my healing, if just a small part, but I was thankful. I hurried the rest of the way, wanting to be inside the second James arrived.

"You have a visitor," a nurse told me and my heart skipped a beat. I half-ran, half-jogged to my room. I opened the door and with a sharp intake of breath, I halted.

"Why are you here?" I demanded.

Lisa stood from the bed, tears streamed down her face, and her shoulders shook. "I'm so sorry, Corinne. Please. I never meant to hurt you."

How dare she show up here? How did she even get inside? I shook my head. "No. I told you I couldn't do this. We can't be friends. You hurt me more than you could ever imagine. I was so weak and you took advantage of that. You lied to me about James and Amos. You made me think there was no one else but you."

"That's not true. You met Will—."

"Why Lisa? Why did you do it?" I raised my voice.

She gave me a long look. "I overheard your parents talking about how you needed to heal without needing James or anyone so much. Your mom mentioned how attached you were to him and how he shouldn't be the only thing that made you happy so I took it upon myself and I told him not to call anymore, per your parents. I thought I was doing the right thing."

"Did you not ever stop to think how much it hurt to hear you say James never wanted to talk to me? I can't believe I even trusted you."

"I was jealous of what you had with him," she cried. "You were the only friend I had and I hated not having you around. Yeah, I had a boyfriend, but I didn't see him every day. I have no one now and I hurt my best friend and I don't know what to do."

That wasn't my problem, I wanted to say. But the nurturing side of me took over. "When's your next therapy session? Or are you even going?"

She wiped her eyes and her face crinkled. "This week."

"I'm going to give you some advice that helped me through all of this. Tell him everything, Lisa. And really *try* this time."

"I will. So does that mean we're okay?"

"I'm getting out of here. And I'm going to live my own life. I think you should do the same."

Her chin quivered. "I hate myself for what I did to you."

"Then, you should talk about it with your therapist." I opened the door wider and motioned for her to leave. "It's time to go. Time to move on."

She stared at me in disbelief and then her eyes moved to the entrance. I felt tension emanating from behind me, so I turned and looked.

"What are you doing here?" James demanded. He glared at her, and I'd never seen such a look on his face. I took his hand and pulled him closer to me.

"It's okay," I said. "She was just leaving."

Lisa grabbed her purse and walked slowly passed us and out into the hallway. I closed the door and exhaled.

"Are you okay?" James asked, his expression immediately changed to concern.

"I'm better than that. I have good news."

"What?"

"I'm going home."

James raised his eyebrows and picked me up and squeezed me. "I knew you could do it. I'm so proud of you." He set me down and gave a smile that made me feel as though I'd lost all bone mass. I felt a little dizzy.

"Thanks. I'm proud of myself, too. I still have to see Dr. Meisner and I still have to take my meds and I have to figure out what I'm going to do."

"What do you mean?"

"Like go to work or school. First, I'd like to get my diploma. Or GED."

"We can do that." He kissed my cheek. "What do you want to do after that?"

"College. Definitely psychology. I wanna help people. Now more than ever. I want to be a good doctor, and compassionate and patient. Just like Dr. Meisner was with me. I just feel like there aren't enough doctors out there who care and can get through to people."

"Then, you'll be that person. I've said it before, but you have so much heart and you are so genuine and caring. You might even care a little too much. But you are so strong that you can accomplish anything. And Emory still has a good psychology program." He grinned.

I rolled my eyes and playfully patted his shoulder. He kissed me with so much passion that I thought I was going to pounce on him, but I didn't.

CHAPTER THIRTY-NINE

My last night in the hospital arrived. I was being released the next day to live my life once more. A second chance. I remembered being scared and lonely that first night. How I dreaded it. But being there made me appreciate things and made me realize just how strong I was. I had been a girl disappearing from everyone including herself.

Mom and Dad came and got me the following morning. I had my own little party, but was a little sad that James wasn't there. I thought for sure he would have come. We met with Dr. Meisner and she explained that they were weaning me off the antidepressants, but I still had to take my headache meds.

I said my goodbyes and made promises to keep in touch with a few of the other girls I'd met. Mom took my hand and Dad placed his arm around my shoulder.

"Let's go home." Mom smiled. She no longer had bags under her eyes and she looked happy.

I bit my lip. "Actually, there's some place I need to go first."

With a simple nod, Dad knew what I meant.

An hour later, we arrived at the cemetery, and Dad pulled the car next to the curb. It was a beautiful September day. The cloudless sky was that deep blue color and the temperature was just right. Those were my favorite days. I followed Mom and Dad up the small hill, through the black, iron gate, and on a beaten path. We stopped once we saw a gravestone with fake yellow roses on either side. I read the granite headstone:

David Leigh Elliot
loving son and brother
Born: May 30, 1992
Died: January 7, 2012

It was the first time I had seen it since the funeral. I felt guilty, but only because I knew I should have visited sooner.

There was no use in trying to hold back the tears since my parents were crying as we held each other. Not much was said at the gravesite since we were all rather in our own heads. Remembering David in our own ways I supposed. Our beach trip suddenly came to mind and I laughed to myself as I remembered him tossing me into the water. Or him belting out a song on the guitar. And how he'd get so excited about football. Or how he always protected me and was there for me. I would never forget my brother, my hero, and my protector. I remembered my promise to him in my dream to live my life and I was determined to keep that promise.

Mom, Dad, and I talked the whole way home and I wondered why there were several cars in the driveway and on the side of the road.

"Who's all here?" I asked.

"Just a few people," Dad said with a silly grin. He took my suitcase and then I followed Mom inside.

"Surprise!" A group of people shouted. Balloons were all over the place, which scared Booger, but he still ran up to me, wagging his tail and smiling. After I petted him, I looked around at all the faces. Maw, Paw, Abby, Emma, Amos, Charles, and James.

I couldn't help but cry. I gave Charles a tight hug. I wasn't expecting to see him at all. I'd forgotten just how much he looked like David, but maybe that was my mind playing tricks. I hugged everyone and got lost in all the commotion. James took my hand in his and gave me a discreet kiss on my temple. I glanced up at him, feeling a smile on my face, and I squeezed his hand tighter and leaned into him.

Mom and Dad came into the room with a cake and lit candles on top. Mom placed it on the table in front of me and it read, *Welcome Home.*

I glanced up at all the smiling faces that looked back at me. I was overcome at how they never gave up on me and how lucky I was to have so many people in my life who loved me. I never wanted to take them for granted again. I was stronger because of them.

My eyes locked with James's, and it overwhelmed me that he had waited for me all that time. I was very lucky to have survived.

"I-I just want to say that it means a lot to me to have you all here," I said. "I know times weren't always easy and I'm learning to find peace again. But I couldn't have done this without you all. Thank you so much."

"Oh hurry up and make a wish," Mom wept. "I don't want the candles to melt the cake." She smiled.

I didn't need to make a wish because I had already gotten mine. To live and be happy.

While it was the hardest choice I'd ever had to make, looking at all the faces of the people that I loved, it turned out to be the easiest decision.

Just listen to the music
And always wait for that someone
Who never came
You never know what it's like
To be there
There- a place with no life
A darken mystery
You think you'll never find
Your way home

PIECES OF ME

Just open your eyes
And you'll see the pain
It's easy to feel, but hard to express
It's easy knowing than to say it
I've been there-but here I am-home
To where someone awaits me
Listening to the sweet music
That calms the soul
Holds the heart
And never let you go

PLAYLIST

"Fix You" – Coldplay
"Some Surprise" – Gary Lightbody & Lisa Hannigan
"This Years Love" – David Gray
"Hear You Me" – Jimmy Eat World
"Brand New Day" – Joshua Radin
"Into Dust" – Mazzy Star
"Perfect Memory" – Remy Zero
"Breathe Me" – Sia
"Everything" – Lifehouse
"Hold On to What You Believe" – Mumford & Sons
"Sober" – P!nk
"Girl Disappearing" – Tori Amos
"Give Me A Sign" – Breaking Benjamin
"Pain" – Jimmy Eat World
"Breath" – Breaking Benjamin
"Like You" – Evanescence

ABOUT THE AUTHOR

Carrigan Richards was born in Cullman, Alabama, but grew up in Birmingham and eventually moved to Atlanta, where she received her Bachelors of Arts in English from Kennesaw State University. She lives near Atlanta with her dog. For more information, please visit www.carriganrichards.com.

Printed in Great Britain
by Amazon